Aftermath

by

ROBERT ER[illegible]

ISBN: 1480178225
ISBN-13: 978-1480178229

Bob Aldridge has two "good guys"-v-"bad guys" e-books:
Aftermath and *Maelstrom,* available on Amazon.
A third, provisionally titled *Turnabout*, is nearing completion.
He has also had a number of short stories published
in popular magazines and broadcast on radio.
Please visit his website at www.penandbrush.co.uk and his blog at
http://bobaldridge.wordpress.com

Robert Eric Aldridge

CHAPTER 1.

The fog swirling about the shabby Pelican had thickened so that the rocks, a hundred feet to starboard, were now completely hidden.

I cut the engine speed still more until the boat was barely making headway against the falling tide and stuck my head out of the wheelhouse to peer through the murk.

The gentle rumble of the engine trembled up through the weather-beaten deck planking, through the soles of my feet, spreading to the tips of my fingers and the backs of my eyes, so that the Pelican and I were one, breath held, listening, watching.

From ahead, and a little to port, came the reassuring double-clang of the breakwater fog bell, followed by six seconds silence and then clang-bang again, over and over. I checked the compass heading and steered another point east.

The unseen rocky shoreline to starboard would soon open out into a wide bay, and on this heading I was a little over two miles from safe harbour.

Familiar smells mingled with the wreathing tendrils of fog, the sea itself, old fish and diesel. Then, faint at first but growing rapidly stronger, the stink of petrol.

Somewhere ahead of Pelican was Dave Gregory's Garland: Steel-hulled, she was almost five feet longer than Pelican's fifty, and had more beam. She was powered by petrol, and judging by the rainbow streaks decorating the smooth sea, she was losing a hell of a lot of it!

I put the strap on the wheel, took the loud-hailer from the cuddy and went into the bow, straining my ears vainly for sound of Garland's engine.

I lifted the loud hailer, wishing I'd bothered to pick up my radio from the repair shop.

'Hey Dave –ahoy Garland—Da-a-ve!'

There was no answering hail. I went back to the wheelhouse and switched off the engine, the better to listen.

With the Pelican swinging and drifting with the falling tide I tried hailing again and again ... Nothing!

So great was the smell of petrol now, it was as if the fog itself was made of the stuff. The only sound was from the fog-bell, and that was worryingly close. I re-started the engine, and headed shoreward again.

It was then that the explosion came, erupting to port with brain-jarring red anger, tearing the fog to shreds, setting Pelican over on her beam and bundling me into the scuppers.

Head ringing and heart racing, I dragged myself upright and stared, stupefied to where, about four boat lengths away, a plume of black smoke and flame roared fifty feet into the air.

In thirty seconds it was all over: -- no flame, no smoke --- and no Garland.

Daggers of glass littered Pelican's deck, some embedded in the cuddy's side. Half a lobster pot was wedged in a shattered sidelight, and two white plastic fenders, which weren't mine, lay in the cockpit. One of the fenders had Garland's name roughly painted on it.

Then the fog rolled back over the spot and it was as if it had never happened. That is if you ignored the damage to the Pelican and the fact that I now seemed to be stone deaf. Also my face felt as though it had been skinned.

As the initial shock wore off, I became aware that I should be doing something: like looking for Dave Gregory for instance; or rather what was left of him.

After ten minutes slow circling, a fresh engine noise heralded the arrival of the RNLI's rigid inflatable. I told them what had happened and one of the crew, Gus Newbold, came in over the rail with a first aid bag and started pulling needles of glass from my face and neck while the r.i.b. made a wide circle then began a slow zigzag down tide.

Gus gave me a pad to hold against the worst damage, and after a last, futile, wide circle, I headed Pelican homeward.

To my surprise I realized I was shaking and felt icy cold. The fog, which had previously been just a nuisance, had become alive and menacing and I wanted to be ashore.

Pelican poked her short bowsprit out into glaring sunlight quite abruptly. My spirits started to rise and, guiltily, I let them. I let myself smile at the questing gulls diving to meet me, at the cobalt blue sky, and breathed deeply of the fog-free air.

A man fishing from a rowing boat glanced up, called out something that sounded like a question and pointed back into the fog bank as his craft bobbed in Pelican's bow-wave.

Closer inshore, small yachts and sailing dinghies reached gently back and forth in fitful zephyrs while beyond, on the esplanade and the rising green behind, families — lovers — children — walked, talked and laughed.

Behind me, not very far, fish would be taking the first tentative bites into the mutilated remains of Dave Gregory.

The lock gates were on free-flow and, as I eased Pelican through, the duty lock-keeper, leaned out of his window and stared at me.

'Bloody 'ell Mike, your face is a right mess.'

Gus called up to him: 'Anything new on the short-wave?'

He shook his head, making his specs flash in the sunlight. 'Still searching,' he said, 'what the 'ell was that bang?'

I told him about the smell of petrol and the explosion; he said 'bloody-'ell' again and ducked back out of sight.

After helping me make Pelican fast, Gus took another look at my neck, told me to get myself up to "Casualty" for a couple of stitches, then headed back to the life-boat station.

Pelican didn't seem to have suffered any structural damage, but she was going to need a deal of cosmetic attention to bring her back up to scratch.

Originally built to sail, she usually carries her sails furled, but right now, thankfully, her full set were hanging in my lock-up. Otherwise Garland's flying debris would have made quite a mess of them.

I had a cursory tidy up before leaving the dock and making my way through the candy-floss and hot-dog stalls inhaling kebab fumes, mingled with those from the Chiperama and the wide-open double doors of the Jolly Lobster.

On my way up the short, cobbled street with its jumbled gift shops and chandlers, people were looking at me curiously over their ice-cream cones.

Catching sight of my face in a mottled mirror in an antique shop window, I could see why. They probably thought I'd been in a drunken punch-up.

A pair of elderly ladies asked anxiously if I were all right; I tried a reassuring grin, which hurt my face and left them tut-tutting and shaking their heads.

I crossed Custom House Square and up the three steps into the police station.

Sergeant Tom Prentiss was behind the desk, tunic undone and a pair of rimless half-spectacles on the end of his nose. Looking up from the ledger in which he was writing, he regarded my battered features for a moment, then pushed the ledger aside and lifted the counter flap.

'Come through and sit down,' he said, 'Is this something I should know about?'

I sat in a swivel chair behind the desk and watched him take a bottle of Bell's from under the counter and pour me a generous measure in a thick tumbler.

I took too-big a gulp and coughed and spluttered as white-fire jagged from the corner of my mouth to my left eye.

After listening to a brief account of events, he had me tell him again while he wrote it down. Then he called a young constable from a back room and bade him run me up to Casualty.

As we crossed to the door, he stopped me with an 'oy!', pointed at the bloody dressing which I still held to my neck and then at the waste-paper basket. As I dropped the dressing in, he took a fresh one from the first-aid cupboard, told me not to bleed inside the Panda, and saw me to the door.

On the short drive to A & E, I repeated my story yet again for P.C. Saunders' benefit. He listened, apparently unimpressed, and when I got out of the car, said that as I hadn't broken a leg, I'd probably be able to make my own way back.

In the waiting room a tubby man with his arm in a sling and a cigarette in his mouth, stood under a no-smoking sign glaring at a bright-lit tropical fish tank: put there to distract folk from their woes and bruises.

For a few moments I watched the fish too –the fantails and angel fish – then turned away, wondering what unspeakable things their cousins were doing to Dave Gregory.

Besides the man with the arm, there were a couple of bee stings, and a sprained ankle in front of me but, when the efficient looking girl with the clip-board noticed the blood-soaked wadding I held to my neck, she fast-tracked me into the care of a jolly-faced colleague who did a deft job with needle and gut, congratulated me on keeping my jugular intact and sent me home.

From the hospital gates I looked down across the grey, tiered roofs of the town to the sea.

The fog had gone altogether, leaving bright waters sparkling happily as far as the horizon.

Too far out to be audible, a creeping search-and-rescue helicopter circled and hovered like a kestrel. I guessed that the shoreline too, was by now being combed by coastguards and volunteers.

Dave Gregory and I had not been exactly ‘mates from way back.’ We’d shared a way of making a living that’s all. Inshore fishing for whatever was in season; taking out angling parties and a little light salvage work when the opportunity arose. We’d had a loose working arrangement and teamed up when it was to our mutual advantage. But that, apart from drinking an occasional pint together, was it.

He was taciturn and a loner, with no regular girl friend and no family living locally as far as I knew.

I thought I’d better go round to his basement flat and try to find an address. Someone, somewhere would need to know what had happened to David Gregory.

Number seventeen Bayswater Crescent, pleasant enough though a touch run-down, backed on to the main London to Penzance line. I’d been here a couple of times when I’d had to rouse Dave for an early start. I opened the squeaky area gate, picked my way down the worn, littered limestone steps and retrieved the key from a crack above the door frame.

On entering the passage, the second door on the right is the living room and I went in there first.

The lower sash of the window was open, the catch hanging by one screw, and a faint breeze billowed the thin yellow curtains into the room. A settee was upended with its hessian base cut out, and a couple of pictures, their backs removed, lay on the table.

The drawers of the small bureau lay empty on the threadbare carpet, surrounded by their contents. In the corner of the room the carpet was folded back, and two short floorboards had been taken up.

I stepped over and looked down the hole. A pocket-torch lay on the damp earth – still burning brightly. Whoever had done all this was not far away.

Stepping quietly to the open window I inched my head out, trying to see both ways at once. The yard was as hot as a baker's oven; the head-high limestone wall to my right blazed with scarlet campion and buzzed with a hundred bees.

On the other side of the spiked railings a strolling green shunting-engine wheezed to a stop, gave a double toot on its whistle and eased slowly back into a siding.

I slid over the low sill and stood in the heat, listening. To my left the rear door to the house was shut. Further down, past the small-paned kitchen window, another door, partly open, showed part of a lavatory pan. I walked towards it slowly, carefully, watching for the slightest movement.

When I reached the door I let my breath out with relief. There wouldn't be enough room behind it to hide a beanpole.

How wrong can you get?

There's small diamond shaped vent cut in the top of the door and involuntarily my eyes went to it. Immediately the door was jerked open from within and a figure hurled itself violently at me, arms flailing. I sidestepped instinctively, stumbled against an edging stone and went down on one knee, grabbing a handful of leather jacket as I went. My other hand was twisted beneath me, doing its best to hold me up.

The occupant of the leather jacket was as tall as me but thinner, with a head like a fuzzy billiard-ball and a very pink face. As I pulled myself upright; one of his wild punches caught me in the short ribs and it hurt. I jerked the leather jacket towards me and gave his pink nose a short sharp butt with my forehead, at the same time managing to rake his shin with the heel of my shoe.

He didn't waste his breath in swearing, just hauled off and gave my thigh a hearty kick before vaulting the spiked barrier onto the railway track

As he went, I picked up a fist sized stone and hurled it after him with more anger than accuracy. Then he was over the lines and down the far bank out of my view and I was left with a few more bruises and holding an epaulet from his jacket.

Seconds later the London to Penzance train rattled through, putting paid to any ideas I might have of following him.

Thrusting the epaulet into the pocket of my wind-cheater, I climbed back through the window, pulling the lower sash down behind me.

Down the hole, the hand torch was beginning to dim and I got down on my knees and stuck my head between the boards, wondering what he'd been after. Whatever it was he hadn't found it, or he wouldn't have been hanging about in the karzy waiting for me go away.

Finding nothing beneath the floor but a damp smell and a lot of cobwebs, I stood up. I'd come for an address and with the room such a shambles, I wondered where to start looking.

Stirring the spilled contents of the drawers with my foot, I looked for something that might be a diary or address book.

There were three mauve envelopes among the mess, bearing Dover postmarks. I opened one and looked at the return address. It was c/o Y.W.C.A., and was signed 'Love Sandra', with two kisses.

'Oh my dear Lord, what an awful mess!'

The woman's nervous voice behind me made me jump, more-so because I was reading someone else's letter.

A pair of glasses glinted at me from the shadowy doorway then their owner edged into the room. She was small, thin, and sixtyish.

'Oh my,' she said again. 'Whatever's 'appened?'

She looked anxiously at my face. 'I saw you and that young man fighting. I rang the police.'

'Thanks,' I said.

She was still staring at my features.'Did he do all that to your face?'

I shook my head and felt the stitches tug. 'That was earlier to-day. —I had an accident. What did the police say?'

'They said I was to stay in my room and they'd send a Panda.'

I had visions of Chi-Chi climbing the steps and knocking at the front door.

'You didn't though, did you?' I said, in the voice I use for frail elderly ladies, 'You came down to have a look. It could have been dangerous.'

'Oh no!, I knew it was the other one's fault, 'cause he was a skin-head. Besides, I've got this.'

She'd kept her right hand behind her but now she brought it

forward and pointed a pistol at my middle.

'It's a Luger,' she added.

I didn't care what particular make it was. My stomach was doing flips and I just wished she'd point it somewhere else.

'My husband brought it back from the war.' she said, then, reading my expression, 'Oh it doesn't work. He did something to it. It's only for frightening burglars.'

It had done a pretty good job on me. 'You are not supposed to tell people that,' I said.

'Oh, I know you're alright, 'cause I've seen you with Mr. Gregory.' Her mind came back to the chaos. 'My – he will be annoyed. All this *mess!*. Did that skin-head take anything?'

'I don't think so. He wasn't carrying anything when he ran.'

How do you tell someone their nearest neighbour has been blown to pieces? She'd called him Mr. Gregory and not David, so perhaps they weren't all that close. I decided on directness, and then fluffed it.

'Dave won't be – er – Mr Gregory has had a bit of an accident. He – er – he is dead, actually.'

Why the hell did I have to say 'actually'!

The hand holding the gun went to her cheek.

She said, 'Oh my dear Lord,' again, very quietly, turned and went up the stairs to her own flat on the ground floor.

I dropped the letters on the bureau and after poking my head quickly into the bedroom and kitchen, which looked relatively undisturbed, I followed, finding her in her tiny tenement kitchen.

She was sitting at the table wringing her hands as though they were cold. I didn't like her color and asked if she was all right. A silly question; I could see that she wasn't. She nodded towards the kitchen cabinet and her voice was a whisper.

'Tablets... in the right hand drawer.'

I found them and drew some water from the tap, which I set beside her. Whatever the tablets were, they were pretty potent. Within two minutes, she looked almost normal and she sat up straight with a long in-drawn breath.

'Poor Mr. Gregory. What happened to him? Do you know?'

I didn't want to start her off again with the details. I shrugged.

'I'm not exactly sure,' I answered. That was true anyway.

I heard a police car siren way off and wondered if it was for us. Through the kitchen window I could see right across the railway line to where the main road snaked up between sunlit "Bed & Breakfast" signs. A blue, winking light sped north on its way to some traffic accident and the siren's note trailed off.

The Luger lay on the velvet cloth in front of its owner, a fly carefully inspecting the muzzle. I picked the pistol up carefully.

'Well Mrs - sorry I don't know your name -?'

'Thompson, -- Lilly Thompson..'

'I'm Mike Peterson. We'd better put this away before the law arrives. I'm not sure it's legal..'

I opened the breech and looked in. Most of the mechanism had been removed and a plug of lead wedged into the breech.. I put the weapon in the drawer of the kitchen cabinet.

Above my head, the doorbell gave a faint, hesitant "brrr".

'It needs a new battery,' said Mrs. Thompson.

I went along the passage and let in P.C. Saunders who looked surprised to see me there.

'Well well!' he said, ' You're certainly "where it's all at" to-day.'

In the kitchen MrsThompson and I gave him a brief outline of events, then I went with him to the basement flat where he viewed the damage stoically.

'How did he get in?' He asked at length, 'Back-door open?'

I told him about the window, then I remembered about the torch and took it from my pocket.

'There may be prints on it,' I suggested.

He sucked his teeth. 'Yours probably,' he said, 'That's if they haven't all rubbed off in your pocket.'

I bridled a bit. 'Well he's bound to have left some somewhere. He wasn't wearing gloves.'

He gave a professional sigh. 'Trouble is Mr. Peterson: you didn't actually see him – or anyone else – in here, did you? And we don't know if anything is missing do we? — And Mr. Gregory is in no position to help us in that connection, is he?'

His attitude was beginning to rile me. I waggled an arm at the mess.

'What do we do about this lot then? Just forget all about it?'

'Not up to me sir. It depends on the 'Super'. By the way, – your neck is bleeding again.'

'Pig-face!'

'Sir?'

I touched the wound and felt protruding gut and stickiness. 'I must have pulled a stitch when I was fighting with him, – with 'Pig-face'.'

'I see Sir,' He took his notebook from his top pocket, 'Now if you would give me an accurate description of your assailant, we may be able to apprehend him.' He nodded at the mess. 'If we do, we can ask him about this little lot.'

I told him what I could remember. 'His nose could be bleeding,' I added feeling a little more cheerful at the thought, 'and he's missing an epaulette from his right shoulder.'

I handed the scrap of leather over and P.C. Saunders put it in a side pocket.

Back upstairs, Mrs. Thompson had made a pot of tea.

'You'd better undo your collar button young man,' she said to Saunders as he sat down with a sigh. 'Getting too hot is no good for anyone.'

'You're so right Madam,' he agreed, and tugged his tie loose as well.

As he read through his notes, Mrs Thompson dabbed at my neck with cotton wool and Dettol.

'Is there anything else you can add Mrs. Thompson?' Saunders asked.

She shook her head doubtfully. 'No... no I don't think so... It was all over very quickly.'

'And you'd never seen the man before! Nor you Sir?'

'Not as far as I know.'

He put away his notebook and stood. 'Right then. Thank you for the tea, Mrs Thompson. If we do catch up with him, we'll be in touch.'

'That will be quite all right,' she answered.

I got up to go too. 'Are you feeling okay now?' I asked her.

'Oh yes – fine.' She glanced up at the wall clock. 'My daughter will be here shortly and then Fred will be home by six— Fred's my husband.'

I asked P.C. Saunders if he'd give me a lift back to the harbour.

He thought about it just long enough to make it an official favour before saying yes.

I suddenly remembered why I'd come in the first place.

'Shan't be a second.'

I dropped down the stairs in three strides and went into the bedroom. On the mantle-piece above the boarded-in fireplace was an assortment of gaudy paperbacks. Among them was a desk diary with a red plastic cover. I flipped through it quickly, saw that it contained some addresses and took it with me. In the Panda, P.C. Saunders was giving H.Q. The big "O.K. Out". He hooked up the mike and looked at the diary suspiciously.

'It's what I came for,' I explained, '— addresses, — someone to write to about Dave Gregory.'

'I'm not sure you ought to be taking anything from the scene of the crime,' he said.

'But your Super' hasn't decided yet that there has been a crime,'I protested, 'and anyway, Sergeant Prentiss said it would be okay.'

He gave me a "look" and let in the clutch with a jolt

When I got back to the Pelican, Sam Wilkins was there, sitting on a bollard and looking down at a bicycle wheel sticking out of the mud. Sam had been sitting on that bollard since before Noah's flood. When it came, he'd just lifted his feet and turned his pipe the other way up.

'You 'ad a visitor,' Sam said.

'Oh? Who?'

He shrugged one shoulder; the other one was barely movable: the legacy of an argument with a trawler winch in his youth.

'Never seen him before,' he said. 'He was poking about on deck but 'e sheered off when I came out the store.'

'What did he look like?'

'Yobo,' Sam said disgust.

'Skin head?' I asked.

'You got him.'

'Well I'll be – I just chased that bastard out of Dave's flat. He was taking it apart.'

'What's 'e after then?'

'Lord knows,' I looked south to where three miles out, the breakwater was now a long black ridge, sharp in the westering sun, ‘but I’ll bet it’s connected with what happened out there.’

Sam screwed his cap down another thread and squinted his eyes to follow my gaze.

‘What ‘zackly *did* 'apen out there?’ he asked.

‘Garland... she just went up with a bang, I smelled petrol— then up she went.’

‘You was pretty close ‘cording to your paint work.’

‘Forty yards or so ... What’s the depth just there?’

‘Eastern end? Ten or twelve fathoms at low springs, but the channel’s too fast for anything to settle unless it’s heavy enough to sink fast.’

'What about Dave's body?' I said

Sam removed his pipe. A sure sign that he was giving the matter considerable thought.

'Take your pick,' he said, 'It's a big world.'

I nodded. ‘That’s what I thought. You know Sam, there’s something damned peculiar about that explosion!’

‘Aye; -like as not, like as not.’

I turned to look at him closely but he was shuffling back towards his store, his shoulders rounded and arms hanging like an orang-outang.

Fishing out my keys from their hiding place, I let myself into the cabin below the wheelhouse, opened the roof lights and tipped the contents of three cans into a saucepan and lit the cooker. As the sweet smell of Calor, mingled with the bouquet of meat and two veg filled the tiny cabin, I tried again to pinpoint what it was that had been *wrong* with Dave Gregory’s explosion.

Then suddenly, as I turned down the flame a little, it was too obvious, There should have been a fire before the explosion, I recalled the strong petrol smell that had first made me uneasy. Not just the smell of an engine running rich, but the stink of gallons of the stuff, swilling about lose.

Okay, freak accidents *do* happen. But why hadn’t Dave Gregory answered my hails? He’d been close enough to hear, that was for sure!

Deciding to dine informally, I swung my feet onto the bunk and ate my meal straight from the saucepan, wiping it clean with a hunk of dry bread. Then, after letting my belt out a notch, from force of habit reached a hand up the shelf above my head for my tobacco tin, before remembering that I'd stopped smoking.

Three whole weeks had passed since rolling my last cigarette, and to my surprise the craving was gone. I felt a surge of relief. I'd licked it, and it hadn't been so bad after all.

I lit one mantle and flipped through the diary I'd brought from Dave Gregory's flat. It contained a variety of information, mostly advanced dates of angling-party bookings for the Garland. Half way through July there were half a dozen firm bookings indicated between then and the first week in September.

Somebody ought to write and tell people it was all off: that there was no Garland any more. Trouble was there were no addresses, only names. I wondered if Dave had taken any deposits. Oh well – none of my business.

There were several names and addresses in the back:-- girls mostly. Sandra was there from the YWCA Dover, Jean from Harrogate and Sheila from Nottingham. Holiday romances all. They had flowered brightly in the sweet summer air of the south coast but would any of them mourn Dave Gregory? ... Or would he just be 'that fellow with the boat'?

I found his cousin's name and address on the last page and it brought a mental image of Frank Gregory, standing in the bow of the Garland with one hand shielding his eyes from the sun; like a big blond Norseman in the prow of a Longship.

That had been Frank's favourite stance; as if he was always searching for new horizons. Frank was twenty years old and about the clumsiest thing ever let lose on the cluttered deck of a small fishing boat. He'd worked with Dave for three months, and for the first three weeks he'd been a mobile hazard. If it was moveable Frank would break it and if it wasn't then he would fall over it.

Gradually though he'd learned to control his hands and feet in their new environment, and his strength and his unbelievable keenness had been a real asset.

I wrote a short note telling him what had happened, and put it aside for the post next morning.

Of it's own volition, my left hand started it's upward journey to the shelf in search of nicotine. I stopped it, and instead directed it to a small locker.

Inside were two sticky sweets in a paper bag, left over from the early days of my self-denial. I removed as much paper as I could and put one of the sweets in my mouth.

Scrooge mayhave been right, I thought: 'Bah.— humbug !'

CHAPTER 2

I woke to grey light, and lay listening to the wind. What with one thing and another, I'd neglected to listen to the forecast the previous day. I switched on the small transistor set hooked to the bulkhead. I'd timed it just right,

'Wight-Portland-Plymouth. North west six to gale-eight imminent, increasing to storm force ten later to day.'

Something slapped rhythmically above my head – a loose halyard probably. And from the posh end of the harbour came the tinny rhythm of stainless steel rigging striking a hundred alloy masts.

Before I'd finished shaving I'd decided what to do with my day. May be with the next few days. Why not? I was a free agent, I had no angling parties for the next seven days or any work at all for that matter.

Pelican's engine had bust a gut three weeks before and I'd had to cancel the few bookings I'd made.

Yesterday's unfortunate trial run had satisfied me that the engine was fit and well again but, – the hell with it... I'd treat myself to a little quality time

On deck, the wind hit me from all directions at once: tunneling between the pink-green limestone buildings, -- busy, -- buffeting, -- bouncing off walls, -- tangling with itself and whirling suddenly upwards sucking up scraps of paper and plastic bags.

It was almost low water again, and a sudden inquisitive dart of sunlight bounced back from the bicycle wheel, which hadn't been there long enough to go rusty.

Looking over at the marina I noted one of the vessels, all bright-work and fibre glass, preparing for sea.

I watched the yacht move out from the pontoon stern first, and a yellow clad figure step smartly aboard as she cleared. Then she was nosing under power towards the wings of the exit from the inner harbour, the vee of her wake making a wide curve.

Two gulls got up from the mud and followed her for a while,

then dived after some scraps thrown from her stern.

As I climbed the iron ladder, Sam came out of a nearby cobbled alley, his half-fastened melton jacket ballooning out at the back. He waved his good arm in greeting and let himself into his store, leaving one half of the double doors open.

I unlocked the doors of the adjoining store: the one I'd shared with Dave Gregory, and switched on the light. Dave's Bedford van took up most of the room in there and, not having the keys, I had to push it back far enough to get out my personal transport: an elderly 350 cc B.S.A., and then let it roll forward again. I locked up, buckled on my skid-lid and went in next door.

'All right then Sam?'

'Right then Mike?'

'I'll be away all day; – maybe tonight and tomorrow too.'

'Depends on your luck I suppose?' Twisting his his head he gave me a knowing leer.

'You could say that. Could you keep your eye on the boat for me please?'

'Allus do, don't I?'

Over at the police station, Tom Prentiss had not yet come on duty I left Frank Gregory's address with the yawning night man and told him of 'pig-face's' interest in the Pelican so soon after he'd raided Dave Gregory's flat.

I posted the letter to Gregory's cousin, and ten minutes later was leaving the northern outskirts of town and opening the throttle a little to take the gradual climb up to the high moors.

Ahead and on both sides, clumps of bright green bracken spread among sheep-cropped turf. Then, higher, purple heather, washed with pale pink mist by the early sun, faded to the horizon. It was going to be a hot day.

The road dipped slightly near the top of the incline. In the bottom of the dip, just by the A.A. Box, a big Honda whispered past, it's rider, all black leather and shiny helmet flicking me a glance which I thought was probably a challenge.

Instinctively my hand tightened on the twist grip, then I firmly resisted the temptation to open up. Not that I had a hope in hell of catching a machine like that anyway.

Seven miles on, a steep winding road branches off to the left and

this was the one I took. Two more miles and the road divides again.
I inclined left, twisting and turning, dipping and climbing, slowing for blind corners hiding narrow bridges over tumbling streams.

High banks conceal the cultivated fields of this tongue of farmland which licks into the wild moors and on one side a dense beech wood throws its arms in a protective arch over the lane.

At the end of this wood the lane bends sharply right, but straight ahead is a rough track and it was along this track that I gently rode. Sun-baked wheel ruts and pot holes took all my concentration for the next few minutes until, coming to a five barred gate, I dismounted and pushed the bike through, letting the metal catch clatter shut behind me.

From the gate, the track climbs round the shoulder of a bracken-clad rise, hiding briefly in a shallow valley, then showing itself again half-way up the next slope, a mile distant.

It finishes at the small rambling group of granite and limestone buildings which is "Highfields":—Jenny McLaine's farm.

I could see Jenny moving around the farm, clanging buckets, her feet scuffing in oversized 'wellies', an untidy bundle of energy with a heart as big as a barn.

Kicking the engine into action, I motored on along the track into the dip, through the water splash and up to the first of the straggling buildings.

Jenny came out of a low doorless opening at the sound of my engine. She looked just as I knew she would. Man's shirt, buttoned wrong and half pulled out of scruffy jeans, thick red hair tied back.

'I saw you come through the gate,' her voice was low and had a built-in husky laugh. Green eyes, squinting against the sun, signaling a welcome to match her wide smile.

Even dressed like this, she's the most womanly woman I've ever known.

Cutting the engine and leaning the bike against the wall I reached out for her suddenly, urgently, hungry to feel her warmth.

'Hallo Jenny!'

She took a step back in mock alarm, which turned to the real thing when the state of my features registered with her.

"Your face, what on earth have you done to it?"

'Oh' - I tried to sound casual, '- a bit of an accident. It looks worse than it is'.

Her expression was dubious. 'I doubt it – anyway, if you want to fool around, you can take off your space helmet first.'

I did so and tried again, this time with more success letting the well-remembered feel of her shape soak in through my arms and chest as we kissed, wondering vaguely why she only held me with her elbows, keeping her forearms and hands clear.

Then she stepped back and I saw that she held three eggs in each hand.

She tilted her head. 'I think you really needed that.'

I nodded without speaking.

She held up the eggs. 'How about these? With some bacon and whatever.'

'Great!' I said. 'That's the second thing I need.'

The kitchen was large and airy with a lived-in and worked-in look. I sat at the scrubbed table and watched Jenny prepare the fry-up, enjoying the mingled smells coming from the frying pan.

'Seems quiet,' I said, 'where's Jimmy?'

Jimmy is Jenny's son. He's fifteen and has been the "man of the house" since his father died in a tractor accident five years before.

'Gone over to Coombe Barton.' Jenny threw over her shoulder. Then 'Damn!' She flicked pieces of eggshell out of the pan with the tip of her knife.

'Oh? For the day or what?' I tried to sound as though it didn't really matter.

She nodded. 'Uh-huh. To help with the hay making.'

Then looked at me over her shoulder and caught my eyes going to the ceiling, above which I knew her bedroom to be. She grinned.

'And I have to go shopping.'

'Shopping? On a day like this? I thought you'd come riding.'

'Some of us have to work. I'm surprised that you are not steaming out past the breakwater loaded-to the gun'ls with intrepid anglers.'

I suddenly remembered why I wasn't doing just that. She put a stacked plate before me and, between bites, I told her what had happened to Garland and Dave Gregory. She sat opposite during the telling, her face registering concern, shock, horror.

'But you were so *close*! It's a miracle you weren't blown to pieces.'

'That's what I keep thinking. But, apart from the broken glass and some blistered paint, the Pelican is undamaged.' I swallowed a mouthful of tea, hot and sweet. 'All the blast seemed to go upwards, and the fire was very brief although it was so fierce!'

Jenny shuddered. 'And Dave Gregory wasn't – washed up on the rocks?'

'Not locally. Depends where the tide takes him.'

She gathered the plates and took them to the sink. 'Was he married?'

'No, not married.'

I told her about writing to Frank about my visit to Dave's flat and the run-in with the yobo and about Mrs Thompson and her Luger.

'It wasn't your day, was it?' The question was flip but the sympathy was real.

'It wasn't Dave's. And it's a funny thing, but the same character was trying to get into my cabin later – after l chased him off from the flat. ... Sam told me.'

Jenny turned, drying her hands on the tea towel. 'Then he must know you. He must have known the boat would be empty while you were occupied with the police.'

The top two buttons of the man's shirt she was wearing were missing and the next had come undone. I lost track of, what she was saying.

'Er – yes the police.' I floundered. Then I reached out and grabbed her by the wrist and pulled her onto my knee.

Minutes or hours later I was brought back from a pink haze by a toot – toot' from outside. Through the window, I saw a red GPO van turning in the yard. Jenny patted my cheek. I twirled an imaginary moustache.

'Bah – foiled again!'

When she came in with the post, she waved a hand vaguely. 'I think there are some cigarettes in the drawer.'

'I've kicked the habit.' I said virtuously.

That got me a grimace of disbelief, which changed to a worried frown as she picked out one envelope from the half-dozen she had brought in.

'I know what this is. A threatening letter from my friendly bank manager.' She skipped through it quickly, then her eyes went back to the beginning.

'Is it bad?' I asked.'

'Bad enough. He's insisting that I make a substantial deposit or he'll be "most reluctantly" compelled to stop further payments on my cheques. Here, read it yourself!'

I took the single sheet from her and looked at the figures mentioned. 'Two thousand four hundred and twenty. That's not so much these days.'

'It is if you haven't got it.'

'I know that. I mean it's not enough for the bank to get shirty about.' I made a quick mental tally of my own resources. 'I've got about six hundred you could have if you are pushed.'

Jenny gave me a sidelong look. 'What would I have to do for it?'

'Or... you could marry *Boscawen* !'

Ralph Boscawen farmed Coombe Barton where Jimmy had gone hay making. He was a big man, in his late forties and drove a new Jaguar with a calf on the back seat. I didn't like him much.

'Yes I could always do that.'

Her voice sounded deliberately non-committal, and with a twinge of jealousy I wondered how far things had gone between her and Boscawen.

She'd been a neighbour of his for twelve years, which was a lot longer than I'd known her. For the past five of those years, Boscowan been intermittently paying court to Jenny in a ponderous, unromantic fashion.

Sourly, I reckoned he was as much after her few moorland acres and her stock as after Jenny herself, prize though she was. She was reading another letter now: one written on blue note paper. I read the upside down postmark on the discarded envelope. It said Chester and I knew that was where her mother lived. When she'd finished, I tried to recapture the mood that the postman had interrupted but Jenny twisted away and made for the stairs.

'Down boy. I told you I've got to go shopping. You can go and saddle up Rosalie while I get ready.'

'I'd hoped you'd come with me.'

Her voice slid down round the curve of the banister. 'Can't be done. This evening perhaps – if you are still here.'

'0h, I'll still be here. You can count on that.'

I picked up my helmet from the floor and went out into the yard.

'She hasn't been out for three days so she'll be a bit keen.'

Jenny's voice had come from under the eaves and when I looked up at her open window she was just pulling something floral and flimsy over her head.

'And don't stare – it's rude.' she said.

I grinned, waved and left her attacking her tangled curls with a hairbrush.

Apart from a small flock of hardy moorland sheep and a few cattle, Jenny keeps a half-dozen or so horses at livery, and whenever I could take a break from the Pelican, I came up here, sure of a ride.

The doors of four of the boxes stood wide and I could see two of their usual occupants grazing a small walled-in paddock just beyond the buildings. I exchanged a polite word with inquisitive heads, which poked over the next half-doors at my approach, and went to look at Rosalie. Her hindquarters, which were all I could see, didn't look at all keen. She wrenched another great maw-full of hay from the net, and turned her head to look at me as she chewed.

'You and me are going for a bit of a ramble, okay.?' I told her.

Rosalie snorted loudly and stamped a hoof.

I went into the tack room and climbed the rickety treads in the corner, remembering to miss the wobbly fourth one. The room above was about six feet by eight and held a wooden bunk, with a mattress which I'd rescued from a thrown-out "put-u-up" one Guy Fawke's night, a small-cupboard and a coat hook. This was my home-from-home when I was not aboard the Pelican.

From the cupboard I took my jodhpurs and boots and changed into them while I planned my ride. Outside, the wind had risen a notch and a half since I'd arrived and the driven clouds, which I could see through the tiny end window, looked rain laden. I thought about the heavy waterproof hanging in the cupboard, then settled for a rolled neck pull-over. If it rained, so what? It wasn't permanent.

Picking up Rosalie's saddle and bridle as I passed through the tack room, I wondered vaguely about the two empty loose-boxes. Then I remembered that there was a point-to-point on that day at Flax Park, the large estate that adjoins Barton Farm at it's eastern end. That gave me an idea. Instead of wandering aimlessly across the moor, I'd hack over to Flax Park and see something of the racing.

I lowered Rosalie's saddle onto her and, sighing deeply, she leaned on me as I reached under for the swinging end of the girth. I gave her a push in the ribs and told her to cut it out. She responded with a playful nip at my elbow. These formalities over, she allowed me to fit her bridle with no more than a disdainful sneer and I led her out into the yard.

The clouds were heavy now and low, but even in this poor light, the mare's liver chestnut hide shone with good health and good grooming. I mounted and walked her towards the gate as Jenny backed the Landrover from it's shed.

Jenny stuck her head out of the window and looked up at the sky, calling something that was blown up and away by the wind.

I surprised myself by cupping my hands and yelling, 'Marry me Jenny !' at the top of my voice.

My words went the way of hers, out over the gorse, dancing along with wisps of hay and straw.

Jenny made smiling 'Can't hear you' signals, swung the vehicle around and bumped off towards the out-of-sight water splash.

I turned Rosalie the other way, towards the gate which opens out onto the two hundred square miles of unrestricted moorland.

At the feel of turf under her hooves, her step lightened and her ears pricked forward at the sight of the gate.

Rosalie is a big girl, sixteen one, and to her, gates are for jumping. Not for her the nonsense of easing up to them gently and then helping her rider to open and close them. I sat back, keeping her on a firm rein as she went into her usual dance routine: A pirouette, "chassez left, honour your partner and a do-se-do". I'd ridden her a half dozen times up till then, and although she'd not actually taken me over the gate, it had always been a battle of wills and wits.

She pushed her shoulders into the gate impatiently as I leaned down for the spring catch and I cursed her as it trapped my fingers. When I finally got it open, I gave up the pretense that I was in complete charge and let her blunder through, allowing the gate to do its own thing.

'Off you go then,' I told her, easing the reins and touching her lightly with my heels.

She started with a great arching leap, then, stretching out to a full gallop across the flat springy turf, had the blood singing as it raced through me. A little left rein guided her into sparse gorse, where the ground rose. Bounding over two dry stream-beds without checking her stride, she was quickly over the crest and haring down the other side with increasing speed, the wind whipping the tears from my eyes.

I began to question my own wisdom in coming this way: There is a stream at the bottom of the slope, some eight feet wide with sheer banks which, for the most part, are boggy. Rosalie made unerringly for the one firm take-off point and went over without demur. Fifty yards on, she kindly allowed me to take charge.

I opted for a quiet amble up the next rise, disturbing a pair of carrion crows which rose from their secret meal and flew away low, cursing me loudly.

Crossing the next crest and ducking my head against a sudden fierce wind gust, I looked back at Highfields. A vehicle was approaching the buildings from the water splash: a small white pick-up, raising dust which was snatched away by the wind. I wondered whether to go back and see who it was, then decided it was none of my business. Whoever it was could wait for Jenny – or come back later.

I entered Flax Park the back way through a twenty year old conifer plantation which sighed and whispered to me as I passed.

Once through the conifers I was immediately among horse-boxes and the comings and goings of an event day. I tied Rosalie up, loosened her girth and gave her water in a borrowed bucket.

Mrs Amanda Wainwright was sitting on a straw bale, rubbing the muddied knee of her otherwise pristine breaches, and cursing 'Sailor Boy' who was dribbling saliva down the back of her jacket.

'Sailor Boy' was one of Jenny's charges, and now I knew why some of the loose boxes at Highfields had been deserted.

Mrs Wainwright looked up at my approach and I fitted on a sympathetic expression and asked her which fence she'd tumbled at.

'I haven't been round yet,' she said with some exasperation, 'this misbegotten idiot,' she jerked her tiny white thumb at the gelding, 'This son of a camel ran orf and I tripped over a tent-peg trying to catch him!'

She squinted at my face more closely

'My, oh my! You look as though you've taken a tumble yourself: - - into a thorn hedge perhaps?'

Without waiting for an answer she began 'oo-ing and ah-ing' as she stood up and flexed her knee joint. She held out a hand to me, fingers stretched and wagging.

'Now if you will kindly give me a cigarette, ... I've left mine in the car.'

I patted my pockets and shrugged. 'Sorry, I've given them up.'

Mrs. Amanda Wainwright gave a snort of disgust and pushed away from me. Her large china-blue eyes slid past my shoulder and lit on someone behind me.

'Oh Ralph, do give a girl a cigarette! This frightfully boring person has stopped smoking!'

I turned to see Ralph Boscawen strutting towards us. He was dressed the part of gentleman farmer — good tweeds and knobbly walking stick

I wondered sourly why he wasn't helping with his own hay making. We nodded to each other civilly enough and I left him fussing over the lady, with cigarettes and matches, while I wandered around for a while enjoying the ambiance.

Winning five pounds with a little cautious betting I then put the lot on 'Hot Potato', who was at twelve to one in a field of eight, for no better reason than it's jockey, Freddy Fletcher, sometimes came out fishing in Pelican. I watched with rising hope as Freddy, moving Hot Potato up from fourth to second place approaching the last fence but one, cleared it beautifully while the leader took a tumble.

Three lengths clear now, Freddie steadied his mount and positioned him for the final jump. Then, instead of taking off, Hot Potato stiffened his forelegs and buried his nose in the birch twigs.

From his new position, astride the fence, Freddy aimed a wild swinging punch at the horses nose. Hot Potato flinched and jerked his head back, causing Freddy to miss, topple from his perch and hang head downwards, his legs still enmeshed in the brushwood.

By now the rest of the field was over and away so I ducked under the rope and helped the cursing, thrashing tangle of limbs to right itself while Hot Potato cropped grass from next to a fence post.

Freddy's face was red with anger. 'The sod always does that,' he said, flinging his crop to the ground in disgust, 'Every bloody time!'

Hot Potato stepped tentatively forward and nudged Freddy in the small of the back sending him lurching forward. I caught his bridle

'Why do you keep him then?' I asked. Freddy grinned as he swung back into the saddle

'Well, we're mates aren't we?' He rode off at a walk towards the horse boxes; a faint ironic cheer from the small group near the fence following him.

I went and untied Rosalie and started back to Highfields. I reckoned she'd had a good rest and took a wide circle, letting her have her head whenever we came to sound going, free of rocks.

At the farm, the pick up I'd seen earlier was still in the yard but there was no sign of Jenny's Landrover. I untacked the mare, gave her water and rubbed her down with dry straw while she munched a bowl of horse nuts.

When I stepped through the door of the tack room, saddle and bridle over my arm, I was brought up short by the sight of 'Pig-face' standings facing me.

He was wearing black motor cycle leathers and knee boots. His clenched fists were planted on his hips, and w ith his bullet-head thrust forward and his teeth showing in the beginnings of a snarl, he looked the archetype of the Nazi storm troopers depicted in childcare's comics.

His presence had barely registered when I found myself on all fours, wondering what the hell was going on. A voice came dimly from far away :

'He'll tell us bugger-all if you kill 'im.'

Then there was the feel of leather under my chin, my neck was jerked painfully and I flipped onto my back. There were two of them looking down at me. Pig-face's pal was a short barrel of a man of about forty, wearing what was once the Englishman's national costume: – sports coat and flannels, very worked-in, and a flat cap, dead square on his head. The cap bent the tops of his ears over.

This one carried a rubber cosh in his right hand, and I realized what had laid me low.

Bone and muscle behind my right ear began to throb painfully, I blinked up at the skinhead who was swinging a stirrup-iron slowly back and forth by its leather. He drew back one of his heavy-booted feet and looked at my ribs. I raised a feeble hand. If I was going to get kicked, I'd like to know the reason.

'Hang on, hang on' I wheezed, — 'why don't you just *ask*?'

Pig face jerked his wrist slightly and the heavy nickel-plated iron hit me smartly between the eyes. I had the feeling that when my head stopped swimming, I was going to be very angry.

'Don't get bleeding funny!' he said. His voice had a strong Estuary flavour. 'Just tell us where you've hidden it and your troubles will be over, - right? '

'Hidden what, for God's sake!?'

'The gold buster, the gold.' He rattled the stirrup-iron on my forehead in rhythm with his words. This was beyond belief; this was pure 'B' picture.

His wrist jerked again but this time I grabbed the leather and pulled hard, managing at the same time to get halfway to my feet.

He loosed the leather and, as I sprawled again, came in with a swinging kick which caught me on the backside. Then flat-cap joined in: plying his cosh with a will.

I curled myself into a tight ball, covered my head as best I could with my arms and wished I were off somewhere laying crab-pots.

Quite suddenly the pounding and the kicking stopped. I counted to ten and opened my eyes. I was alone.

Fresh noises came from outside – a lorry engine and a woman's voice shouting directions. I staggered to my feet and limped to the door.

Mrs. Amanda Wainwright left off directing the horse-box driver and stared at me in puzzlement. I gestured weakly towards Pig-face and Flat-cap who were getting hurriedly into the cab of the pick-up.

'Stop them,' I yelled foolishly.

Mrs. Wainwright ducked her head to look into the side window of the pickup and waved her hand at Pig-face

'I say there: you're wanted,' she cooed.

The pick-up shot away in a tight turn and the lady executed a smart hop, skip and jump to avoid it.

'Well of all the ill-mannered...!' She turned on me then, 'I don't think much of your *friends*-!'

Jimmy McLaine jumped down from the horse-box and walked towards the kitchen door. Then, strangely, there were two of him. My knees buckled and I was down again, with Amanda Wainwright kneeling beside me, holding my head to her generous bosom.

Jimmy came running out of the kitchen, shouting something about burglars and suddenly I was sitting on Jenny's settee, spluttering as neat brandy burned my throat. I made myself think; found Jimmy's face and focused on it.

'Where is your mother?'

'She's not home. She hasn't come back yet. Just look at this mess ---'

I tried but things started to skip away again. Fresh voices— uniforms -- and I was being lifted on a stretcher. A gentle swaying, and a low engine-note which gradually increased as the swaying motion smoothed out. Ages later came the sound and feel of rubber wheels on tiles, and a slight jar as we pushed through swing doors, followed by the draught of their closing. Then silence.

I lay blinking at too-bright fluorescents, and suddenly she was back: my "angel of mercy" in starched white: the nurse who had picked the glass from my face. There was professional concern in her brown eyes and in her voice.

'What on earth happened this time?'

I licked my lips and tried on a brave smile. My voice sounds croaky and slurred.

'I just had to see you again,' I said, 'and there seemed no other way!'

Chapter 3

I was helped to sit up, given me something fizzy to drink and told I had visitors.

As they stepped round the screen the nurse announced them as would a parlour maid, and withdrew.

Detective Sergeant Oldacre was in his mid forties, slow moving, tall and bulky in a dark grey suit. His expression suggested that he'd seen it all before and didn't think much of it.

His colleague on the other hand, detective Constable Copeland, (zipper jacket, jogging pants and trainers) had the look of an eager Jack Russell terrier.

Oldacre glanced around and pulled a face. 'I hate hospitals,' he said, '...It's the smell.'

His voice was as north-country as his name.

He took the one available chair, pulled a pipe from his pocket looked into the bowl and put it away again reluctantly.

'Now sir,' He fixed me with his world-weary eyes, 'what can you tell me about the men who attacked you?'

I had felt fine until then, at least relatively so. But at his question a dull aching throb started behind my right ear.

'One was Pig-face-- you know about him.'

The terrier had laid the brief case he was carrying on the foot of my cot and his button-bright eyes quizzed me over his notebook.

'He was the one who wrecked Dave Gregory's flat,' I prompted, 'Your Constable Saunders took the particulars.'

DC Copeland nodded and wrote.

As I was describing my other attacker Oldacre leaned over for the brief case and extracted from it a slim file, which he handed to me.

'Would you have a look through this lot sir? And see if there is anyone you know?'

There were a dozen shiny photographs in the file and Pig-face was the third one down. I stabbed at it with a finger.

'That's him.'

The sergeant took it from me and read the details aloud: 'Bennett, Percival, aged twenty seven, no fixed address. Anyone else?'

I flipped through the rest without finding Flat-cap.

As I passed the photos back, I shook my head: That was a mistake and I screwed my eyes up in agony.

'Now sir, the next question is "Why?"

I opened my eyes slowly and waited until the throbbing reduced to an acceptable level.

'No idea!' I kept my voice to a whisper in self preservation and he noticed my pain

'Am I tiring you sir?... This won't take very long.'

I almost shook my head again but remembered just in time.

'No – my head hurts a bit that's all.'

'And you cannot think of a single thing that you or David Gregory might have that these men want?'

'Not a thing.'

'Mr. Peterson, were you or Gregory engaged in smuggling?'

I looked from one to the other. They both stared at me fixedly. I thought guiltily of the odd cartons of Gauloise and bottles of Martel.

'No ---' It sounded weak and unconvincing.

'Drugs, for instance?'

'Certainly not !' Firmer this time.

'People?'

'No' There was an itch between my eyes and as I lifted a hand to scratch I heard Bennett's voice, as he'd cracked me with the stirrup-iron.

'*Gold,*' I blurted,

'Gold?' Copeland's nose and ears twitched. 'You've been smuggling *gold* Sir?'

'No,' I said impatiently, '*Gold* is what they were after.'

'What gold would that be sir?" This was Oldacre.

'I don't know what gold. There isn't any as far as I know. Bennett just said: "Tell us where you've hidden the gold", and hit me between the eyes.'

'That's all?'

'Well no, he kicked me as well, and then there was the other fellow's cosh.'

'I mean was that all he said?'

'Yes.'

'So you don't know what form this gold is in? Jewelry or coin or what?'

'No idea at all.'

Another picture came back to mind now: Jimmy McLaine's face and the mess in the farmhouse living room. I sat up quickly and looked at the wall on either side of the bed. On one side there was a telephone socket, I pointed to it and asked Oldacre if he'd fetch me a handset. from reception.

'I'd better ring Mrs McLaine,' I said ,'She must be feeling pretty rotten.'

Oldacre and his constable exchanged looks. Then the Sergeant said quietly: 'I'm afraid that won't be possible sir. At least not at present.'

A sudden cold lump in my chest grew and spread. I waited, without breathing, for him to go on.

'We don't seem to be able to find Mrs McLaine sir.'

CHAPTER 4

To the nurses' disapproval, I discharged myself from the hospital half an hour after the two detectives left.

In the taxi I tried to piece together what had happened. I made my mind go back for another look at it. There was lead in my stomach at the thought of Jenny being missing. The police had been looking for her Landrover all day, in and around Plymouth. All the public car parks had been checked, also her bank, solicitor and accountant.

She had visited none of these.

It was almost dark as I paid the taxi off at the quay side. I watched its stoplights brighten and fade as it turned out through the rusted iron gates that had been jammed open since the war ended.

Oldacre had told me that Jenny had not been seen at the farm since I'd watched her drive away the previous morning, and that son Jimmy was frantic with worry. They'd also told me that the raiders had ripped out a large section of telephone wire at Highfields, so that it was no use trying to ring him. There was a police radio car at the farm and it would stay there until the G.P,O. fixed the wire.

Before I'd taken the first iron rung down to the Pelican's deck, a pair of headlights chased shadows in a wide arc across buildings and moored boats, coming to rest, shining straight into my eyes. I put up a hand to shield them and they dipped immediately. My heart had begun to beat faster. I was tensed up, poised either for flight or fight, but as my vision recovered, I saw that the car was a blue and white.

PC Saunders unfolded from the driver's seat and came towards me.

'There's been a development sir. Mrs. McLaine's vehicle has been found.'

'Where?,' I shouted, 'where was it found?'

'On the farm. Her son found it hidden in a small overgrown quarry. But there's no sign of his mother'

My mind churned, recoiled, and tried to escape the conclusion that harm had befallen Jenny. I felt sick at the thought that they may have hurt her... tried to make her tell what she did not know.

She must have come back while they were searching the farm.

But what had they done with her? Bundled her up and put her out of the way? Was she now trussed up in one of the out-buildings? Unconscious may be? Or out on the moors?... Dead?

‘I’m going out there.' I turned away from the quay- side and walked towards the store.

‘Message from Sergeant Prentiss sir: he says there’s enough people out there already, and come morning, we”ll have soldiers if necessary. He also says you should have stayed in hospital and you’ll just be a nuisance if you start collapsing all over the place.’

‘Does he now?’ I fumbled in my pocket for keys and put my hand on the padlock. I could feel that it was unlocked, just hooked in place. I swung the doors wide, flicked on the switch and the fluorescent tube blinked itself awake.

'Saunders had followed me over and now stood in the doorway, looking at Dave Gregory’s battered Bedford. The fact that its back doors and driver’s door were wide open meant nothing to him, but to me, coupled with the loose padlock, it meant that an intruder had been here too, I took a quick look around without comment.

'The place looked no different to any other untidy quayside store but I could see that things had been moved: Coils of rope, crab-pots, timber and spare sails – none of these things were how I’d left them.

'I opened my mouth to swear but closed it again. If I told the Saunders, there would be delay and I had to get out to Highfields.

‘Do you propose to drive this vehicle Mr. Peterson?’ Saunders asked.

‘Yes. My bike's still at the farm.’

He was squatting now. ‘This back tyre looks near the limit. Has the vehicle got a current em oh tee?’

I climbed into the cab. The key was in the ignition and I gave it a twist. The engine spun without firing and then the starter motor faded. I cursed and thumped the steering wheel. Saunders was looking at me, waiting for an answer.

‘What – oh, yes – it's somewhere.’ I got angry ‘Look – those thugs have got Mrs McLaine and you’re asking about bloody forms. For Christ’s sake, help me start this heap.’

Outside, the car radio spoke in an almost human voice. Saunders went outside to attend to it.

I had another fruitless try with the starter then looked around for the starting handle. It was not in the van so I jumped down to look under the workbench. There is a big ammunition box under there, which serves as tool chest, and this was lying open on it side, the tools scattered. There were quite a lot of them and I scraped my foot impatiently through the heap. No starting handle, but there was something else, something that at first did not register:

The floor of the store is of cobblestones, and one of the cobbles under the bench had an unusual bright streak running across it where something—the tool box probably—had scratched the surface. I knelt, picked a file from the heap of tools and ran it over the stone. More bright streaks appeared and I felt excitement well up inside me. There was no doubt in my mind that I was looking at gold.

I was about to yell for Saunders, when it dawned on me that if Bennett and Flat-Cap had Jenny, then I could bargain with them.

I kicked a sack over the tell-tale brightness just as the constable came back through the door.

'I've got to shove off,' he said, 'Bit of a punch-up at the Crown and Cushion. If I were you, I'd forget about trying to start the van and get some sleep. Get somebody to drive you out there in the morning.'

'Yeah, you're probably right.' I let my shoulders sag and he looked at me suspiciously, doubtless thinking I'd given in a bit too easily.

The radio crackled again and he went back to it. Thirty seconds later he was driving quickly out through the iron gates.

I untangled the frayed wires of the battery charger hanging on the wall, fixed the crocodiles to the van's battery lugs and switched on. The needle stayed infuriatingly inert until I'd thumped the instrument twice. When it came to life I clicked to rapid-charge and said a quick thank-you prayer.

I crossed towards Pelican, knowing with depressing certainty I was going to find chaos aboard, and switched on the lights.

Freshly splintered wood showed stark around the cabin door lock. The inside of the cabin looked like the morning after a teenagers' party.

From the debris I pulled a thick pullover and a woolen cap and put them on. With a last disgusted look around I turned to go.

That's when I saw the note pinned to the inside of the cabin door.

It said simply, in block capitals: 'FOUR EAGLES'.

The words seemed meaningless... But then: they must mean something or why were they there?

Ripping the paper from the door and ramming it into my pocket, I went back to the store without bothering to look into the hold or the chain locker.

If I *had* checked, I could have saved Sam Wilkins a good deal of pain and distress.

With hammer and chisel, I attacked what was probably the most valuable cobblestone in the world, and in a few minutes had levered it clear of the ground. It was painted a muddy-grey colour, but now more bright streaks showed through, caused by the tools I had used. It was the size and shape of what I'd always imagined an ingot of gold should be, and, though I knew gold to be heavy, its weight for size surprised me.

I carried it round to the back of the van and dropped it inside, pushing it well forward and covering it with a sack before closing the rear doors.

The engine spun freely when I tried it again, spun and coughed once, – twice. I pulled out the choke and tried again. It fired this time, caught, ran unevenly, then smoothed out. I pressed the accelerator gently, set the choke halfway, disconnected the charger and scrambled back behind wheel.

Flicking the gear lever into reverse, I glanced in the rear view mirror.

Standing just inside the store doorway, hands deep in duffel coat pockets, was a thin man, bare headed and with an untidy fringe of sandy hair round a bald pate. I leaned out of the sliding door and looked back at him, annoyed.

'Out of the way, Stoker, I'm in a hurry.'

He had a cigarette in his mouth and he removed the ash by blowing along it, then he was walking towards me, sliding his feet along almost as if he were skating. I started to reverse the van past him. He took one hand from his pocket and, grabbing my arm, walked beside the moving vehicle, speaking round his cigarette.

'Hang on a minute.' he said.

I depressed the clutch, annoyed. 'What do you want Stoker? I told you I'm in a hurry.' He half turned his head and spat out the dog-end, then nodded to the interior of the van, over my shoulder.

'I know where there's more of that,' he said. 'Lots more!'

I grabbed a fist full of duffel coat and jerked Stoker towards me, lifting him up on his toes. 'What do you know about it? What do you know about this whole bloody business?'

I scrambled from the van, and pushed him back, hard against the vise on the corner of the workbench.

There wasn't much of him to push. It was like handling a sack of dry sticks, and fear came into his eyes when he saw what was in mine. He clawed at my wrist, and flinched his head aside from my raised fist, then surprised me with a hard kick on the shin. I stamped on his foot and swung him around, finally pushing him away so that he sprawled over the toolbox and fell in a heap. I picked up a chain-wrench from the floor and held it threateningly in front of his face..

'Where is Mrs McLaine?'

He sat up slowly, anger replacing fright on his face. He started coughing. When he stopped, his voice was angry too.

'There was no call for that.'

'Where is Mrs McLaine?' I repeated.'Where is she?'

'How the hell would I know?' he yelled,'I don't even *know* any Mrs-bloody-McLaine.'

I crashed the wrench down on the workbench and felt rage draining away.

Stoker got painfully to his feet and leaned on the bench, coughing again, holding his chest, eyes closed.

I was feeling guilty at treating him so roughly. 'So what do you know about... what's in the van?'

He grinned weakly 'Like I said – I know where there's lots more. And I know there's some poisonous bastards after it.'

'Who? –Bennett ?'

He nodded, 'Bennett and Joe Harris and another bloke.'

'Joe Harris? Does he wear a flat cap?'

Stoker said he did. The inside of the store was thickening with exhaust fumes. I got back in the van and drove it outside. Stoker followed me. I called to him to switch the light off and get in the van.

He swung the double doors together and got in beside me. 'Where are we going? 'ave you got a fag?'

'No I haven't.'

'Where are we going?'

We were outside the iron gates now. I slammed down the foot brake and Stoker lurched forward, hands grabbing the dashboard.

'You tell me!' I said, 'You seem to know what's going on. Tell me where I can find Bennett and Harris.'

Stoker shrugged. 'They've got a boat they're living on but they keep moving it around.'

'What's the name of the boat?'

'Hasn't got a name. Or if it has, it's been painted over.'

I wondered if they'd got Jenny aboard their boat and my stomach churned afresh at the thought.

It was no use looking for an unnamed boat in the dark. I let in the clutch.

'So where are we going?' Stoker said again.

'Up on the moors — To Mrs.McLaine's farm; the police say she's missing.'

There was no more talk until we'd cleared the dock area, then I jerked my thumb towards my cargo.

'If you know all about that, and about Bennett and Harris, how come they keep knocking *me* about?'

He peered at me in the light of the passing sodium lamps.

'They do that to your face?'

'Some of it... I suppose Dave Gregory planted that gold brick under the bench?' I glanced at him and saw him nod.

'Dave was a good bloke,' he said, 'He was going to help me get the rest of it. … And what are we going to this farm for? Do you think she's around there?'

'I don't know, I can't think where else to start looking.'

I gave him a brief run down on events and told him I'd use the ingot to bargain for Jenny if I had the chance.

'She must be some bird,' he said.

We were out in the country now, approaching the turn-off.

'You say there's more of that stuff?'I said.

'More than you ever dreamed of,'

'Where?'

'Under the sea mate. Davy Jones's Locker.'

'Sunken treasure?' I scoffed. 'Do me a favour!'

He laughed, a rasping sound, and started coughing again. 'Would you have believed your store was paved with gold?'

He had a good point. Then another thought occurred. 'How do I know it's genuine?' I asked.

'Those hard cases wouldn't go to all that trouble for a lump of painted lead.'

'All right, how do they know? And how do you know?'

'I don't know about them,' he said, and his voice became bitter. 'But I've known for forty years. Forty long years!'

'Forty years ago', I thought, 'War time!' Something scratched the surface of my memory. A brief news item either heard or read. Then I had it.

'Is this anything to do with that gold shipment to the Russians?' I asked.' The one that went down in the North-Sea? The navy are diving on that wreck aren't they?'

He shook his head. 'It's not that bloody big, And not the north sea neither.' He started rummaging in the dashboard locker. 'Are you sure you haven't got a fag?'

He clammed up then and, despite my prompting, would say no more about the gold.

When we got to the moor gate, I could see that lights burned at Highfields. For a self-indulgent minute, while Stoker opened and closed the gate and I drove through, I let myself believe that all was well and that Jenny herself would open the kitchen door when we drove into the yard.

The rough track set the jumbled contents of the vehicle sliding round behind us with a loud racket. The van's headlights threw back the green and yellow of the gorse, and ruby flashes from the eyes of disturbed sheep as we nosed down into the water-splash and up the other side.

When we turned into the yard, Jimmy's border-collie came out of the kitchen door like a noisy, black and white projectile.

I slid my door back, and his threatening barking changed to a 'woofle' of welcome, Jimmy followed the dog out, pausing in the doorway as he recognised the van. Then the bright beam of a hand lamp came in through the passenger window, blinding me as I turned that way. That door was slid back from outside and the lamp was shone briefly into the back of the van. I had a quick mental image of the light setting on a bright new made block of gold and a voice saying 'Ello, ello!'

Instead, the light was extinguished and the voice said 'Hallo Stoker, and what can we do for you?'

'I'm with him,' said Stoker, pointing to me with his thumb.

'Have you found Mrs.McLaine yet?' I tried to keep my voice even.

In the reflected headlamp glow, the young policeman's eyes moved from Stoker to me. '

'And you are, sir?'

'Peterson... Michael Peterson.'

'Ah yes, Mr. Peterson, we heard you were on your way. There is no news yet sir.'

There were other vehicles lurking in dark corners of the yard, a police personnel carrier, a 'jam-sandwich' and two cars without marking. I switched off my lights and went into the kitchen. Stoker stayed put.

The kitchen was full of people, mostly men and mostly in uniform. I suppose I should have felt satisfaction that so many were here; reassured that things were being done to find Jenny, but at that moment all I felt was resentment. This was Jenny's kitchen and I was a privileged visitor, but not these strangers, lolling against her dresser and sitting tipped back on her kitchen chairs. I resented the young WPC., who was opening a fresh packet of tea from the kitchen cabinet.

Jenny should have been there, doing the homely things.

I sought Jimmy's eyes, saw in them an echo of my displeasure, but knowing that his was directed at me.

It always had been. He'd been the man of the house for almost half his life time, and he'd seen in me a threat to his status.

Now he probably saw me as being the cause of his mother's disappearance.

'She'll be okay, Jimmy.' I said.

He recognised the futility of the words and lowered his eyes, frowning in irritation. The collie leaned against his leg and rolled his head back to look up at him, shooting out a quick red tongue and giving a little whimper.

Two more men came in from the living room. Det. Sergeant

Oldshaw was one of them. At sight of the other, the uniformed constables, sat straighter, their faces stiffening into alertness.

Oldshaw brought the other man over.

Even in a kitchen full of large policemen, he was a very imposing figure, standing about six feet four inches and looking half that wide. His face was square, craggy and topped by a thatch of grey hair.

'This is Detective Chief Inspector Cawardine – Mr. Peters.'

Cawardine extended a hand like a builder's shovel and shook mine. He glanced at the papers he held and at the cluttered kitchen table, then suggested that I follow him back into the other room. As he turned his back, there was a collective exhalation of breath and previous postures were readopted.

The living room had been tidied up after a fashion but I could sense, almost smell, the presence of Bennett and Harris. The lump behind my right ear began to pulse. I asked the chief inspector why there were so many people in the kitchen, when Jenny had not yet been found.

Oldshaw interrupted from a window seat. 'That lot have come in for a break. At the moment there are some twenty men out looking – and three dogs.'

Through the window that overlooked the open moor I could see distant pinpricks of moving light . Cawardine sat on the long comfortable settee and arranged his papers on the coffee table.

'Bennett is living on a boat,' I said, 'It's got no name and he keeps moving it about. He could have taken Mrs. McLaine there.'

Without looking up Cawardine shook his head. 'We know about the boat,' he said, 'there is no one aboard. It's being watched, and if Bennett goes back to it we'll have him.'

I was surprised. 'How did you find out about that?'

He allowed himself a satisfied smile. 'One of my sergeants used to be with the Met. He was out sailing one Sunday, when he recognised Bennett in a passing boat. Bennett being an old customer from the 'smoke', my sergeant decided to keep tabs on him. He guessed Bennett would not just be down here on holiday. Now it seems he was right.'

He sat back and ran his great banana like fingers through his hair. 'Now, Mr. Peterson, 'how do *you* know about the boat?'

'From Stoker Figgin.'

'Ah yes, the Stoker,' he waved a hand at a chair, 'Please sit down, Mr. Peterson, I'm getting a crick in my neck looking up at you.'

I walked towards the hall door. 'I'm going out to help with the search.'

'Mr. Peterson, I will not have you out there getting in the way. If you try to leave this room, I will have you restrained. Do I make myself clear?'

He was now very much the senior police officer. I turned back reluctantly.

He went on as before: 'Now, where does Stoker Figgin come in? What's his connection with Bennett?'

This was a tricky one. The wrong answer could lead to the ingot in the back of the van and I couldn't imagine the authorities exchanging that for Jenny.

I shrugged. 'I don't know... I told Stoker I'd been attacked by a man called Bennett and Stoker said he knew him and that he and Harris lived on a boat but he didn't know where.'

'Why did you bring Stoker out here with you?'

'He just happened along as I was leaving. I know he sometimes worked on Dave Gregory's boat. I thought I might find out more from him.'

'And have you?'

I shook my head carefully. Sunken treasure was Stoker's problem. I just wanted to get Jenny back and I was beginning to regret coming out here.

Cawardine was right when he said there were enough people searching. And I reasoned, a little late perhaps, that if she were a hostage they'd have taken her away in the pick-up.

I took a deep breath.'Is that all? I'd like to get back to the Pelican.'

He shuffled his papers. 'Ah yes, you live aboard her I believe. You have no other address?'

'No — look, I came here on impulse. But now I see I can do no good. I've got quite a lot of clearing up to do on board. Bennett paid the Pelican a visit while I was in hospital.'

He raised his eyebrows at this. ' You didn't mention it.'

'I'm mentioning it now.' My head was throbbing again and I was getting irritable.'

‘Quite so.’ He consulted his notes again drawing his brows together. ‘I’m not happy about this Mr. Peterson, not happy at all.’

‘Happy!’ I exploded. 'Who the hell cares whether you’re bloody happy or not?... Mrs. McLaine’s missing, I keep getting hammered, and houses keep getting wrecked, and you’re moaning about not being *happy*!'

I was shouting at the top of my voice, Oldshaw got up from the window seat and took a couple of nervous paces forward. The kitchen door opened and a moon face appeared, stamped with a question mark. The pain behind my ear was almost intolerable. I groped for a dining chair and sat, half-on half-off it, not seeing, not hearing.

Somebody was urging me to ‘take these’. I felt something pressed to my lips and licked it in, then crunched up the taste of aspirin, ‘and another,’ the voice said, 'now drink’. I drank and opened my eyes.

‘You should have stayed in hospital,' Oldshaw said.

I got up very gingerly. My voice came in a croaking whisper ‘I’m going back to my boat.’

‘You can’t drive in that state,’ Cawardine said

‘Stoker can drive.’

‘I shall need to see you again Mr. Peterson.’

I didn’t try to nod or speak, just concentrated on putting one foot in front of the other.

In the hall, I was surprised to see Stoker sitting on the stairs. He’d scrounged a cigarette from somewhere and as he looked up an inch of ash spilled down his duffel coat.

DC Copeland was there too, seated at the telephone table. He put away his notebook and stood up, looking beyond my shoulder, ears pricked attentively.

Inspector Cawardine spoke from behind me. ‘Have you finished with Mr. Figgin, Constable?’

‘Yes sir. All done.’

‘Have you got a driving license Figgin?’

Stoker said. ‘Er – yes, I got a license.’

‘You don’t seem too sure.’

‘Well I ain’t exactly got it on me, but I got one.’

‘Very well, you’d better drive Mr. Peterson home.’

Neither of us spoke until the moor gate was behind us. Stoker took matches and cigarettes from his pocket and lit up. 'Want one ?' He offered the packet.

'No thanks. Did Copeland give you those?'

He let in the clutch. His gap-toothed grin was gleeful in the reflected light.

'Not exactly,' he said.

When we got back to the Pelican, it must have been past midnight. Sweeping an armful of belongings from my bunk and crawling into my blankets, I couldn't remember feeling worse in my life.

Stoker said he'd like to sleep in the hold. He didn't want to go back to his lodgings because Bennett knew where he lived. I told him he could go to hell if he liked.

He said he'd prefer the hold, and left the cabin.

Two minutes later he was back. He stood by my bunk coughing. I waited for him to finish.

'What's up now, Stoker?'

'There's a body in the hold.' he said.

CHAPTER 5

Poor Sam Wilkins had been alive when the ambulance had taken him away.

Not "and kicking" by any means, but you couldn't expect much when he'd been lying bound and gagged in my sail locker for for the best part of two days. Also, according to one of the paramedics, he probably had a hairline fracture of the skull.

I'd run out of sugar, and the milk had been spilled during Bennett's rampage, so it was a lousy cup of tea.

Stoker passed his opinion of it and I told him, he could go round to the Cozy Cave Cafe if he didn't like it. He said theirs was usually worse.

I sat on the edge of my bunk trying not to think of Jenny. My head was still full of the tangled sounds and visions of the night hours: Of sirens, –flashing blue lights, –blue uniforms.

Morosely, I pondered the 'ifs' of the situation: If I hadn't asked Sam to keep an eye on the boat... If I'd looked in the hold when I'd found the cabin ransacked... If Sam's wife hadn't gone to her sister's for a few days...

Stoker mouthed some profanity which brought me back to the present. I realised that the gnawing inside me was partly due to hunger and I tried to remember when I'd eaten last.

Unless I'd had something at the hospital without remembering it, my last meal had been breakfast with Jenny two days before. My stomach had every right to complain.

I found a tin of bacon and one of tomatoes and mixed them over the Calor flame. There was half a loaf which had gone a bit green but with the outside crust cut away, it was just edible.

I also found a tin of condensed milk, which cheered the tea up no-end.

When he'd finished his share, Stoker sucked his teeth.

'Ave you got a fag ?'

'No – I keep telling you. – Look, forget the cigarettes. We've got to get things sorted out.'

'Such as what?'

'Such as what to do when Bennett and Co get in touch again. I doubt if they'll come calling in the open, but – well, the way I see it: they think Dave Gregory and I were sitting on a golden egg. And because they couldn't find it they've taken Mrs McLaine in order to do a deal. Okay so far?... Right then, when they do get in touch we'll do a swap.'

'There's just one thing though,' Stoker said hesitantly.

'Oh? What's that?'

'Well –it's my gold, innit?'

'That's no problem. When Mrs McLaine is safe you can go to the police and tell them that Bennett has pinched your gold brick.

'Come off it Mr. Peterson! You know I ain't gonna do that. There'd be too many questions. Look... are you interested in more of the same or not?'

'At the moment all I'm interested in is getting Mr s McLaine back, safe and sound. When that's done though...'

I thought of Jenny's constant struggle to make her few moorland acres pay their way and the ups and downs of my own existence.

'How about telling me more about it?' I said.

'Are you sure you ain't got a—? Okay , okay. The rest of the loot is no more than five fathoms down at low springs. Dave Gregory was helping me salvage it. He was diving off the Garland.'

‘Where?’

Stoker’s face took on a cunning look. ‘I'll tell you that when we've come to some arrangement.’

'And what about disposal ?’

‘Dave was in touch with some people.’

‘Who did the gold belong to originally?’

‘The gov'ment.’

‘So why not recover it openly and claim salvage?

Stoker got up and started fumbling in his duffel coat pockets. His face brightened when he found a half-smoked Gitane. He lit up before he answered.

‘Two reasons,’ he exhaled half a cabin-full of smoke, ‘First, it’s in French waters and second,' He paused, 'I’m a deserter from the Royal Navy.’

‘Well,’ I said, ‘I won’t shop you. Go on.’

‘It was in nineteen forty-one, – early autumn. I was a “killick” on M.T.B.’s. We had this special job lined up –supposed to be landing guns and ammo on the French coast –for the resistance fighters.

'I thought there was some thing fishy about that cargo from the beginning. Well, you don’t usually get a full captain handling boxes of ammo himself, do you? And squeezing below decks in an M.T.B. and helping to stow it?'

'Anyway, as soon as I had a chance I took a closer look, –on the quiet of course, – I prised opened one of the ammo boxes, and under a layer of loose rounds was a gold brick. The next two I opened was just the same.

'So I thought: “who’s a lucky sailor then?” Except I couldn’t do nothing about it, seeing as we was well out into the Channel by this time. I couldn’t get the bigger boxes open without being caught at it, but I can tell you they was too 'eavy to contain just guns.’

There was the sudden rattle of heavy rain topsides. Stoker paused to take a last drag on his Gitane and looked regretfully at the stub. Then his brow furrowed as he squinted up through the rain-spotted cabin sidelights.

‘I’ll have to go and get meself some fags. You couldn’t lend me a couple of quid I suppose?’ He nodded up at the van, ' –till pay day?’

‘Finish the story first,’ I told him.

But he was still looking up at the Bedford. ‘You sure we ought to leave it just lying in the back?'

'Safest place I can think of,' I said, 'It's just junk among junk. in there. Anyway, I threw a sack over it.'

His voice rose to a squeak. 'A sack? What the 'ell is the use of that?'

'Relax, the doors are locked.'

He looked really worried now. 'Any villain worth 'is salt would have it open in a flash. They carry bunches of *keys*. What about if somebody 'ad just driven it off during the night?'

I reached up to the shelf over my head and took down the distributor head, complete with plug leads, and put it on the table between us. It sat there like a complacent spider.

'They'd have had a job,' I said, 'now, please, get on with it.'

'Oh yeh,--well –you should have said. –Where was I?'

'In mid-channel, –you'd just found the loot.'

'Well anyway, guns or gold, we'd still got to land the cargo on the French coast, right? There was plenty of heavy cloud and not much of a sea. –Ideal conditions for our job. Then the cloud began to break up; the moon shone through and we were spotted by 'E' boats, – three of 'em. They chased us all over the flaming 'oggin, banging away at us all the time; -- and us twistin' and twirlin' —,' Stoker's face had become excited; his eyes gleamed as his weaving hands described the vessels' movements. 'We loosed off a coupla tin-fish but they dodged ,em'

'And what were *you* doing?' I was interested, 'What was your job?'

'Me – oh I was on the twin Lewis guns mounted on a swivel.' His gnarled hands grasped imaginary machine-gun handles and he aimed through a side-light at the van. 'Tat-tat-tat-tat----'.

He stopped speaking, still squinting at the Bedford, then got to his feet.

'I'll nip out and 'ave a look through the back window,' he said, '… just to satisfy myself.'

'Sit down,' I said, 'if Bennett or Harris have their eye on us they'll cotton-on to what's in there.'

He sat down again, reluctantly.

Another thought occurred to me. 'If you know all about this gold business how is it that *you* don't get thumped?'

Stoker looked uncomfortable, then gave a sly grin, ' 'Cos I keep on the 'op, don't I?'

'Come off it, there's more to it than that.'

He chewed his lip. Then raised his hands defensively, palms outwards. 'Look – don't get me wrong but, well, —they think I'm on their side.'

'They *what*?'

'They think I'm on the inside working for them. They think Dave and you was working together and I was only the paid help. They think I don't know nothing but they're expecting me to find out.'

'What did they offer you?'

'They offered not to knock me about, and five hundred quid on top.'

'Generous... What happened with the E-boats?'

'Yeah well, pretty soon we started listing and going round in circles.' He gave a dry chuckle, 'We nearly rammed one of them by accident and that didn't 'alf confuse 'em. Two of the stupid bastards started firing at each other and by the time they'd sorted themselves out, we'd managed to scarper.

'We sorted out the steering problem but some of their cannon shots had punctured us below the water line and we were going down.'

He paused again as if to gather his thoughts.

'We was nearer France than England so the skipper put us back on course for our rendezvous and we all started baling and pumping, fit to bust. After about an hour, it looked like we might make it.

'We were right up to the coastline, and I was on watch on fore-deck. Then we hit something, -- a half- submerged rock most likely,–and I was pitched into the water. By the time I got my breath back to shout, the current had got me, and I was too far away to get back. I could hear them revving, the engines for a long time after, trying to get free of that rock.'

The Pelican had risen on the tide till her cabin was above the edge of the rain-swept dock, and I had a clear view of the gates. When contact was made, as I knew it must be, that was the way it would come.

'Are you listening or not?' Stoker sounded offended, 'Cos if you're not —!'

'Sorry, yes I'm listening –go on. –No, don't. Somebody's coming.'

Stoker leaned over and wiped condensation from the glass, 'Paper boy,' he said with relief.

The boy jerked the front wheel of his bike up off the cobbles a couple of times, attempting a 'wheelie', stopped by Sam Wilkins' store and shoved a paper through the letter box, then came over to the Pelican.

I went up into the cuddy, slid the door back and stuck my head out into the rain. 'Who are you looking for son?'

'Are you Mr. Peterson?'

'That's right.'

He took an envelope from his pocket and leaned over, still astride his bike. I took it from him.

'Man gave me two quid to bring it,' he said.

I felt in my pocket and handed over a fistful of loose change.

'Cor... thanks mister!'

The message read: 'Go to the call box outside the gate and wait for the phone to ring'.

'Was he a skinhead—the bloke who gave you this?'

The boy shook his head 'Old bloke,' he said, 'a bit fat.'

It sounded like 'Cosh' Harris'.

Stoker's head emerged into the cuddy. Passing him the note I stepped ashore and jogged across the cobbles, head down against the rain, out into the road. The call box is twenty yards beyond the gate and the phone started ringing as I pulled open its door. One or two panes of glass were still intact and afforded a little shelter as I picked up the receiver. The voice was not that of Bennett or Harris, but of someone more cultured. It also had a slight foreign inflection.

'Mr. Peterson?'

'Yes.'

'You know what we want Mr. Peterson and we know what you want. So if you will just follow my instructions you can have the lady back safe and sound. Are you listening carefully?'

'I'm listening,' I said, but at that point I stopped listening.

Instead, I was watching Jenny McLaine walking along the opposite pavement and my mind was doing a sideways flip. Then the voice in my ear became louder, urgent. Are you still there Mr.

Peterson?'

I shouted 'Get knotted!' down the phone and crashed it back on it's cradle. Then I was running across the road calling Jenny's name. She looked my way and came to meet me. We met in the middle of the rain-swept carriage way, and I picked her off her feet with a yell and swung her round and round.

A van swerved by, splashing us, the driver shouting something unprintable. Then we just clung tight for a spell, her face pressed close into my chest, while I sucked in deep the feeling of having her back.

'How on earth did you get away?' I could scarcely ask the question, so great was my elation.

'Dead easy,' she said with wide grin, 'I just hit him with my handbag.' She held the bag up by the handle. It was of shiny plastic and an offensive shade of mauve.

'That's never yours!'

'How can you tell? —No, you're right. Actually, I pinched it.'

She raised her face, half closing her eyes against the raindrops. 'If you'll take me somewhere dry, I'll tell you about it.' She prodded my chest with a forefinger. 'And you can tell me how I got involved. Come on, the boat!'

After a few step she hung back and pointed back at the phone box. 'I must ring Jimmy. He'll be *frantic.*'

I hesitated. I suddenly realised that the phone box must be watched. Probably from one of the rented offices above the shops and warehouses that lined both sides of the dingy street.

Somebody had had to watch me approach the kiosk, in order to ring at the right moment.

More people were moving about now, on their way to work. There was more traffic. A lorry turned into the narrow lane leading down to the fish quay.

'We'll go to Violet's,' I said, 'she's got a pay phone.'

The Cosy Cave Cafe was hot, steamy and nearly full. I pushed Jenny through the curtain at the back to where the wall phone hung and went over to the counter.

'Morning Vi – two teas please.'

Violet, young-old, hair and eyes dark like a gipsy's, filled two thick, patterned mugs, I put my hand in my pocket to pay and remembered that the paper boy had had the lot. ‘Can I owe you Vi?’ I asked.

‘Trade that bad my lover?’

‘Yeah,’ I said,’ I’m waiting for my ship to come in.’

I carried the tea over to a corner table. When Jenny joined me,

I waited until she’d taken a deep drink, then clasped her hands. ‘Now tell me what happened.’

'A policewoman answered the phone.' Jenny sounded indignant at the idea of a strange woman answering her phone.

'She let me speak to Jimmy though. Poor lamb. He sounded terribly manful but I think he was crying a bit.’

‘Tell me what happened when they took you away.’

She frowned. 'That wasn’t funny. I was on my way home. They were obviously coming from Highfields and stopped me as I came through the ford... They were polite at first, -- said they were looking for you, and asked what time you'd be back. I said I didn’t know, but if they’d leave a message, I’d see that you got it. Then they started to get nosey. Did you come often? Did you stay the night – and had you left anything with me?.'

'I told them to go then but they turned nasty. They dragged me out and bundled me into the front of their pick-up then drove it into the old quarry. I was flaming angry, I screamed at them at the top of my voice, and leaned on the horn button.

‘That made them mad, so they gagged me, and tied me hand-and-foot to something heavy in the back of the pick-up.'

She paused and looked at me quizzically. ‘What were they after Mike? They acted as if I should know.'

‘A gold bar,’ I told her, ‘What happened then?’

‘Oh yeah? Studded with diamonds I suppose. Look I’m not saying another word until you tell me the truth.’ She sat back and folded her arms, the awful handbag clasped to her.

‘It is the truth,’ I insisted, ‘I found it last night by accident. I'll show it to you in a minute.

‘Wo-ow!’ Jenny breathed out the word like a long sigh.

‘Go on,’ I prompted, 'where did they take you and how did you get away?'

'They took me to this big rambling house, on the outskirts of Plymouth. An hour ago, the younger one went out and I got the other one to untie me so that I could go to the bathroom. The window was nailed shut, so I couldn't get out that way but when he tried to tie me up again, he got a bit careless. I grabbed the poker from the hearth and clonked him with it.'

I touched the back of my head gently.

'Poetic Justice,' I said, 'Then what?'

'I just let myself out of the front door and hopped on a bus.' She spread her hands, 'So, what's new with you?'

'Not much except that I found a gold mine in my lock-up. —This house you we're in: did you see the number? Or the name of the road when you left? If we go round to the police station now, they could raid the place and get Harris if he's still out cold.'

'You're too slow', Jenny said, 'I've just given all that information to the WPC. on the phone. They'll have the place surrounded by now and somebody will be shouting: "Come out Bugsy, you ain't got a chance".'

I sighed and relaxed. 'Which one of the lads did the handbag belong to?'

Jenny looked blankly at the bag. 'Oh – this? This is Sandra's. I picked it up from the hall table on the way out. I thought it might contain clues.'

She opened it and dumped out the contents among the tea stains. Three five-pound notes, scent, lipstick, key ring, etc. And a few business cards. I picked these up and read them. "'Zippy Dry Cleaners',-- 'Able Taxis'-- 'Stonefort Securities'.

Nothing much there. But what did we want with clues? We knew who the villains were and two of their bolt holes. We knew what they were after and roughly where it was, which was more than they did. I tapped the cards together and handed them back to Jenny.

'Who is Sandra?' I asked her.

'The young one's girlfriend. She was still in bed when I got away. What are you looking at me like that for?'

'I was wondering how you managed to be tied up all night and end up looking like that?'

'Like what?'

'Like the answer to a sailor's prayer. You look great!'

'I tidied up in the bathroom before I slugged my jailer. You wouldn't expect me to escape looking a mess would you?'

'Of course not; the very idea! Come on.' I got to my feet. 'We'll get a taxi back to Highfields.

Jenny remained seated. She shook her head and her nose twitched. 'I'm starving,' she complained, 'and the smell of that frying bacon is driving me mad.'

I caught Vi's eye and called for two thick bacon sandwiches and some more tea. Vi made a caustic comment about my slate, so I opened Sandra's bag, took out one of the fivers and held it aloft.

Jenny was horrified. 'But that's stealing.'

I shook my head, 'Receiving,' I said, '*You* stole it!'

The bag was still open between us, and as we munched our bacon sandwiches I found myself studying the protruding corner of one of the business cards and wondering why a little bell was ringing in my mind. I withdrew the card between two fingers, and the little bell became a telephone bell. 'Stonefort Securities', 27 Albemarle St. Plymouth Tel: 2437.

Albemarle Street was the one that ran past the dock entrance; the one with the phone-box.. I had a mental image of the fruit- and- veg wholesaler's near to the box . Their number, painted boldly on their shop front, was twenty four. Twenty seven therefore, would be roughly opposite.

I told Jenny I wouldn't be a minute, that I had to fetch something from the boat, and left the coffee house quickly, before she could object.

It was raining heavily now, and as I skipped across rainbow puddles and dodged leaking gutters, I thought again that I must have been watched as I'd approached the kiosk earlier. I turned into Albemarle Street and started looking at numbers.

Twenty-five was a betting shop and twenty-nine a sorry-looking launderette. Between the two, twenty-seven was a wide-open doorway exposing a depressing squalor of peeling paint and torn, cracked lino. On the wall were half a dozen letterboxes each with hand-scrawled or type-written title. One of these read 'Stonefort Sec' Room 7,Top floor.

I walked towards the flight of wooden stairs, which ascended into a dim limbo and started to climb. The treads were bare and worn paper-thin in the middle.

On the first floor I stopped to listen. The doors leading off the landing were tight closed and secretive. Two more steps and a board creaked under my right foot. I hesitated and heard a sudden noise from above, like a drawer opening and closing. Twice more the same sound, then a cupboard door slammed and there was the murmur of voices.

I went up the next flight in three long, silent strides. The door of number seven was ajar and I put my eye to the crack. Pig Face Bennett was standing by the rain-lashed window looking down into the street. Next to an iron safe a very fat man knelt, stuffing papers into a blue Pan-Am bag.

'I don't see why you've got to leave this place,' Bennett's voice was truculent, with the hint of an impatient whine.

'Because the police are not as stupid as you are my dear Percival,' the fat man answered, 'there is bound to be something in the house, or on Harris, to connect me with your ridiculous kidnapping caper. I cannot take the risk of becoming involved.'

I'd only heard the voice say a few words on the phone earlier, and had been distracted by Jenny's unexpected appearance, but I was sure that this was the same man.

Bennett turned from the window and there was a sneer on his porcine face and in his tone. 'It wasn't so bleedin' ridiculous when you thought it would work, was it? And don't call me Percival.'

The fat-man stood up and pushed the safe door shut with a highly polished shoe. He was well over six feet –half a head taller than Bennett –and there was hardness beneath the fat which showed in the way he held himself.

'Watch the window and don't get lippy,' he said.

Bennett looked an if he'd have liked to argue further, but turned back to the window and spoke over his shoulder: 'Where will I get in touch with you? At Windbeck?'

The fat man picked up the bag and began taking a last look round the drab room. I thought it was time to get out of sight but I had to hear this.

'You will not get in touch with me. *I* will get in touch with *you.* That is, of course, if I continue to employ you. Your gratuitous violence is becoming a bit of a liability you know, Percival.'

Bennett swung around –annoyed again. The other said 'The window,' sharply, and Bennett turned back to it, his face like thunder.

There was a draught blowing through the crack of the door, making my right eye water. I changed eyes, and wondered what I could do to stop these two leaving.

To walk blithely in and ask them politely to submit to a citizen's arrest would be to invite another belting. To creep away and hide – letting them walk out –was unthinkable.

Bennett straightened, and turned quickly to the fat man.

'A police van just stopped outside—come on!'

I flattened myself against the wall. When they came through the door I'd maybe have time to say 'boo' before they shoved me down the stairs. With thumping heart I waited—and waited.

After about three years, I put a tentative eye back to the door crack. The room appeared to be empty.

Low voices and the squeak of loose treads wafted up the stairwell: Reinforcements!

Feeling braver I pushed the door wide. The room was empty and a door in the back wall stood partly open, showing the top of a fire-escape. I went to look. A car started up in the back lane, then a motor bike.

Well – that was that. I turned back into the room to greet the cavalry. It was just my bad luck that the first two constables on the scene were young, keen and didn't know me.

Then Sergeant Prentiss and PC Saunders wafted through the door and released me from the arm-lock that the bigger one had on me. I'd collected a few more bruises and I had a sneaking impression that Saunders was enjoying the situation. The smile on his face gave him away.

By the time I'd explained which way the pair of fugitives had gone, four of the policemen had clattered down the stairs to give chase.

To Tom Prentiss I recounted the conversation I'd overheard between Bennett and the big man.

'Windbeck?' he looked at the ceiling and repeated the name twice. 'Nope. Never heard of it. Could be the name of a village –or a farm perhaps. Or a house name.'

'Could it have been *the* Windbeck?' Saunders said, 'It sounds as if it could be a boat.'

I pondered the question for a moment but ‘No.’ I told him, ‘I would've noticed that. There was no “the” and he said “at”, not “on”.’

We collected Jenny from Vi’s caff and went to the station to look at the “family album” The big man was not in it. Jenny’s lips tightened and she gave a small shudder when a turned page revealed Bennett’s bristle-topped face. I squeezed her hand. She looked up quickly at Tom Prentiss as a thought struck her.

‘What about the poor man I hit with the poker?’ She asked anxiously, ‘Will he be alright?’

I couldn't believe what I was hearing. ‘Poor man?’ I yelped. 'Jenny, that poor man kidnapped you!’

‘I know but, –’ She screwed her face in distaste and pointed at Bennet's picture, ‘he wasn’t as bad as that one. He was more—gentle somehow.’

I sighed and remembered just how gently Harris had laid into me with the cosh. I decided not to disillusion her. After all, this was Jenny, and I loved her.

Tom Prentiss chuckled wryly. ‘Well, he’s in the casualty ward but he’s not badly hurt. They’ll probably let us have him back tomorrow morning.’

I looked innocently at Jenny. ‘We could take him some flowers. If you like,’ I said.

Her face brightened. ‘Oh that’s a good — *Beast* !’

Tom Prentiss nodded towards the door in the corner. ‘We’ve got Sandra Green in there. She’ll probably be charged with being an accessory.’

‘Oh poor girl – I think she was frightened of Bennett.’ Jenny’s face was concerned. She suddenly remembered the handbag and pushed it towards Tom. ‘Will you give her this back? I only borrowed it.’ She pointed at me. ‘He owes her five pounds’

'Tom raised his grey eyebrows. ‘You took money from the bag?’

‘We had to eat,’ I said defensively. I took a handful of change and paper from my side pocket and spread on the counter. ‘Here's the change. If you’ll lend me the rest, I can square it.’

‘I think I’d better. We can do without that kind of complication.’ Tom took a five-pound note from his wallet, put it into the handbag and pocketed the loose change.‘You owe me,’ he said.

'Sure.'

I picked up the remaining crumpled piece of paper from the counter, smoothed it out, read it and pushed it back into my pocket.

We'd left the police station and were half way across Custom House Square when Jenny forced a halt by gripping my arm and digging her heels into the cobbles.

'What is it? What is on that paper? I saw your face change.'

I glanced back at the watchful windows and started walking again. 'Not here,' I urged, 'wait untill we get back to the boat.'

Then I remembered that Stoker was on the Pelican. I led Jenny into the nearest cross-alley and stepped into the doorway of an antique shop. I handed her the note. She read it and looked up, puzzled.

'Four Eagles! What does it mean?'

'It means that David Gregory is alive.'

I wondered why I had not recognised the writing immediately and why I had completely forgotten the note's existence. Too many bangs on the head, I concluded.

'How do you know? Where does this come from?'

'I found it in my cabin, pinned to the bulkhead. When I got back from Highfields.'

I put both arms around her and pulled her close, remembering the emptiness I'd felt when I'd thought I'd lost her.

She put a hand on my cheek, then round the back of my neck and pulled my head down to kiss me. Two jolly holiday ladies squeezed past us, giggling.

'Don't mind us, love – give him one for me.'

Their laughter harmonized with the jingling of the shop bell and at the same time, the sun came out, so that bright jewels dripped from the eaves instead of raindrops.

I took her hand and started up the alley. 'Come on, I'll show you gold.'

She took long leaping strides over the puddles to keep up.

'What does it mean? Four Eagles?'

'It's the name of a cafe in Roscoff. It looks as if he wants me to contact him there.'

We were walking along a wider thoroughfare now, lined with gift shops, restaurants and ice cream parlours, with here and there, struggling survivors from the past: a small chandler's and a family grocer.

Ahead of us the harbour waters sparkled, and multi-coloured sails spread themselves to the sunlight like butterfly wings.

When we got to the Pelican, Stoker was sitting on the fore-hatch, soaking up the sun His eyes were on Jenny but it was to me that he spoke.

'Did you bring me any fags?'

'Who, me?' Jenny said, surprised.

'No, him,' growled Stoker, 'Who are you?'

'This is Mrs McLaine, Stoker, and I'll thank you to mind your manners.'

'Oh, – Mrs *McLaine*!' Stoker grinned, 'You'm supposed to be kidnapped. Was it all a mistake?'

'I *was* kidnapped,' Jenny told him casually, 'but I didn't like it, so I left.'

I unlocked the back door of the Bedford. There was no gold brick. I looked at Stoker.

'Okay, what have you done with it?'

Stoker's face would have done a choirboy credit. 'Done with what Mr. Peterson?'

'With that dirty old cobblestone, that's what!'

'Oh – that! I've put it somewhere a little safer Mr. Peterson. Anyway, you won't be needing it now you've got the lady back, will you? On the other 'and though, if you was still thinking about helping me with that little salvage job... ?'

'I'll take Mrs McLaine home,' I said, 'We'll talk about it when I get back.'

'Okay, – look, I'm gasping... '

'There's some money in the locker under my bunk, in a tobacco tin.'

'Ta –I'll pay you back.'

'That's right.'

As we drove out of the gates, Jenny asked me. 'Is there really a gold brick? Or is this one of those "in" jokes.'

'It's real alright. After all, Bennett and Harris snatched you for it!'

'Yes but – they might have only thought it existed.'

I shook my head and re-lived the whole story as I told it to her, watching her excitement grow.

At Highfields, Jimmy helped me load my B.S.A. into the back of the van. He thanked me for bringing his mother back, but his manner said: if it hadn't been for me, she wouldn't have been taken away.

I called in at the hospital to see Sam Wilkins when I got back to Plymouth. He was sitting up in bed, wearing a big white turban and looking through a large window, which gave him a view over the outer harbour and beyond.

Dinghys were racing each other around the buoys. Sam's glasses winked as he turned his head to greet me. He waved a thin limp hand at the window.

' 'Lo Mike. From up here you can definitely tell the sailors from the farmers.'

His voice was weak. He didn't look too good to me, and the ward sister had warned me not to stay more than five minutes.

'Hallo Sam,' I felt uncomfortable, 'Sorry to get you knocked about like that. I shouldn't have asked you to keep your eye on things.'

Sam shrugged and tried to grin. 'I've had wuss. They was busting open your padlock. I poked my 'ead out of my door and told 'em to sheer off. 'Stead o' that, they come into my place and laid me out.'

'Wasn't anyone else about?'

'There was folks further down the dock, but them two acted so casual, nobody'd think they was doing wrong – not 'less they was looking close.'

'Was it the skinhead? The one that came before?'

Sam nodded. 'The other bloke was older – 'e wore flat cap. He's the one that 'it me.'

I pointed down the ward to a screened portion. 'If you want to get your own back, he's in the end bed.'

Sam looked as if he'd like to believe it. 'Go on, you're pulling my leg !'

I told Sam about Jenny being kidnapped. When I told him how she'd escaped, he lay back on his pillow and laughed in silent spasms while tears welled. A worried looking nurse came over and told me I'd have to leave as I was exciting her patient too much.

Sam waved his hand in protest. 'No, no,' he gasped, 'he's just done me the power of good.'

He struggled to sit upright again and the nurse plumped his pillows, gave me a severe look, and went away.

When he got his breath back, Sam insisted I tell him the whole story.

'Folks don't gen'rally get kidnapped 'less there's a lot of money involved,' he said, 'So what were they after?'

'I can't tell you that yet Sam, but if things go right, your lump on the head could earn you a good bonus.'

Sam grinned, 'I'll believe that when I see it.'

But there was a light in his eye that hadn't been there when I arrived. I'd given him something to look forward to. I rose to go and when I turned back at the foot of the bed, his speculative gaze was on the screen, lower down the ward. I shook my head.

'On second thoughts, you'd better not,' I advised. 'Little boy-blue is behind there with him!'

CHAPTER 6

When I got back to the Pelican Stoker Figgin wasn't there. I waited for two days before I went round to his lodgings. His landlady said he'd taken some of his clothes and told her he'd be back.

He hadn't said when, or where he was going.

That was normal for Stoker though. For as long as I'd known him he would appear at intervals, pick up a few days casual work and then lose himself again.

I hung about, aboard and around the Pelican, cleaning up the mess, repairing the damage and becoming more and more certain that this time, enriched by the gold bar, Stoker wasn't coming back.

I began to feel depressed: The sight and thought of gold had poked a stick deep into my well of avarice and stirred the waters.

I thought of taking Dave Gregory's note to the police and letting them sort it out but the memory of the gold brick kept getting in the way.

That and Stoker's tale of more of the stuff.

I wanted to make inquiries about the status of recovered gold but I couldn't figure who to ask without stirring up bubbles of speculation.

Sometime in the near future there was going to be a Coroners inquest on Dave Gregory, and I would have to give evidence.

Well, so what? I could only swear to what I'd seen – and smelt.

The note about the Four Eagles was neither here nor there, was it? Just because the writing was similar to Dave Gregory's, didn't mean he'd written it, did it? Anyway – if Dave wanted to be dead for a while, I'd seen enough of the opposition to understand why.

Naval divers had been down in the deep channel off the breakwater and reported that Garland's steel hull was in two pieces and neither piece was a danger to navigation. They were reasonably sure that Dave Gregory's body was not trapped in the wreckage, but had been washed out to sea.

But I knew now that he was alive and over in Brittany.

Smoothing the note out again, I compared the writing with that in Dave's diary. It was more hurried and untidy but there was no doubt in my mind that it was his.

I searched the boat again, looking for Stoker's gold, then examined the floor of the store, scraping likely looking cobblestones with a file.

I was poking about in the rafters, annoying innocent spiders and scaring pigeons when Frank Gregory turned up.

He spoke from the doorway making me jump.

'Hallo Mike – I got your letter.'

I was glad to see him. I jumped off the workbench and dusted myself down before shaking hands. He had no suitcase, so I guessed he'd already booked in somewhere.

'The 'Red House' in Breton Street' he told me. Then, with forced casualness, 'I don't suppose they've found Dave's body yet?'

'No, they haven't. I'm sorry.'

He followed me aboard the Pelican and I started making a brew.

'I'm surprised you could get time off,' I said, 'or is this your holiday?'

Frank beamed. 'I was made redundant last Friday. 'That's three times. Trouble is: I never work anywhere long enough to get a golden handshake.'

I sympathised. 'What were you doing?'

'Driving. Not much of a job but it paid the rent. I don't suppose you need an extra hand aboard? I could pick up my dole money down here just as well as in Leicester.'

The kettle started to boil and instead of answering, I changed the subject. 'Frank, how are you at hypothetical problems?'

'It's a big word.'

'It's a big problem. Suppose you knew the whereabouts of a great deal of loot, right? *Somebody* owns it, but as soon as it shows up, all sorts of people are going to lay claim to it.'

'What sort of people?'

Good guys and bad guys. -- And two governments.'

'Ours and—?'

'The French.'

'Could this have anything to do with the Garland blowing up?' Frank said, 'Did the bad guys kill Dave?'

I poured tea into thick mugs and pushed one to him. Then I laid the note beside it.

'I found this pinned to the bulkhead couple of days ago. I don't think Dave *is* dead!'

Frank studied the note silently, chewing his bottom lip – then said: 'What does it mean – Four Eagles?'

'It's a cafe in Roscoff.'

'And you think Dave came here and left the note so that you would go and see him in Roscoff?'

'Looks like it.'

'But that doesn't make sense. If he came to the boat, why didn't he wait and see you aboard?'

I shrugged, 'He probably wanted to get clear of Plymouth before he was seen.'

Frank scratched his head. 'Do you think,' he asked, 'that you could start at the beginning?'

I did. And when I'd finished, Frank sighed and put the matter in a nutshell, 'So now, he mused. Dave, Stoker, and the bad guys have disappeared in three different directions; you are minus the one piece of loot that you had your hands on, and you don't know where the rest is.'

'That's about the size of it!'

'And you reckon Dave blew the Garland up deliberately?'

I nodded. 'To make it look right.'

Frank whistled. 'A bit expensive though.

'Not if the reward is great enough. Stoker didn't say how much was down there, but it must be a substantial amount.'

I left Frank aboard the Pelican and went round once more to

Stoker's lodgings, on the off chance that he had returned.

Mrs. Cook, his landlady, a friendly widow nearing seventy, opened the door before I knocked.

'I saw you come through the gate. Ronald hasn't come back yet.'

'Ronald? Oh, – Stoker.'

I'd forgotten he had a proper name.

'Would you like to come in for a minute? I've just put the kettle on.'

I didn't really want to, but this was my only link with a fortune. The front parlor was neat and overly warm, with a bright coal fire blazing in the grate. Mrs. Cook explained about her arthritis, and asked if I wouldn't mind filling up the two scuttles before I left.

The small coal cellar was half-full and the top of the pile of fuel reached up to the grating. I filled the two scuttles and as I set them side by side in the hearth I commented to Mrs. Cook that she was well stocked up for the winter. Her face glowed with pleasure.

'That was Ronald. He insisted on buying a ton of coal before he left, so I wouldn't be short. Wasn't that generous of him?'

I agreed that it was and I could have laughed at the craftiness of it.

'I'm keeping his room for him,' she went on, 'I don't think I could get used to a stranger, I do hope he'll come back.'

I told her she could bank on it. 'He'll be back long before you get to the end of the coal,' I said.

When I got back to the Pelican, there was a red post- office van on the quay, I watched the postman put something through the flap in the door of my store.

It was a letter, from Stoker, suggesting that I ring a particular phone number at seven that evening. Frank said he'd come back at that time: that was if I didn't mind.

I didn't. If eventually, Stoker and I were going to go after the bullion, then we would need help. Frank Gregory would be an ideal recruit. At seven, I rang the number from the Albemarle Street kiosk and as I listened to the ringing tone, I squinted up at the window opposite: the one that had housed Stonefort Securities, and wondered where Bennett and the fat man had gone to ground.

A voice in my ear crackled 'Unicorn' and I asked for Stoker.

'Who?'

'Stoker Figgin!'

'Your name Peterson?'

'That's right.'

'You're to ring Mr. Smith at 2729.'

I rang that number and another voice claimed to be the Duke of Cambridge.

'Is Mr. Smith there please?'

'Who's calling?'

'Mike Peterson.'

'Just a sec!'

When he came on the line I was feeling exasperated. 'Stoker, there's no call for all this cloak and dagger stuff. Bennett's done a bunk.'

'Yeah? I bet he ain't gone far. Listen – are you interested in that proposition?' His tobacco laden wheezing was anxious.

'I'm interested.'

'Yes, but *really* interested. Are you in?'

I took a deep breath. 'I'm in!'

There was a five-second silence from Stoker, I could hear glasses clinking and a juke-box screeching *"Yeah baby, oh--oh--oh--!"*

Stoker made up his mind.

'Okay. Pick me up from Commercial Wharf a week today at noon.'

'In the van?'

It was Stoker's turn to sound exasperated.

'In the Pelican. We can't sail a bleedin' Dormobile across the channel can we?'

'Stoker, --what is the melting point of gold?' I said.

'How do you mean?'

'Well, supposing some was put on the fire in mistake for coal?'

Stoker sighed loudly. 'Okay, but you must admit it's a pretty good hiding place.'

When I came out of the phone box, Frank was coming up the street from the town end. He spotted me and hesitated outside the 'Crown & Cushion' pointing at the door. I gave him the thumbs up and he disappeared inside. When I got to the bar, he'd got two pints on the counter.

I raised a glass. 'Cheers.'

'Happy hunting.'

After the first swallow we went to a corner table, away from the juke-box and the fruit machine.

'I spoke to Stoker,' I said.

'And?'

I started to make beer-ring patterns on the tabletop. 'How would you like a share of a fortune, Frank?'

'Just so long as it doesn't affect my "supplementary benefit".'

'I'll leave that to your conscience. Stoker wants me to pick him up, in the Pelican, in a week's time. We'll need help, and as you're here...'

'Okay,' he said, 'Anything for a laugh.'

Two girls came into the bar and the draught from the door set the smoke clouds swirling. They perched themselves on high stools and scratched about in their voluminous handbags for cigarettes and lighters.

They gave Frank and me a brief professional appraisal, then set their sights on two gold-cuff-linked cigar-puffers standing at the bar.

The next time the door opened, it was Tom Prentiss who came in. He was in civvies but by the time he reached the counter, the girls had stubbed out their cigarettes and were making for the exit.

Tom spotted us and brought his drink over. I introduced him to Frank – stressing the 'sergeant'.

'Frank's here because of Dave,' I explained.

'The inquest is on Friday,' Tom said, 'you'll be expected to give evidence Mike.'

I nodded and took a pull at my beer.

'There's no doubt it will be adjourned,' he went on, 'What, with there being no body.'

Frank slowly twirled his glass. "What happens if my cousin's body isn't found?'

I began to feel a little nervous. I hoped Frank wouldn't say, or ask, too much.

'You can apply to the High Court to assume his death,' Tom told him, 'in the circumstances, it would probably take a month to six weeks.'

Frank kept his eyes on his glass. The conversation stopped there and didn't seem to want to get going again. I asked if either would like another drink.

Tom said no thanks – he wanted his supper. Frank said no thanks – he thought he'd go to the pictures.

'Oh – what's on?' Tom was interested.

'"Gold !" said Frank, 'Roger Moore, --you know?'

I glared at him, but his face was completely innocent.

Back aboard the Pelican, I felt depressed. Jenny was safe and I thanked God for that, but poor old Sam was in dock, Stoker was hiding down some rabbit hole, and Bennett and his boss were out there somewhere, planning villainy.

It was raining again too. A vindictive, vertical downpour, which hammered on the deck head, and found a dozen ways into the cabin.

I switched on the radio, but there was too much static, then found a damp, half-read paper-back and tried vainly to get interested in it.

Eventually I threw down the book and thought about Jenny. What I really wanted to do was go out there and stay until it was time to meet Stoker.

So why didn't I? Well, for one thing: my presence at Highfields might well put Jenny in danger again. And for another: I didn't think I could stand several days of Jimmy's truculent scowling.

Something would have to be about that lad. I wondered if they'd ever bring back National Service. Twelve months or so of uninterrupted Jenny would suit me fine.

The thought of National Service led logically through a succession of mental images to Aunt Carrie, resplendent in her Wren's uniform. Not that Aunt Carrie had been called up. Caroline Grantley had volunteered in nineteen thirty-eight, and had been a prop to the Senior Service for over twelve years.

I must have been five when I last saw her in uniform, and I have a clear recollection of knocking her blue and white tricorn hat askew, when she helped me mount my first pony.

Now "Lady Grantley" -- Aunt Carrie lives at Merritor, on the northern edge of Dartmoor. Over the years, the estate has been whittled down in size by death duties, until now it is a tight commercial farming enterprise of about twelve hundred acres, poking like a green fist into the brown heath land.

Maybe three times a year, I go and stay there for a short spell, as I have done ever since I left the place seventeen years ago to make my own way.

It was still raining, I put on my oilskins and went once again to the phone box in Albemarle Street. When I picked up the receiver, I found I'd come out once more without money.

I reversed the charges and heard Aunt Carrie's faint voice as she accepted the call. There was a click and she came through loud and clear, her accent rich and fruity.

'My dear boy, if you are so impecunious, then it is about time that you came home and lived in a civilised manner.'

'Sorry Aunt Carrie; I'm not broke, I just came out without change. And... it's raining.'

'Are you alright Michael? You sound in rather low spirits.'

'No – I mean yes. I am all right Aunt Carrie. But I'd like to come and stay a few days. — If it's not inconvenient?'

'Of course it's not inconvenient. The very idea!'

'Thanks Aunt Carrie – oh, and I'd like to bring Jenny with me, if she'll come. You remember Jenny McLaine?'

'Michael, – what is the matter with you? I am not senile, I remember Mrs McLaine perfectly well.'

'Oh – sorry!'

'Michael – when you are at sea, the rest of the world does not stop turning you know. People are running into each other all the time!'

'Yes, Aunt Carrie.'

'I shall expect you tomorrow Michael. Do try and be in time for lunch.'

'Yes Aunt Carrie. Goodnight Aunt Carrie, God bless.'

'God bless you, dear boy!'

When I rang Jenny, Jimmy answered. I heard him say no, he would not accept the call, and I wished I was close enough kick his backside. Then I heard Jenny's voice, distantly, asking who it was. Jimmy reluctantly handed the instrument over.

'Come to Merritor for a few days? Are you potty? I'm a farmer Mike, which means I have to *farm.* — Know what I mean?' She sounded indignant.

'Not for just two days?' I lowered my voice, 'I need you Jenny'.

She didn't answer that, and in the brief silence heard the drone of a man talking.

'Am I interrupting television?'

'No, that's Ralph's voice you can hear.'

'Oh, is it?' I heard the jealous stiffness in my own.

'Mike!' There was reproof in her tone. 'Ralph and Amanda have very kindly come over to make sure that I am alright.'

'Amanda Wainright?'

'Yes, – just a minute.' The background rumble stopped, and I guessed that she'd closed the hall door.'That's better. They've become very close you know.'

I remembered the way he'd fussed over her at the point-to-point; and what Aunt Carrie had just said about the world still turning when I was at sea. Suddenly my spirits were soaring.

'Jenny – when I come back from the Spanish Main, with the Pelican loaded to the gunn'ls with gold plate, will you marry me?'

'Fool!'

'Will you Jenny?'

'Mike - ?'

'Yes Jenny?'

'I'll be at Merritor tomorrow.'

CHAPTER 7.

At Merritor, I'd found my room ready as always, had luxuriated among the ornate Victorian plumbing in the large, draughty bathroom and was now standing at the drawing room window looking out through the avenue of beeches.

I was wondering what it would be like to live here all the time. To do what Aunt Carrie had wanted of me for years.

Jenny would fit this place perfectly. There was a curved stairway in the large hall and I pictured her standing at the top, in a green silk dress, red hair piled up high and the hall below filled with guests: white shirt fronts, gleaming shoulders, --- all watching her.

Aunt Carrie's voice rippled my reverie:

'Michael dear, do you think you could pop into the conservatory and help Charles pull off his boots? Hawkins seems to have disappeared.'

'Certainly Aunt Carrie.'

'And lunch will be in ten minutes. I'll go and see if Evelyn will be coming down.'

Evelyn is Sir Charles Grantley's sister and she seems to have been very old and very frail for the thirty-five years that I've known her.

I found Charles in the conservatory as Aunt Carrie had said. Charles is a few years younger than Evelyn, and is himself approaching ninety. He was snipping away purposefully with a pair of secateurs and leaving a trail of mud from caked wellingtons.

He spotted my reflection in the window glass, turning to greet me with a vague smile.

'Ah Michael my boy – good to see you, good to see you. Sorry I didn't greet you when you arrived; I was in the... ,' He gazed at the mud on his boots, '... in the vegetable garden, helping Hawkins.'

He turned and walked carefully to a cane chair under a spreading palm frond, settling into it with a wheeze like a concertina.

'I say – I wonder if you'd give me a hand with these boots?' He bent his head to look under a bench, 'Used to be a boot-jack in here somewhere.'

'How are you keeping Charles?'

'Well, they haven't put me under yet – I'm keeping one step ahead.'

I pulled off the boots and he wriggled his toes luxuriously, took something like a small button from his shirt pocket and popped it into his ear.

'Lunch is in ten minutes. Aunt Carrie said to tell you,' I said loudly.

'No need to shout my boy. I can hear perfectly well.' He gave the button in his ear a prod with a forefinger, then gazed sorrowfully at my muddy hands.

'You seem to have got yourself into a bit of a state. Never mind – there's a water tap in the corner.' He pointed, then levered himself from the chair, cane-work and joints cracking in unison. 'Better hurry, I think lunch will be ready shortly. You are staying to lunch aren't you Michael?'

'I'm staying to lunch Charles.'

I swilled my hands and turned off the tap. There was a tea towel lying between the plant pots and I dried my hands on that before following Charles..

Four places were set, but the meal had been under way for five minutes before Aunt Evelyn put in an appearance.

Tall, thin, and only slightly stooped, she stood framed in the doorway, leaning on a silver topped cane.

I rose from my place and went to guide her to hers. She offered a parchment cheek to be kissed. Old she may be, but there is nothing wrong with her eyes, and her mind is a deal sharper than her brother's. Half way across the room she stopped, her look lasering to a spot under the table.

'Charlie, why are you eating luncheon in your stockinged feet?' Her intonation was piping, tremulous.

Aunt Carrie looked up. 'Where are your slippers Charles? — And you have dirt under your finger nails.'

Charles gave a shrug of magnificent indifference, chewed and swallowed. 'Soil Carrie, not dirt; good rich soil.'

Aunt Carrie snorted. 'And we know what makes it rich!'

She found his slippers behind a chair and insisted that he put them on.

I wanted to guide the conversation round to Aunt Carrie's time with the Wrens but Charles was happily bent on torment. He gave me a broad wink. 'Know what's the best thing for tomatoes Michael? The very best thing?'

I shook my head warily.

'Sheep muck that's what. You put it in a bucket of water, and –'

'Charlie!' His sister rapped the table with the handle of her knife,'Not while we're eating.'

'It's good basic organic husbandry,' Charles protested.

Carrie tried to quell him with a look. 'If you insist on being basic Charles, then you'll have to take your lunch into the potting shed.'

'Now that's not a bad idea Carrie.' Then in a stage whisper to me. 'Hawkins has a jar of scrumpy in there.'

He held up his glass and looked at the pale contents critically. 'Far better than this 'Plonk'.' He sipped, pulled a wry mouth, took the hearing aid from his ear and dropped it into his pocket.

Evelyn had been regarding me sharply since sitting down. Now she said: 'Will someone tell me why Michael's face looks as though he's been dragged through a briar-patch?'

I'd already told Aunt Carrie about my proximity to the Garland when she blew up, and added a cock-and-bull story about having surprised burglars at Highfields and being battered as a result and now I repeated the account for Evelyn's benefit.

I hadn't mentioned anything about Stoker Figgin, Jenny's abduction or sunken gold.

Charles dozed, woke with a start and an apology, and wanted to know what we had been talking about.

Evelyn told him that at his age, he should lie down after lunch. She herself would retire to her room. Not to sleep of course, but to finish her book, — "though heaven knows, after Michael's story, it will seem terribly flat."

Charles rose too and made for the hall door, commenting that: although Evelyn was talking nonsense as usual, forty winks would be rather enjoyable.

As he passed me, he peered closely at my face, then took a pair of heavy horn-rimmed spectacles from his side pocket and used these to look again.

'My word Michael, your face is in a state. Horse throw you ?'

He didn't wait for an answer. 'Never mind, tell me all about it at tea my boy.'

He followed Evelyn from the room. Aunt Carrie gave a deep sigh of amused resignation and rang for coffee to be brought to the terrace.

I followed her out through the French casement and we sat at a small table in the sunlight.

When the coffee had been put before us, Aunt Carrie leaned back and tilted her face to the sun's benediction, her eyes closed. At seventy, she looked fifty. A beautiful fiftyat that.

This is what my own mother would have looker like had she lived, had her life not been cut short by some vindictive bug, ten years before.

Aunt Carrie broke in on my reverie.

'...So Michael, — suppose you now tell me the full story.'

I reflected that not much gets past Aunt Carrie..

I now gave her an almost complete run-down of events to date.

'Recovery of the gold shouldn't be much of a problem,' I said, ' – provided the French don't catch us doing it.'

'What about *our* authorities? — When you bring the gold ashore here.'

'I could declare it openly – you know – claim salvage!'

'What would you get? Ten per cent?'

'Probably. But ten per cent of what? I don't even know how much is down there. For all I know, the ingot I saw might be the only one. I'd rather know how to get the full market value, without sticking my neck out.'

Aunt Carrie snorted and reached for her coffee cup.'Your neck will be stuck *right* out. You know very well that that gold belongs to the Admiralty – or the Government.'

'I'm not so sure. By now it could legally belong to the French.' I smiled at the thought. 'If I remove it quietly, I could be averting an international incident.'

'You know,' Aunt Carrie said, 'What intrigues me is: what was it for? What was the gold going to buy?'

'Search me!' I hadn't given any thought to that aspect. Too much had happened too fast. 'Weren't you in Naval Intelligence at one time? I seem to remember you mentioning it.'

'That was from forty-two onwards. Your loot went missing at the beginning of, — forty-one, did you say?'

'So I'm told.'

Aunt Carrie leaned her elbows on the arms of her chair, put her hands together as if in prayer and tapped her chin with her finger-tips.

Her next words came slowly and drawn out. 'I – wonder!'

'You wonder what?'

'If he's still alive... My old chief. His name was Poplar. Commander Poplar. He'd been stationed at Devonport since before the war. -- I was moved there from Chatham in forty-one but I didn't transfer to Intelligence until a year later.'

She went off into a reverie again, then spoke almost to herself: 'It would be rather satisfying to find out.'

'To find out if he's still around you mean?'

'And to find out what it was all about. I seem to remember he lived somewhere near the Lizard.'

I had a sinking feeling. If Aunt Carrie started digging up "old comrades" and stirring things, it could jeopardise future prospects.

She went into the house, returned with a telephone directory and started riffling the pages.

'Aunt Carrie!'

She looked up and laughed aloud at my expression. 'Don't worry Michael, I shan't do anything silly like "giving the game away",' her eyes went back to the book. 'Ah, here we are; there are three.' Her voice became excited 'And one has a Helston number: D.J.Poplar, Windbeck, Helston 2478. Michael I'm sure his name was Desmond, so the initial is right -- Why is your lower jaw hanging open?'

I couldn't believe I'd heard correctly. Did you say Windbeck?

She glanced down at the page. 'That's right. A house name probably. Is it significant?'

'I'll say it is!'

I told her about the fat man saying he'd contact Bennett at "Windbeck".

Aunt Carrie was aghast. 'But what would these men have to do with the Commander.'

'I don't know, but I smell fish,' I said.

We both lapsed into thought. At length I broke the silence, hesitantly:

'Supposing, –just supposing–: that your old boss is employing that heavy mob to find the MTB.'

Aunt Carrie thought that one out.'That would mean,' she said, 'that he knows the gold is recoverable... Would your informant have contacted him?'

I couldn't think of a reason why he'd have done that. But then: there must be a lot he hadn't told me.

Speculation was interrupted by the sound of an approaching vehicle.

'Sounds like a Land-Rover' my aunt said.

'Could be Jenny,' I said.

I walked to the end of the terrace and looked around the corner of the house. 'It is Jenny! Why on earth is she dragging a horse-box behind?'

'Too far to hack over. Oh, didn't I tell you? We're holding a one-day event tomorrow. I've put your name in as a late entry.'

'You have?'

'Yes – and Jenny McLaine's. She's riding Rosalie.'

Again my face must have mirrored my thoughts, for Aunt Carrie went on:

'I do hope you are not going to be difficult Michael. We were frightfully short of entries and it is for a very good cause.' Then, as she remembered that I'd been somewhat knocked about, she was immediately contrite. Her hand flew to her mouth.'Oh my dear, whatever must you think of me. Of course I had no idea when I entered your name. I'll ring the secretary at once and scratch you – '

'No – no.' I protested. 'In fact, it's probably what I need to blow the cobwebs away.' I smiled at her – I hoped reassuringly. 'I'll go and help Jenny with Rosalie.'

Jenny had the ramp down and had backed the mare half way out by the time I reached the stable yard. Her green eyes flashed me a smile and my heart did it's usual flip at the sight of her warm, untidy, femininity.

Kenny, the stable boy, came and took Rosalie. As soon as his back was turned, I bundled Jenny back into the concealment of the horse-box and pressed my mouth to her lips, her eyelids, her neck. At first she laughed and made a show of struggling, then suddenly she was responding passionately and we were floating.

We were brought down by a cough close at hand. Kenny was standing at the foot of the ramp, staring up at us, a mesmerised smile on his sixteen year old face.

'I was just wondering if there's any special instructions,' he said.

'Yes,' I growled, 'Shove off !'

Jenny squirmed free from my embrace, skipped down the ramp and over to the loose box, which now held Rosalie.

Aunt Carrie came into the yard and caught my arm as I reached the cobbles.

'I'll show you the horse I'd like you to ride in the cross-country, Michael. I may buy him if he does well.'

She led me past the dozen loose-boxes to the paddock gate, beyond which two bay geldings were quietly grazing. The nearer one, almost sixteen hands, had white socks on the off-fore and near-hind, a star, and as I could see now that he'd raised his head and stopped chewing, a tremulous lower lip.

I thought I knew him, but to make sure I climbed the gate and went to examine him more closely. It was the mark of an old scar on his near shoulder that clinched it. I went back to the gate and Aunt Carrie with a heavy heart.

'That,' I said accusingly, 'is Hot Potato!'

'There – I knew you'd recognise him.' Aunt Carrie sounded pleased. I know he used not to be reliable but Mr. Fletcher assures me that he's cured him of all that nonsense.'

'Aunt Carrie,' I said patiently, 'less than a week ago, I saw Freddy Fletcher trying to swap punches with that animal, and he was definitely un-cured.'

Later, in the library, I told Jenny of the new twist: Of what I'd found out from Aunt Carrie about 'Windbeck'.

'You mean that those people are working for this Commander Poplar ?' she asked in surprise.

'It seems that way. And before you suggest going to the police – I think I've persuaded my Aunt that I ought to try and get hold of at least some of the spoils first.'

Jenny tilted her head sideways and put on a comic expression. 'Too right!'

'I've got to pick up Stoker Figgin at Plymouth, in a few days time,' I said, 'and then: – well, let's hope the weather stays fine for diving.'

Uncle Charles, fresh from his nap, breezed into the room. His craggy face lit up when he saw Jenny. 'Ah Mrs McLaine, what a delightful surprise.' He took her hand and brushed her fingers with his moustache.

'I do hope you'll forgive me my dear but I must go and find Hawkins. It's time he started taking up some of those potatoes.'

He went out onto the terrace, leaving the glass door open. Clouds had thickened up from the south-west, and a cool breeze had developed. I closed the door and told Jenny about Hot Potato. She thought it was funny.

Then Aunt Carrie came in and suggested it was time for tea. The three of us ate tiny cucumber sandwiches and drank from translucent china while we rolled the subject of the sunken bullion around.

'I must say,' Aunt Carrie's expression was intense, 'that I can't imagine for a moment Commander Poplar employing *criminals*.'

I'd given that aspect some thought too. 'I can suggest one possibility,' I said, 'Supposing my contact went to the Commander saying he knows the whereabouts of the booty and wants finance to recover it. Poplar has two options. One: he can remember that he is an "officer and a gentleman" and pass this info to the government, or two: he can get greedy.

'He plumps for “greedy” but now he has to find out if it's a scam, so he gets a security firm –Stonefort Securities – to check up on Stoker. When Stonefort find out that the story has substance, they go gold-crazy, and people start getting hurt.’ I glanced at Jenny.‘And abducted!’

‘Look,’ said Jenny, 'if the Commander employed those men, as you say, just to find out if he's being conned: then he would presumably pay them off and talk business with the first man, wouldn’t he?’ She ran her fingers through her thick red hair, puzzled.

‘The only men as far as I am aware – who know where the stuff is, are Stoker Figgin, who was there when it went down,' I said, ' and Dave Gregory, who is supposed to be dead but isn’t. And I don’t think we can deduce the extent the Commander's involvement until I’ve heard the rest of Stoker’s story. There must be plenty he hasn't told me.’

A few minutes later Aunt Carrie left the room to look in on Evelyn. As she went through the doorway, she said: ‘Dinner will be at seven thirty. Ralph and Amanda should be here soon.’

‘I didn’t know anyone else was coming,’ I said to Jenny, ‘I wanted you to myself for a couple of days.’

She smiled and came over to stand in front of my chair, arms outstretched. ‘Come on, you re getting too fat and lazy. Take me for a walk..

' Instead of letting her pull me to my feet, I pulled her into my deep armchair and spent a brief but happy interlude counting her ribs.

A cool draught of air struck my cheek as the terrace door opened and Charles was saying cheerfully: ‘Don’t get up,’ as he trailed mud across the library carpet.

Jenny struggled free with a laugh and made for the still-open door.

****

When I went to my room later, Mrs. Beddows was just coming out. ‘I’ve laid out your clothes Sir.’

‘Thank you Mrs. Beddows.’

She’d always been there, like Aunt Carrie and Charles and Evelyn. Other staff came and went over the years, but Mrs. Beddows went on forever and did practically everything.

A little later, when I was between bathroom and bedroom, I heard voices down in the hall and peered carefully over the ballustrade

Amanda Wainwright was oozing free of her wrap, and telling 'darling Caroline' that it was 'frightfully sweet' of her to invite them, and wasn't what had been happening to dear Jennifer 'too awful'.

Ralph Boscawen – florid and beaming – hovered possessively.

Funny: but I felt quite benevolent towards him now that he was no longer pursuing Jenny. I made my way to my room thinking: 'Good old Ralph; grand chap'. If there was time before dinner, I'd see if he'd give me a hundred up at billiards.

I finished dressing and gave my tie a last twitch in the mirror.

At the head of the stairs, another mirror, I checked the tie again. Only an eighth of an inch out of true, but it makes –

A melodic, church-bell-like summons, diverted my attention down the stairs. I watched Mrs Beddow's reflection crossing the hall to the front door and Aunt Carrie emerging from the drawing room. I wondered if this was another dinner guest arriving.

It was.

Aunt Carrie stepped forward to greet him as Mrs Beddows swung the door wide.

'Mr. Ruyter, I'm so glad you could come.'

'Lady Grantley – it's very kind of you to invite a stranger into your midst.'

'One must make new neighbour feel welcome, Mr. Ruyter.' She took his arm. 'Come into the drawing room and meet the others.'

Their voices faded as they went from view. Mrs. Beddows went into the cloakroom with Ruyter's hat and coat and I started slowly down the stairs.

There was no doubt about it: the man who had just arrived was the man I'd previously only seen through the crack of a door.

He was 'the fat man' from Stonefort Securities

'Are you all right sir?'

'All right? Oh yes, – thank you Mrs. Beddows.'

I was at the foot of the stairs deciding how to handle the coming meeting.

Ruyter didn't know that I'd seen him, and as far as I knew, the only time he'd seen Jenny and me had been as a fore-shortened view through rain-distorted glass that day in Albermarle Street.

I crossed the hall to the dining room, and as I gripped the door handle, the obvious hit me: Ruyter may not know our faces but he was bound to know our names.

Right, let's see how *he* handles the meeting.

Ruyter, Ralph Boscawen and Amanda were grouped by the window in the, as yet, unlit drawing room, admiring a spectacular sunset.

Jenny, dressed in something long and shimmery, was talking to Aunt Carrie, and Evelyn; the latter sitting regally erect in lace and jet, her blue-veined, transparent hands folded on her silver topped stick.

Aunt Carrie led me to the group by the window and introduced me to Ruyter. His greeting was formal and his handshake just on the right side of limp. If my name or my face meant anything to him, his expression didn't show it. I decided to probe a little.

'Ruyter: that's an interesting name, — Dutch perhaps?'

'I've always believed so Mister Peterson.'

The others had moved away to talk to Evelyn.

'And what brings you to Devonshire, Mr. Ruyter? Are you on holiday?'

I kept my tone light, as if only mildly interested. In the approaching dusk it was difficult to see his eyes and I may have imagined the hint of a challenge as he answered.

'I'm far too busy to take a holiday Mr. Peterson. No – I represent Stonefort Securities.' He smiled disarmingly.

'Oh? -- would that be about finance? -- Investments and such? Or Armoured wages vans? --That sort of thing?'

His smile broadened and I caught the glint of gold far back.

'We do act as agents for the latter,' he explained, 'but our speciality is in enquiries. Vetting people who apply for positions of trust for example.'

'I see – or people with diamond making machines, I suppose, or cranks with tales of buried treasure.'

He did not answer straight away, just looked at me intently and I thought I had over reached myself. His next words were pitched low, for my ear only.

'I think we may have a subject of mutual interest to discuss, Mr.

Peterson. — After dinner perhaps?'

'After dinner Mr. Ruyter.'

The meal was more of a success than it should have been: considering Ruyter's presence. In fact, he turned out to be a most entertaining dinner guest: contributing just the right amount of light, but interesting, conversation to balance the parish-pump topics of the rest of us.

Of course, what had befallen Jenny and me came in for its share of attention.

Amanda, who sat at Ruyter's right, and was soon calling him Eugene, gave him a blow-by-blow account of what those 'perfectly odious people' had done to 'dear Michael' and 'Poor Jennifer', and all for 'a pot of gold' which she was quite sure was the merest figment of someone's warped imagination.'

A feeling of unreality seized me as I listened to Ruyter's sympathetic interest. He spoke directly to me.

'And what of the police, Michael? What are they doing about all this?'

I shrugged and sipped my wine. 'As much as they can in the circumstances,' I said, and watched his face closely as I added: 'I believe that an office they were using as a base, was raided but there was no one there. They picked up the man named Harris and a girl friend after Jenny escaped — They'll probably sing like canaries.'

Ruyter chuckled and started to peel an apple. 'Sing like canaries,' he repeated, 'That sounds like "Raymond Chandler". I think I read all his books when I was younger.'

'Probably where you got your crooked ideas,' I thought sourly.

At this point, Charles asked Ruyter what profession he followed and under cover of the verbal confusion that followed, I asked Aunt Carrie how she had come to meet her new neighbour.

She told me he'd taken the gate lodge on a half-yearly lease. I reckoned this must be pretty high in the coincidence league, even for a narrow peninsular like this.

It occurred to me that Aunt Carrie was going to be less than pleased when she found she was nurturing the proverbial viper.

When the ladies left us, my eyes followed Jenny with regret, realising we had hardly exchanged two words during the whole of the meal.

Charles fetched cigars from the sideboard and for a moment I was sorely tempted to accept one. The other three were soon wreathed in clouds of Havana and we all took our first sip of brandy.

Then Ruyter said he must have a breath of air and went out onto the terrace, leaving the door open a little.

Two minutes later, when Ralph and Charles were deep into the subject of warble-fly, I slipped out to join him. He was at the far end of the terrace and his face glowed briefly dull red as he sucked in on his cigar. He spoke quietly when I drew near.

'I don't think there's any need for us to beat about the bush Michael, I believe that we can be of service to each other.'

It irritated me that he should use my given name. It smacked of 'all pals-together' and thinking of what Jenny had been put through, I began to smoulder.

'Ruyter, before you go any further, tell me if there is any reason why I shouldn't flatten you?' I raised my right fist, 'Mrs McLaine has suffered a great deal of distress and indignity at your hands and--'

He raised a placating palm. 'Please believe me – I had nothing to do with that.'

'Can you deny that you spoke to me on the phone? Attempting to bargain for Mrs McLaine's release?'

The night became perceptibly brighter as the drifting clouds thinned a little, and I saw the podgy white hands fluttering as he gestured. His tone was earnest, urging me to believe him.

'When I spoke to you, I had only just found out that Mrs McLaine had been abducted. And what's more, I had immediately ordered her release.' he tried a faint smile, 'I didn't know she'd taken matters into her own hands.'

'Then why all that nonsense on the telephone?'

'Bluff, pure and simple, I thought there was still time for us to do business before you realised she was free.'

I thought back. It would have worked if Jenny had gone to the police station first instead of coming to find me.

Ruyter went on: 'When my colleague went back to the house to release Mrs. McLaine, he found policemen all over the place.'

'What exactly is going on, and what's your proposition?' I said.

Ruyter stabbed out his Havana in an ornamental urn and became business like: 'There is a solid gold ingot, value about twenty eight thousand pounds, somewhere close by. I believe that you have it. I have been retained to recover it.'

'I *don't* have it,' I said.

He ignored the interruption: 'My – employees, are unfortunately impetuous and not very bright, which is why you have been hurt and Mrs McLaine put under no little distress.'

'And Sam Wilkins beaten almost to death, and Dave Gregory blown to bits,' I added bitterly.

He looked up sharply. 'What happened to Gregory was also no of my doing,' he said,'In fact, I have been gravely inconvenienced by it. As to the rest of the needless violence: f I could persuade you to join me it would cease. And you would be well compensated for what has happened.'

'Was Gregory working for you?'

'We were – shall we say – *co-operating!'*

'And look what happened to him!'

He shrugged, 'An accident.'

'Harris is in gaol – and Sandra; and your other "colleague"is presumably on the run. People who 'co-operate' with you seem to be unlucky.'

'Mr.Peterson: the gold ingot I spoke of is only a small part of a considerable fortune. I think that for a ,'- he hesitated fractionally,- 'quarter share, you might be prepared to risk a little ill luck?

'What would I have to do?'

'Dive for it. I believe no more than six fathoms.'

'Where?'

'Ah now, that information is confidential. You would be guided to the location.'

We had been walking slowly back towards the dining room door as we talked, and now it was pulled open and Charles stuck his head out.

'I say you two, – do come along in. We're trying to get a jolly old whist drive going.'

Inside, I crossed to Jenny's chair, kissed her lightly on the cheek and took her hand.

Aunt Carrie said brightly: 'I thought you and Mr. Ruyter were going to jaw all evening out there.'

'Sorry Aunt, we were talking shop. Mr. Ruyter is thinking of hiring the Pelican.'

I caught a flash of alarm in Ruyter's eyes.

'For a fishing expedition,' I explained.

Ruyter's face relaxed. He nodded and smiled.

****

The house was still. At the far end of the passage, where it branched left and right, a low-wattage wall-light burned. I turned right and paused outside the first door, gently closing my fingers round the knob. It turned noiselessly and when I pushed, the hinges gave not the slightest protest. With the door closed safely behind me, I moved quietly across the carpet, guided by the faintest of lights from the un-curtained windows.

'Mike ?' Jenny's voice was low, slumberous.

'Yes darling !'

'I thought you'd never get here.' She turned back a corner of the covers. I dropped my dressing gown and slid in beside her.

'Jenny?'

'Yes darling?'

'You won't doze off on me will you?'

****

It was three in the morning. I stood by the window, a little cold, and watched the white half-moon skip from cloud to cloud. From up here I could clearly see the line of poplars along the river that marks the eastern boundary of Grantley land.

One day it would be my privilege to run this place; a privilege I had not yet started to earn. I had been too busy 'doing my own thing'

In the past fifteen or so years, I'd worked on places in Canada and Australia that would make Grantley Park look like your average back yard. But I'd always taken the minimum of responsibility and moved on when I'd got itchy feet. I needed to stop and learn.

I half closed my eyes so that the moon-washed vista blurred, and imagined that this was our room, Jenny's and mine, and that we'd lived here for years and years.

Then Bennett's face obtruded, mocking – and Ruyter's. I saw Sam Wilkins lying, as Stoker had found him, in the hold. My guts tightened and the sourness of fear was in my mouth. There was a stirring behind me, a soft padding of bare feet on the carpet and

Jenny's hands slid around me, clasping my middle. She pressed close taking the chill from my back. Her voice was sleepy.

‘What are you thinking about Mike?’

‘You and me; and – mortality.’

‘Mm – such a serious fellow.’

She gave me a squeeze and I covered her hands with mine.’

‘Jenny – sell Highfields to Boscawen and come and live here with me.’

‘And what would the neighbours think?’ She asked primly.

‘As my wife – chump. Aunt Carrie’s been onto me for years to take up the reins but I’ve been too... irresponsible, I suppose. I’ll forget the gold, forget Stoker and Dave and Ruyter and – '

She turned me around. ‘You’re not making sense Mike. What has Ruyter got to do with anything?’

‘Sorry – I forgot that you’re not up to date. Look – when the police raided that office in Albemarle Street – '

Jenny put a finger on my lips. ‘On second thoughts, tell me at breakfast. I’m much too sleepy to take anything in.’

She put a hand behind my neck and pulled my mouth down to hers.

‘I’m cold,' she whispered, '– come back to bed,’

****

Mrs. Beddows brought tea to my room at a quarter past eight. I was standing, still in my dressing gown, looking out at the weather and vaguely assessing my chances in the coming cross-country!

‘Good morning Mr.Peterson.’ She put the tray on the bedside table.

‘Good morning, Mrs. Beddows. Wonderful day isn’t it?’

‘It surely is!’ she said.

At the door, she turned and looked at my immaculate bed. - 'And it was a fine night too, no doubt.’

Chapter 8

Jenny and I were alone for breakfast. I told her about Ruyter being the fat man from Stonefort Securities and my reasons for not calling the police.

She whistled in surprise. 'Well of all the brass necks,' she said indignantly, 'What is he doing here?'

'He's taken the lodge, and Aunt Carrie just naturally invited him to dinner.'

'And you knew him from the moment he walked in and said nothing? How could you manage to keep your hands off him?'

I felt a stab of guilt. I had been more intent on playing word games. Trying to find out how far Ruyter had got and how much he knew.

I gave her Ruyter's version of her kidnapping and she was partly mollified.

'Stoker wants me to help him recover the gold from the wreck,' I said, ' I'm to pick him up in the Pelican in three days time, — Ruyter wants to take over the operation .'

'Take over? What can he put into it?'

'He can handle the sale. Get the best price.'

'He's a crook!'

'I know. That's why he'll get the best price. Legally we'd get about ten per cent. Ruyter's offering twenty five if I go in with him.'

'But he's a *crook*!' Jenny repeated. 'Surely you wouldn't trust him.'

'Not an inch – and there's another thing: – why would he need me? He's got a perfectly good boat of his own and he implies that he knows the location of the wreck. He says that I would be 'guided in'.

Jenny chewed on her toast and concentrated hard.

'You said that the police were watching that boat for a sight of Bennett. He probably knows that.'

'Okay,' I concede, 'So may be he needs the Pelican. But he also maintains that Dave Gregory was working with him. I don't believe that. According to Stoker, Ruyter thought that Dave and I were collaborating. He was paying Stoker to watch us. He doesn't seem to be aware of Stoker's importance.'

'Why would Ruyter say Dave was working with him if he wasn't?'

I shrugged. 'Lord knows. Maybe to confuse me, make me more pliable.'

'Well, it's confusing me anyway. More tea?'

I nodded and pushed my cup forward.

'What will you do?' Jenny said.

I stirred my tea. 'Keep out of his way, pick up Stoker, snatch the goods and head for the hills. If Ruyter and Co are still around when I get back, I'll blow the whistle on them.'

'And how will you sell the stuff? Always supposing you don't get an attack of the 'legals'.'

'I believe Swiss banks are pretty accommodating.'

Jenny gave a 'hah' of disbelief. 'And how would clever clogs get it to Switzerland?'

'What about a caravan holiday? I don't suppose the customs search campers much. Not outward bound ones anyway.'

'They might.'

'Don't you want to marry a millionaire?'

She regarded me quizzically. 'Correct me if I'm wrong, but was that you, last night, who was going to give it all up for my sake? Was it you who was going to settle down and farm?'

I reached for her hands across the table. She pulled hers away and sat upright.

'I'll marry you Mike – and I won't say a word against you going after the gold – on one condition.'

'Ah! And what might that condition be?' I asked suspiciously.

'That you let me help. — Take me with you.'

I was horrified. 'Take you? But that's impossible.'

'I knew you'd say that. Why is it that men always want to hog all the fun for themselves?'

'Fun? I like that. It will be hard work'

'Then the more help you have the better.'

'It will be dangerous!'

'Rubbish – you're going to leave the 'baddies' behind. And the wreck is not too deep, so where would the danger lie?'

'We could all end up in a French prison,' I said despairingly.

'Oh, but the French judiciary are very understanding,' Jenny smiled, ' They'd probably give us adjoining cells – with a communicating door.'

'Be serious Jenny.'

'I'm getting more serious every second. Have you thought how you're going to handle the job? I don't mean the actual diving, I mean your 'cover'. How are you going to disguise what you are up to?'

'We could creep in after dark. It may all come up in one operation, depending on how much is down there. And how the wreck is lying.'

'Too sneaky,' she said, 'Too suspicious by far, they probably have – radar bugs or whatever – all over the place.'

I said I thought this was unlikely unless the site was near a naval base. 'Go on then, mastermind, how would *you* go about it?'

'Openly,' she said, 'Drop anchor there like a regular 'Anglais' holiday maker, and while you are beavering away down below – sending up the stuff on the blind side – I'll be sunbathing on deck or doing some shopping ashore. — Diverting attention.'

I was dubious. 'We'll see what Stoker says. He's had forty years to think about this lot.'

We'd finished breakfast by now and still neither Aunt Carrie nor Charles had put in an appearance. With unspoken accord, we went outside and made our way to the stable yard.

'And that's another odd aspect,' Jenny mused, as she put her arm through mine, 'Why has Stoker never tried to get hold of it before? Forty years is a long time to keep the stopper on a fortune.'

'It is. Mind you, I've only heard half the story. Possibly, he only knew the approximate location, and he's only recently been able to pinpoint it.'

It had rained sharply at first light, and now the sun was shining between fresh-washed, high white clouds, making puddles sparkle and drawing steam from heaps of soiled bedding straw outside each loose box. A bucket clanged. Kenny called something from within one of the dark caverns, and was answered from another, by a girls voice, teasing.

This was a mighty good way to start a day.

I gave Jenny's waist a squeeze.'Tell you what: – let's forget it all and enjoy ourselves for a few hours.'

'Brilliant idea!'

We changed and saddled up, then made our way across the fields to the trials area. Walk, trot, canter, the turf springy, firm underfoot; the horses gleaming, keen, and spring-stepped.

From the top of Hanger Hill we could see horse-boxes drawn up in tidy rows. Large self contained lorries and small, neat affairs, drawn by family saloons or Range Rovers. Some had their ramps down with their four legged passengers standing patiently while tails were brushed and legs bandaged.

A minute figure that was surely Aunt Carrie, stepped out from the secretary's caravan and squinted in our direction, her hand shading her eyes from the sun. So *that* was why I hadn't seen her at breakfast!

She waved an arm at us and we headed her way. Kenny and Lisa, the stable girl, riding a pair of likely looking duns, caught us up as we threaded our way through the towing vehicles. Aunt Carrie thrust a schedule at me and I found my name, inked in, at the bottom of the open event.

'Hey what's this?' I pointed at Jenny's name, which was printed.'You were entered all the time, and you didn't say a word.'

She smiled sideways. 'It's a queer thing about being kidnapped,' she said, 'It always drives everything else from my mind.'

'Come on,' I said, 'let's see what's in store for us.'

We handed the horses over to Kenny and Lisa, and started to walk the course. It began with a couple of simple brush fences, and then through and over a variety of ingenious obstacles made up from logs, old motor tyres, oil drums and rope.

Two thirds of the way round we crossed a dry ditch, turned right and angled up over grass towards a stand of conifers.

Two figures, partly obscured, were standing in a gateway some two hundred yards to our right.

One was Ruyter. He moved out of the gateway and angled up the slope as if to intercept us at the top. I nudged Jenny, and her stride checked for a second as she caught sight of the large, lumbering figure

'He's after my answer, I'll bet,' I said

Ruyter reached the trees and paused to look down at us before stepping from view between the trunks.'

'What will you tell him ?' Jenny asked.

'I'll string him along a bit; tell him I like the idea but have to think about it.'

We reached the first of the conifers and looked about for Ruyter. I called his name, then we stood still and listened.

There was no sound except for the faint stirring of the slender treetops.

'He must have walked on,' Jenny said, and led off along the needle-carpeted track. We passed the next two jumps with no sign of him.

A long, gently-sloping meadow now lay before us, sweeping down to the finishing point with its fast-swelling crowd. The public address system was squawking into hesitant life and still more horse-boxes and cars were arriving.

Half-way down, Jenny turned her head to look back up the slope.'Well he's not ahead and he's not following, I wonder where he got to?'

'Beats me! Perhaps he doesn't want to discuss skullduggery in front of a lady. Some crooks are funny that way.'

We found Rosalie and Hot Potato secured to the side of Amanda's horse–box, happily sharing a hay-net. A thin, haughty looking miss of about fourteen, appeared to be looking after them. Jenny knew her.

'Hallo Trish, where are Kenny and Lisa?'

Trish gave me a down-the-nose look as she pointed with her chin. 'Novice jumping,' she said, adding, 'In number two ring.' She got to her feet and moved off. 'I'm going to watch!'

Jenny thanked her for looking after the horses and we sat side by side on the ramp. I took the creased schedule from my pocket.

'What time are we on?' Jenny asked.

'One thirty according to this. I got up and slapped a horse-fly on Rosalie's rump. 'Come on Jen, they'll be okay for a while. Let's watch the jumping.'

We walked carefully round a half-dozen shrill, young Thelwell types, who were jumping straw bales, and arrived at ring two in time to see Lisa and "Chatterbox" complete a clear round. She trotted over to us, beaming happily and patting the dun's neck.

'I'm in the jump off' she crowed.

Kenny went next, knocked a brick off the wall, and refused at the parallels. With seven faults, he was out of it. I saw Freddy Fletcher explaining to him, with waving hands, where he'd gone wrong.

Afterwards, Freddy made his way over to Jenny and me. 'Hallo Mike. Your Aunt tells me you're riding my old mate Hot Potato.'

I nodded a greeting. 'I hope he serves me better than he served you last week. Anyway, why aren't you riding yourself?'

He turned his mouth down. 'Trials aren't really my cup of tea. Too many twists and turns.'

'Aunt Carrie says she might buy him. I can't visualize you two ever parting.'

'I need the money' he said bluntly. 'Bloody tractor's costing a fortune in repairs and I can't farm without it. Then he brightened. 'You'll be all right. Just whisper 'glue factory' in his ear before you start and he'll fly 'em all!'

We watched Lisa win the jump off, then walked along the perimeter track beneath overhanging trees, back towards the official hub. There was the sound of a gently revving engine behind me. I guided Jenny off the path, and we stood aside to let a dusty bronze estate car go by, closely followed by a big saloon, which rolled expensively in and out of the ruts. I glanced idly at the two occupants as the saloon passed, but it was a good thirty yards away, and accelerating, before it dawned on me that Bennett occupied the front passenger seat.

I yelled! 'Oy!' at the top of my lungs, and sprinted after the vehicle, catching it up as it slowed to turn out of the gate. I grabbed the door handle and tried to wrench it open, but it was locked from inside. I poked an arm in through the partly open window, to release the catch, but Bennett told the driver sharply to 'put his foot down' and at the same time rapped my fingers hard with something heavy and metallic.

As he struck, he sucked his lower lip in between his teeth and turned hate filled, pink rimmed eyes to mine. Then the car was gone and I was left standing in the middle of the lane sucking my bloody knuckles.

Back at the caravan, Aunt Carrie got busy with the Elastoplast, while Jenny wanted to know what I thought Bennett was doing there and what was I going to do now? I tucked my hand under my armpit and considered the two questions.

'I can't fathom what's going on, but I don't like the feeling of him and Ruyter being so close. I've changed my mind about not going to the police. In fact, if those two are picked up, we'll have a clear field. I can't see them blabbing about gold to the cops, can you? They'll be too busy trying to wriggle off the hook.'

'What about the driver? Have you seen him before?'

'I took it for granted it was Ruyter. I didn't get a look at him.'

'I did,' Jenny was emphatic, 'At the back of his head anyway, and it definitely was *not* Ruyter!'

An anxious young face under a hard hat appeared at the caravan door, with a query, and Aunt Carrie's attention was suddenly back on the job. I eased out through the opening and stood undecided on the trampled grass. Jenny joined me.

'What now?' she asked.

'Well – there's no phone box near. I could go back to the house and phone from there.'

Jenny said that there was usually a police car somewhere about on show days.'Probably up at the turn off from the main road' she said. 'We could send one of the messengers.

She looked over my shoulder. 'Here comes Kenny. He'll go.'

When Kenny heard the message we wanted him to take, he gave a short laugh of disbelief, but when it sank in that we were serious, he was bursting to go – full of eager self importance.

Jenny nodded to the hedge. 'Go by the fields,' she said, 'You'll be quicker.'

Kenny swung the pony around, and made for a nearby gap in the hedge. We watched them fly up the sloping meadow beyond, the pony's neck and tail at full stretch, and Kenny's heels pounding.

Jenny laughed. 'There goes the news from 'Ghent to Aix' !'

CHAPTER 9.

A police car was now parked between the secretary's caravan and the ice-cream van.

The Grantley limo had arrived at lunch-time, and was taking up half an acre of space on the other side. Uncle Charles dozed in the front seat, while Evelyn sat erect in the back, picking at a picnic box. She called, 'Good luck Michael', as I rode Hot Potato at a walk down to the start. I smiled and waved back, then I turned my back on the starter so that he could read my number.

'You're last to go" he said, 'two more before you.'

While I waited, I scanned the horizon looking for Jenny and Rosalie.

Hot Potato started throwing his head about and trotting on the spot, so I walked him in a brisk circle a couple of times.

Then I saw Jenny and Rosalie, a long way off, moving in and out of sight as the ground rose and fell.

'One minute, Mr. Peterson!'

Rolalie came over the drop-jump at the top of the rise, stumbling as she landed. Jenny slid forward over her neck, recovered, and came on.

'Thirty seconds!'

I turn Hot Potato and walk him, held in, towards the line. He's quivering, taking short dancing steps.

'Ten seconds!'

I throw a glance over my shoulder, Jenny's on my left, moving parallel towards the last fence.

'Three – two – one – Go!'

We're away and over the first brush fence, and making for the water splash. For a nasty moment, I think I've forgotten the way and at the next jump, try to remember what the little arrows stand for. Black for Open? Or is it red? White means 'restricted', or should ---? No, I must follow the black ones.

We drum on.

Over a log we go, a row of hanging tyres beneath, and Hot Potato lengthens his stride through a patch of gorse

Left across the track, spectators straying dangerously close.

A plank fence next, then a sharp descent to a thorn-hedge with a muddy landing on the far side. Each obstacle guarded by a clipboard-wielding judge.

Now we're flying flat-out towards a group of three ancient beeches. I relax and concentrate on enjoying myself.

Under the trees we clear a "picnic table" in fine style, then sharp right over a bank into a sunken lane – brambles clawing and grabbing. Which way is out? Sharp right again, you idiot! Now left – left! Panic – the black arrow is pointing heavenwards. 'Not yet God, please!'

Through an open gate, we erupt from the cloying gloom onto crisp golden stubble. A hundred yards ahead stands a farm wagon with iron-bound wheels – old and dignified. Jump on, "clomp, clomp, clomp "– a fat, hollow sound – jump off –

Gleaming rooks scatter like black rags in a wind storm, and the snorting rattle of the gelding's breath is loud in my ear.

Leaning forward I urge him on, clearing low, rustic poles; into a new-planting of silver birch. Thin, dream-like trunks, flashing, merging, as we twist and turn between them. A stone wall – grass – cows and sheep grazing, just out of harms way and no longer interested.

Another wall, another wood, sombre, dark green, with a heavy pine smell. The track bends slightly and before us are crossed-poles. We race on towards them, my spirit soaring ------.

I don’t remember hitting the ground .... Just waking,-- breathless, --to complete silence and very near total blackness. I'd descended through tightly meshing branches of close-packed spruce saplings, and they had closed after my descent as if to claim me forever.

As my breathing returned to almost normal, I began to get to my feet, stopping short when I reached a kneeling position, to consider what a perfectly good brown brogue was doing not a yard away from me, with its toe pointing skywards.

I moved my head and saw that the shoe contained a sock, dark green like the pine trees, and the sock merged into the pale colour of cavalry twill. I crept forwards on my hands and knees to investigate the phenomenon.

Ruyter’s eyes were wide open, but he was quite dead.

CHAPTER 10

‘But you must admit Mr. Peterson, that for someone who doesn’t know what it’s all about, you do get involved rather often with these people!’

DI Cawardine walked over to the drawing room window and stood with his back to me, looking out at the gathering night. DS Oldshaw was sitting at the spindle-legged writing table, his notebook open, and a look of expectancy on his face.

‘Perhaps Mr. Peterson would care to make a statement Sir,’ he suggested.

Cawardine turned to face me. ‘I think that is a very sensible suggestion Sergeant. What do you think Mr. Peterson?’

I walked over to the wall switches and turned on all the lights. The last of the lingering daylight fled, turning the grey rectangle of the window jet black. I crossed the room again, and closed the heavy velvet curtains.

The delay didn't help.

'Mr. Peterson ?' The inspector was prompting me.

'A statement? Is that necessary? Surely you don't think that I killed him?'

'No sir. A statement is merely a convenient method of recording your part in what occurred

'I had *no* part in it,' I said,' It had happened by the time I found him.'

Oldshaw stopped scribbling and looked up. There was wonder in his tone. 'That was quite a coincidence sir: your falling off your horse at the very place where – '

'I did not fall off: I was thrown. There is a difference.' I was being petty.

'Of course sir !' His voice was conciliatory. He was needling me politely. All part of the treatment.

'You say you'd seen Ruyter earlier in the-day?' Cawardine was now examining a silken Chinese scroll hanging in a recess.

'That's right – walking into the wood.'

'And did you speak to him?'

'No – by the time we reached the wood, – Mrs McLaine and I, – he was gone.'

'Was anyone else around at the time?'

'Several people: riders walking the course, - - one or two spectators, – judges.'

I suddenly remembered the man Ruyter had been talking to in the gateway. I told the Inspector. He went over to Oldshaw and looked over his shoulder at the notebook. I wished he'd stand still.

'Could that have been Bennett?' he asked.

I shook my head. 'No – the man was short and stocky.'

Oldshaw looked up and tapped the table with his Biro. 'Could the man in the gateway have been the one driving the car you saw later? The one with Bennett in it?'

'Possibly. I didn't really see the driver – only Bennett.'

Cawardine asked me why I'd chased the car.

'Because Bennett was in it,' I said

Oldshaw asked if I wanted to drag him out and thump him.

I began to feel like a ping-pong ball. ‘I don’t know. When I realised it was him I just boiled over and ran after him.’

‘And got your knuckles rapped.’ Oldshaw eyed my plaster covered fingers.‘What did he hit you with? Could it have been a gun?’

‘Could have been,' I said, ' I only caught a glimpse.’

‘Ruyter appears to have been shot. Do you own a gun Mr. Peterson?’Cawardine aked.

‘No, – I mean yes!’ Four eyebrows raised fractionally. ‘There’s a ‘four-ten’ in the library that belongs to me.’

Oldshaw made another note. Cawardine sat down on a wheel-back chair and regarded me thoughtfully.

‘Mr. Peterson – when we raided the office in Albemarle Street, you were there first – er – keeping the place under observation as it were...'

‘That’s right. As I said, I found a card in Sandra’s handbag and put two and two – ’

‘A card like this ?’ Cawardine held out one of Stonefort's cards.

‘Exactly like that.'

‘There were a dozen of these in the dead man’s wallet. Now think carefully Mr. Peterson. Was Ruyter the man you saw through the door-crack on that occasion?'

My mouth was suddenly dry as I realised where this was leading. I licked my lips and tried to sound unconcerned.

‘Yes,’ I said.

Their eyes were intent – unwavering.

Cawardine said: 'Lady Grantley has told us that Ruyter was a guest here at dinner last night, and that you were also a guest.’

I nodded.

‘Did you not recognise Ruyter last night Mr. Peterson?’

I could see no point in denying it. For one thing I didn’t know how much Aunt Carrie had told them.

‘Yes I did recognise him,’ I admitted.

‘Then why did you not ring the police immediately? Have you an explanation for that Mr. Peterson?’

I took a good deep breath and prepared to tell them the lot. I was tired of prevarication.Then I had what I took to be a brainwave. I went over to the sideboard and poured myself a drink.

'Would either of you care – ?' I began.

Neither spoke. Neither changed his facial expression.

'Oh, of course not. You're on duty.' I took a sip and changed my tone to one of confidentiality. 'My reasons for not turning him in are quite sound.' I glanced towards the door and lowered my voice. 'You see, there are aspects of the situation that may well be covered by the official secrets act. I watched their faces without much hope. Now I'd said it, it sounded pretty feeble. Inspector and Sergeant exchanged dead-pan looks.

Cawardine lowered his voice to match mine. 'We are bound by an oath of loyalty sir. You may trust our discretion. Or if you prefer it, I can arrange an interview with the Chief Constable. He has direct access to the Home Office ...'

I was being sent up rotten and I had the feeling that I was getting way out of my depth.

'I recognised Ruyter last night – yes. And he knew me. He put a proposition to me.' I went and sat in an easy chair. I was still wondering how much to leave out. 'He said he had a client in Helston who was using him to investigate a possible confidence trick-- Ruyter employed Bennett and Harris.'

'Did he tell you the name of the client?'

'No. But I do know it. His name is Poplar, and he lives at a house called "Windbeck" '

Oldshaw looked up from his writing. 'Can you be more specific about this supposed confidence trick?'

The ground was sticky here--Quicksand!

'Not really, except that it was to do with sunken gold.'

Cawardine's eyes were watching me keenly. 'The gold again. You said Ruyter made you a proposition. Was it to do with this gold?'

'He seemed to think it actually existed. He wanted to use my Pelican to go after it!' I tried to sound indignant.

Oldshaw tapped his teeth with his pen.'He knew it's location then?--- That's if it does exist.'

'He implied as much.'I said.

Cawardine jumped in. 'And how about you Mr. Peterson? Do you know it's location?'

'Of course not. How could I?'

'Well, I think it's a reasonable assumption that you would. Gregory must have been involved or Bennett would not have been searching his flat. Then he went on to search your boat and Mrs McLaine's farm. You worked with Gregory frequently. You may have been working together on this!'

'No!' I was beginning to feel hemmed in. 'I knew nothing about any of it until I went to Dave Gregory's flat and caught Bennett ransacking it.'

Cawardine changed tacks suddenly. 'Did you have anything to do with the Garland's destruction, Mr. Petersen?'

'Good God no!' I was on my feet again, angry. 'That's a stupid suggestion!'

'Stupid? I don't think —'

'Look, it's obvious. Bennett blew the boat up. Bennett and Harris did all the breaking and entering and kidnapping; and I'll bet that Bennett shot Ruyter.'

'And why would he do that?'

'How would I know?' I was exasperated, 'He's a thug! He probably wouldn't need much of a reason.'

Oldshaw was leafing back through his notes. He found a page and held it open. 'You say Ruyter's client lives at a house called 'Windbeck?'

'That's right.'

'And a few days ago you overheard Ruyter tell Bennett he'd contact him at 'Windbeck' '

'Yes.'

Cawardine shuffled the 'Stonefort' cards and dealt them. 'Do you know for a fact that Bennett sank the Garland?'

'Of course I don't. But if it wasn't accidental, then he seems to be the best bet.'

Oldshaw now. 'The car you chased to day, have you remembered any more about it?'

I sighed. 'Maroon Jag; -- 'V' registration.'

'And you've never seen it before?'

'I told you. No!'

A cough from the doorway caught our attention. Charles stood, looking vaguely at the policemen. 'There you are Michael; I thought you might give me a game of billiards. Perhaps your friends would care to play? Cawardine stood up and at a sign from his superior, Oldshaw, closed his notebook and did the same.

'Thank you sir, but we must go.'

The Inspector walked towards the door. Charles turned and led the way into the hall.

'Dobson should be around somewhere to let you out, but never mind, I'll do it – Can't think where the fellow's got to. Fine defensive bat you know, but absolutely useless as a butler.

'Good of you to take the trouble sir.' Cowardine smiled at Uncle Charles, then turned to me. 'If you should remember anything else, Mr. Peterson-?'

'I'll let you know of course.'

'You'll be required to attend the inquest. And the inquest on Gregory is tomorrow, don't forget.'

'What time does it start?'

Oldshaw answered for him. 'Ten a.m. sir.'

When he'd closed the door behind them I grinned at Uncle Charles. 'What was all that about Dobson? He left here a couple of years ago didn't he?'

Charles flapped a gnarled hand. 'Very likely, my boy – very likely!'

We joined Aunt Carrie and Jenny in the large drawing room. Jenny was sitting on a regency striped settee and I gave her a squeeze as I sat beside her. She pecked my cheek.

'How was the third degree?'

'I felt as guilty as hell. It was all very polite, but I don't know... I could almost feel the handcuffs.'

Aunt Carrie was standing at the hearth nervously playing with a glass paperweight. 'What now, do you think?'

'I expect they'll go to 'Windbeck' and arrest Bennett. That's if he's gone back there.'

Aunt Carrie was staring thoughtfully at the phone, which sat on an onyx table by the window. She crossed the room, picked it up and dialed. 'Oh – hallo – my name is Rogers – Deborah Rogers – could I speak to Commander Poplar please ? - Oh I'm sorry, I was told he was still – of course – No, no. I served under the Commander for a while during the war and there is to be a small re-union. Who am I speaking to please ? - I am sorry to have bothered you, Mr. Poplar.

Goodnight!'

We were all waiting expectantly as she put down the receiver.

'He died seven years ago,' Aunt Carrie said, 'That was his brother I spoke to: Dermot Poplar.'

Jenny stirred. 'So somebody finds sunken gold and goes to a retired naval officer's brother with the story. Why would he do that? Why not just raise it?'

We tossed that ball about for another hour, without getting any where, then Charles, who had appeared to be dozing in his armchair, sat up, wondering who the 'blue Rover' belonged to. We all looked at him. He closed his eyes again and folded his hands across his waistcoat.

Aunt Carrie said sharply. 'You are *infuriating,* Charlie – what blue Rover?'

Charles opened one eye a fraction. 'It was parked behind the lodge. I saw the bonnet sticking out when we drove through this morning, to go to the show. Wasn't there when we came back!'

The eye closed, then before I'd taken another breath, they were both wide, and he was halfway across the room.

'Come along Michael, I want that game of billiards.'

I was sucked along behind him by his enthusiasm, and as we set the game up, I asked him if he'd told the police about the blue Rover.

He hook his head. 'I'd forgotten about it untill now,' he said.

I rang the police station from the billiard room extension. The desk clerk thanked me and assured me that he would pass on the message.

Uncle Charles beat me two games out of three.

CHAPTER 11

I sat on the edge of Jenny's bed, combing my fingers through her hair, enjoying the silken feel of it, and the play of light from the table lamp.

'I should have gone back home this evening,' she sounded troubled, 'There's an awful lot of work.. Jimmy will ---'

I gripped her hand and shook it a little. 'He's nearly sixteen

Jenny! He's old enough to run things on his own for a couple of days. And you did ring him.'

She frowned. 'Do you know he actually sounded rather pleased that I'd be away another night!'

I laughed. 'And now you wonder what he's up to. He's grown up now! Anyway – I'm glad you didn't go.'

I bent to kiss her, and she smelled of autumn roses.

Later, I was roused by a door banging outside. I slipped from Jenny's side and was surprised to see, by her small traveling clock, that it was only just after midnight. I switched off the light and looked out from her window to the back terrace.

In the pool of light spilling from the kitchen window, two gleaming red setters stretched and yawned, before beginning a sniffing perambulation from drainpipe to drainpipe. The larger one, known as Pluto, barely had time to anoint a large ornamental urn, when his companion Juno, gave a warning bark, and was away like an arrow, into the solid blackness of the night.

Pluto catapulted after her. I opened the window wider and cocked an ear to follow their crashing progress as they careered through the vegetable garden, to set up loud aggressive barking in the region of the potting shed.

Jenny padded over to join me, the eiderdown wrapped around her. 'What's happening?'

'The dogs are after something. Hark at that racket!'

She yawned. 'Probably a fox or rabbit.'

'I'll go and check. Could be a prowler.'

On my way through the library, I took my old four-ten from the gun cabinet. Letting myself out through the French windows I skirted the house round to the kitchen.

Mrs. Beddows stood framed in the open door, flashing a torch like a small searchlight, out over the vegetables Jenny, now in dressing gown, came through the kitchen and joined her.

The dogs were silent as we moved down the wide steps and along the well-kept paths to the shed.

Pluto sat like a garden ornament, as though hypnotised by the door handle, while Juno lay stretched, gnawing a bone gripped between her paws.

I pointed the shotgun at the single black window. Mrs. Beddows stood to one side to shine the torch through.

It's beam lit up, a man sitting on a stack of bagged compost, the collar of his donkey jacket up and his old woollen cap pulled well down.

Squinting, he held up a hand against the torchlight.

I lowered the gun, pushed Pluto aside with my foot and opened the door.

'Come on out Stoker. The game's up.'

Stoker edged out, tentatively, and glowered down at Juno. 'That bugger's 'ad me supper!'

Mrs. Beddows flicked the light up at him. 'You mind your language!'

'Sorry!' Stoker rumbled, 'Couldn't tell you was a lady – what with the light in my eyes.' Then he caught sight of Jenny. 'Oops – two of 'em!

We went back to the kitchen, where the dogs, after a last, suspicious sniff at Stoker, curled up in their baskets.

I explained to Mrs. Beddows that Stoker was a friend of mine,

'If you're sure he's respectable Mr. Peterson. Though it beats me why he was skulking out there.'

She reluctantly retired to bed. Jenny made coffee and I found Stoker some bread and cheese.

'So what *were* you doing out there?' I asked him.

He chewed and spoke with his mouth full. 'Keeping out of the way 'till the "busies" had gone.'

He swallowed and bit again. 'I fell asleep in that shed. Then I was coming over to the house when the 'ounds of the Baskervilles went for me, so I nipped back sharpish.'

'But you're supposed to be waiting for me in Plymouth.'

Stoker looked uncomfortable. 'Yeah, well, I would've been, only I ran out of money.'

'You shouldn't have spent so much on coal.' I told him pointedly.

His face took on a worried look. 'You think it's safe there?'

'As in the Bank of England!'

Jenny was looking from one to the other of us. 'Am I missing something? Why shouldn't coal be safe?'

'It's what beneath the coal,' I told her, 'An item dear to Stoker's heart.'

Jenny's eyes lit up. "You don't mean the -?' She shaped an imaginary brick with her hands.

I nodded.

Stoker sat back, sucked his teeth, and started groping in his side pockets. Eventually, his careful fingers extracted a dog end, a full inch long. He delicately picked blue fluff from it and critically examined both ends.

I sighed. 'Hang on a minute.'

I went to the library and came back with three or four cheroots which I placed beside his plate.

He said, 'Cor thanks,' and lit up.

Jenny refilled his coffee cup, and Stoker leaned back, his face radiating gap-toothed happiness.

'This is living!'

I was half disapproving, half jealous. 'They'll shorten your life,' I said.

Stoker closed one eye against the smoke and coughed. 'I'm sixty-eight and looking forward, "For the best is yet to come".'

'You don't look it Mr. Figgin! I would have guessed you were much younger.'

Stoker transferred his rheumy gaze to Jenny, lapping up the blatant flattery. 'Thank you Ma-am, but please call me Ronald. All my friends do!'

'No they don't,' I butted in brutally, 'they call you Stoker, and you look at least a hundred. How did you know I was here?'

With difficulty he dragged his eyes from Jenny's face. 'Oh, I went back to the Pelican, but Sam said you was prob'ly at Mrs McLaine's.'

I was surprised. 'Sam Wilkins is out of hospital?'

'Yeah – he wrote himself out. Head all bandaged up and chirpy as a sparrer.'

'Anyroad, I hung about a bit, waiting for you to come back, then I thought I'd better make sure, so I telephoned the farm and the young lady said – '

Jenny sat bolt upright, her eyes wide. 'Young lady, *what* young lady?'

'I don't know,' Stoker faltered, 'I never asked. She said as how –'

'What time was this? Jenny was gripping the edge of the table.

Stoker regarded the ceiling through the tobacco haze. 'Round about twelve... Summat like that.'

'I'll kill him! I *will*! I trust him to behave and he goes---'

The rest of it was lost as Jenny flounced out of the kitchen, in search of a phone.

'Ave I put me foot in it?' Stoker's look was apologetic.

'Both feet!' I told him. 'Her lad was assumed to be alone there!'

Stoker grinned. 'Lad having a bit of nooky on the quiet? 'Ope I 'aven't spoiled it for 'im.'

Jenny came back into the kitchen. 'There's no answer,' she glared at Stoker as though it was his fault.

'Probably worn out and fast asleep,' I said brightly. 'You know how it is.'

Jenny's look practically bored a hole through me, and I added hurriedly: 'Being left on his own with all that work.'

'As I was saying,' went on Stoker, 'It was nearly dinner time by then, so I 'ad some chips and then gave this place a ring, and they said everybody was at the show ground. So then I —'

'Dinner time?' Jenny sounded relieved. 'You mean, you phoned Highfields at a quarter to midday, – not midnight?'

'That's right.' Stoker's face was dead-pan.'Why? What difference does it make?' Getting no answer, he went on: 'I thumbed a lift in an 'orse box and Bob's your Uncle.'

'But that was hours ago!' I poured myself more coffee. 'Where have you been all this time?'

'For a start, I saw Bennett and another bloke in a Jag as we turned off the main road, so I knew there was something up. Then, when we gets into the show ground, I starts looking for you.

'The old bird in the caravan said you'd be about ten minutes, so I hung about, keeping one eye on that copper in the Panda, till this kid comes dashing up on a pony, yelling there was a dead body in the woods.'

Stoker threw his cigar stub accurately into a coal-scuttle and spread his hands.

'Not wishing to be in the way, I sort of faded into the background... Who was it ?'

'Eugene Ruyter, Bennett's boss.'

'Well well. Was that why Bennett was leaving in a hurry? I'll bet he did it.'

'Did you recognise the other man in the Jag? The driver?'

'Nah! It was Ruyter's car-though.'

'Do you know anyone who drives a blue Rover?'

Stoker scratched his nose. 'I've seen Bennett drive a Rover, yeah, a blue one!'

Jenny summed up. 'So Bennett and someone unknown arrive in a blue Rover. They and Ruyter are all at the trials. Then there is some juggling with cars; Ruyter is found shot, and the other two dash off. Both cars have gone too.'

I looked at the marble clock on the mantle piece. It showed a quarter to two.

There was an easy chair by the kitchen range and, after pulling off his boots, Stoker stretched himself comfortably in it.

'This'll do me till daylight if nobody minds.'

He was holding an unlit cheroot between his fingers. I told him nobody would mind as long as he didn't set the house on fire.

When we got to Jenny's doorway, she turned and poked a finger in my chest.

'I don't believe it was a quarter to twelve *midday*,' she poked again for emphasis, and her eye was steely. I believe you made that up between you!'

Then she was gone and the door was between us. I heard the key turn in the lock.

When Mrs. Beddows brought my early morning tea, she seemed surprised to find me asleep in my own bed.

CHAPTER 12

It was still dark when I guided the Pelican through the deep water channel, at the eastern end of the breakwater, and headed directly south towards the beckoning beam on the Eddystone Reef.

Frank Gregory and Stoker, were making ready to hoist sail, and when at last we ran clear of the land and had the easterly breeze square on the beam, I put the strop on the wheel and went forrard to help.

Gaff and jib cupped the wind, held it, and the Pelican heeled comfortably onto a reach. I went back into the cuddy, took the wheel again and cut the engine.

Immediately, with the vibration and noise gone, Pelican took on a different character. Under power she had been stolid, pushing her unfeeling way through the water.

Now though, she was released and became one with the sea and the wind. She was alive, straining eagerly at the darkness, and through my fingers, my wrists and muscles of my arms, she was pulling me with her.

Stoker felt it too. In this thin, phantom mist, which was creeping over and about us, I could see him standing in the bow, hands deep in his pockets, balancing himself easily with the Pelican's motion.

Frank, I wasn't so sure about. He was leaning over the lee rail, in an unmistakable attitude and I guessed it would take him an hour or two to get his sea legs back.. Some people succumb more readily to a steady roll than they would to a gale, and poor Frank was one of these.

The still invisible sun pushed a pale pink band of light clear of the eastern horizon and tinged the Pelican's grey-white sails.

A flight of swallows swooped down from astern, flew alongside for a while and then soared up and away, going south, like us, but further and faster. A couple of them had alighted on the weather shroud and hung there, twisting their heads this way and that, looking at each other, looking at the sky, as if not exactly sure what they were supposed to be doing.

The cabin hatch opened and an arm appeared, swathed in a thick green pullover. From the cuff protruded a slim brown hand, holding a large steaming mug of tea.

Jenny put the mug by my feet, then disappeared to bring two more. I slid back the wheel house door on the lee side and hollered 'Tea up!'

Stoker turned and came aft, leaning against the tilt of the deck.

Frank didn't move.

Stoker picked up two mugs and hailed him with the unfeeling cheerfulness of the un-seasick. 'You stay where you are mate, I can drink yours.'

Nevertheless, he took Frank's tea over, coming back immediately, grinning.

'I think he said: "go away".' He stood by the open starboard door, slurping his tea noisily.

The tall column of the Eddystone Lighthouse slid by. A couple of smart yachts crossed our stern, west-bound. Then two fishing boats heading for the Atlantic and a low black coaster, the 'Greta' out of Antwerp, steadily working her way to Falmouth to pick up china clay.

Jenny came up from below and sat on the bench behind me. She leaned towards Stoker.

Without preamble she asked: 'What happened when you got ashore in France all those years ago?'

Stoker flicked away his cigarette end. It curved high, caught by the wind, and one of our escorting gulls swooped to investigate, decided it was not edible and resumed its station.

'What happened? Well, not a lot. I mostly just kept out of the way.'

'But weren't you captured?'

Stoker shook his head and drained his mug. 'That was a lovely drop o' tea. I don't suppose there's any more?'

Jenny spoke with exaggerated patience. 'I'll make you a pot all to yourself, if you'll just tell me what happened. I'm *interested.* I've led a sheltered life. Now; From the beginning.'

Stoker puffed out his cheeks and directed his eyes at the masthead.... 'Well – when war broke out, I – '

'Are you trying to be funny? — From when you landed on the French shore.'

Stoker looked mournfully into his empty mug. Jenny sighed, took it from him, and went below.

Stoker called down after her.'If the good captain 'as 'appened to bring along any o' them cheroots, — Not for myself, you understand.'

Eventually, Stoker wedged himself to his own satisfaction, in the doorway, with his tea and his smoke. 'Where was I? Oh yes, — well, when I got ashore, it was still dark ... and damned *cold* as well, I can tell you.

'A few yards up the beach, I was into barbed wire. I felt my way along but there was no weak spot as far as I could tell ... So I squeezed through, kind of gentle expectin' to go sky high on a mine, any second, or set off a flare. But nothing happened. Then I came up against a wall, and I heard voices. I moved along for another fifty yards or so, then I could see a gap in the cliff against the stars so I headed for it, up this bit of a sandy track . When I gets to the top, there's a lot more wire ... and iron stakes.'

Stoker stopped talking as Frank slowly pushed himself upright against the rail, took a few deep breaths and walked towards us, a weak lopsided grin on his pale face. Stoker handed him his cold tea. The sun had heaved itself up out of the sea by now and her rays were bouncing off a million whitecaps.

'Go on!' Jenny prompted. Stoker lowered his head further into his upturned collar and shivered at the memory.

'Well, there I was – cold, wet, and bloody browned off, so I crawled in among the gorse bushes, to wait for daylight.

'When it did start to get light, I heard voices again, some way off --like orders being shouted, -- then crunch – crunch – crunch -- boots marching on gravel.

'I 'ad a dekko and there was a couple o' dozen Jerries heading towards me from a dip in the ground. They went by too damned close for comfort, and over to some pillboxes that had started to show up.

'They must have been the day shift, 'cos a bit later, another lot comes marching back again.

'When they'd gone, I crawled through the gorse till I could look out over the sea. There was no sight of the M.T.B., and I reckoned she must have gone down. Any road, I didn't want to 'ang about there, so I starts crawling the other way. I found the place where the soldiers 'ad gone through the wire and just kept going. It was all sand dunes – ups and downs, and then more barbed wire. I've never seen so much of it. How I got through without being spotted or blowing myself up – well it's a flipping miracle.'

Stoker, delicately stroked his scalp and sucked his teeth at the wonder of it. I moved aside, letting Jenny take my place at the wheel, while I thankfully stretched my arms and arched my back. Frank, without comment pointed astern to where the high white bulk of the cross-channel ferry was overhauling us steadily.

Stoker looked at it over his shoulder.

'Easy, nowadays innit? You just walk on and pay your fare.'

'Don't change the subject,' Jenny ordered, 'You were crawling through the wire – '

'Eh? Oh yeah, the wire. Well, suddenly I'm through it and in a field of artichokes, and there's a ditch running straight as a die, right across it.

'I'm into the ditch, along it like a rabbit, and I fetch up against a hedge, with a lane the other side.

'Quick shuftie both ways, then through the 'edge and I'm sitting in another field, and there's this old bloke, with an 'orse and cart, not six feet away, looking down at me, kind of surprised, wondering where the 'ell I'd sprung from.'

Stoker took a tin from his pocket and began to roll himself another smoke. His work-honed fingers fashioned an almost perfect cylinder, fastidiously poking stray tobacco ends back in with a matchstick before lighting up.

Then he coughed till his eyes ran and wiped them on the blue serge sleeve of his donkey jacket and patted his chest.

'Cor – that's better. Anyway, after a bit, the old 'un says "Matelot?" And I says. 'Yes.' And he says "Anglais?" and there wasn't no sense me denying it. He scratched his 'ead a bit, lifted his cap and put it back sideways, felt his ear, then he turns the 'orse round and makes signs. He wants me to lead it by the bridle and follow him, while he walks in front.'

Stoker broke off as the high, white hull of the ferry throbbed noisily past, and the Pelican corkscrewed over her wake He raised a laconic salute, acknowledging the waving children at the ship's stern.

'There was kids at the farm –' he went on, 'Where the old fellow took me. They weren't like that lot though, 'appy and waving. They was like... quiet and watchful even the youngest of them. You could see, it had been drummed into 'em to "see now t', hear now t' and say now t". The old lady was a treat — never turned a hair when her 'usband walked into the kitchen with me; just found me some overalls an' a flannel shirt and gave me a damned good feed – stew!' Stoker closed his eyes and sniffed delicately. 'Do you know, I can smell it now, that stew.' He sniffed again and opened his eyes.

'Damn me, I *can* smell it!'

We all sniffed and sure enough, a strong aroma of cooking filled the wheelhouse. Jenny loosed the wheel suddenly, and shot down into the cabin, with an unladylike oath.

Left briefly to her own devices. Pelican screwed up to windward, and the boom started to swing heavily inboard.

Frank was nearest, and with a laugh, he grabbed the spokes to bring her back on course. Jenny's voice came up from below with a request to keep the boat steady if we didn't want the dinner to end up all over the cabin..

No one attempted to answer that one! She came back, up the steps.

'There – it's cooked. We can warm it up when we want it. Nobody's hungry yet I hope?'

Nobody was.

Frank said: 'Okay, Stoker, so Granny took a shine to you. — What then?'

'Well, they let me kip down in a big feather bed for a few hours, and I'm not kidding you, I thought I was in heaven. It didn't last though. When I woke up, I could hear an 'ell of a row going on downstairs, then this other woman comes into the bedroom and starts yelling at me something horrible. I think she was the old lady's daughter or daughter in law.

'I couldn't understand the lingo, but there was no mistaking, she wanted me out. Well, I goes down stairs and there's another row and the old boy beckons me outside, and off we go, with the 'orse and cart again – miles and miles it seemed: back lanes – fields – woods – and we fetch up at another farm. Miles from anywhere it was – on the side of an 'ill and in amongst the trees.

There was an old couple there too, all bent and nervous. The three of them went indoors and I could 'ear them discussing me while I stood outside, stroking the 'orse. And they kept peeping. First the old girl would come to the door, then her husband would take a dekko through the window. At last, they fetched me in and took me down the cellar. He made 'shushing' signs, then he went back upstairs and blow me if he didn't bolt the door. Well, beggars can't be choosers, I thought, but it was a far cry from that feather bed.

'There was a bit of a grating, high up in the wall, and I watched him lead the 'orse away. It went quiet for hours, then, when it was getting dark, the old man shoved a lump of bread through the grating and some cheese and a bottle of water.

'I'd no sooner finished that than I heard some new arrivals. There were footsteps above my head going back and forth back and forth and voices again, but there was no row this time.

'Then I heard the bolt go back and the door open. A man's voice told me to 'come on up' - in English – and when I did, the lamp was lit and the shutters closed. The man who'd called me up was about forty and he only 'ad one arm. There was a young woman with him, who was his sister.

'Now, she 'ad an 'usband who' done a bunk over to England, on a fishing boat, and he'd left his papers behind; — o'course, I didn't find all this out first-off: it took a while to tell it, 'cos Emile – that was the younger chap's name – well, his English was a bit hit-and-miss like.'

Stoker's cigarette end had gone out and stuck to his bottom lip. He spat it expertly over the lee rail, and straightened up from his wedged position. He seemed suddenly embarrassed.

'You don't want to hear any more of this old stuff. It's ancient history now.'

We chorused ou protest, and he continued reluctantly.

'Well, the upshot was, I took the husband's place, and stayed and worked on the farm till the area was liberated.'

Frank goggled. 'What? - for four years? And you never got found out? What about the neighbours?'

'Well, the husband 'ad a name for being "doolally", He'd pretended to be barmy so's they wouldn't send him on forced labour. So all I had to do was run and hide when anybody called. Not that many did. The place was that isolated, even the Boche never bothered 'em much.'

'Did he come back after the war? — The husband?' Jennie asked.

Stoker shook his head. 'He joined the Free French navy and got killed on D-Day.'

'Lucky for you eh Stoker?' Frank said, 'He might have sorted you out when he got back. Taking his place like that.'

Stoker grabbed Frank by the front of his jacket.

'She's a good woman,' he said, poking an angry finger; and I won't have none o' that talk understand?'

He loosed his grip on Frank, thrust his hands in his pockets, looking at each of us in turn.

'Just so's there's no misunderstanding. I only took his papers, all right?'

Frank said, ‘Sorry Stoker!’

‘And the gold in the MTB.?’ I said,. ‘Why now? Why not before?’ Stoker shrugged ‘All I knew for sure was that the boat had got off the rock. I wasn’t positive she’d gone to the bottom. For all I knew, she could have made the rendezvous after all... And then again, if she *had* gone down in the bay, the Germans had had four years to investigate it.’ He spread his hands. ‘All things considered, I never gave much thought to laying me hands on the cargo. Though I must admit, I often wondered what it was *for* --- what was being *bought* with it.’

‘But now, is different eh?’

‘Now is different.’ He agreed.

He would say no more on the subject.

CHAPTER 13

South of us, the lights of Roscoff were bright against high banked black clouds; and west, a pale blue strip low over the sea, was the pennant of the dying day.

We rolled past the marker buoys and I maneuvered Pelican into an empty berth against the long straight pier.

Frank and Stoker jumped ashore, and made fast fore and aft, as a neat, uniformed figure approached leisurely from the port cabin office block. He read aloud, the carved name above the cuddy door.

‘Pelican eh? And how are you Mr Peterson?’

I smiled at an old friend. ‘Very well thank you Justin, and you?’

‘First class! Have you anything to declare?’

‘Not a thing! I trust Madame is in good health?’

‘Never better. Is this a working visit ?' his eyes went towards the cabin side-light and evidently caught a glimpse of Jenny,

'Or purely pleasure?’

‘Something of both. A little fishing, a little this – a little that! Perhaps you will find time to join me in a drink tomorrow.’?

‘I’ll look forward to it!’

He turned and walked away.

We quickly attended to the small amount of work necessary aboard, then went ashore. I led the way past the fish sheds and beyond the gift shops. Jenny shook my arm.

‘How far are we going? We’ve passed two perfectly good

restaurants already!'

I turned into a dark alley, which opened after a few paces into a dimly lit courtyard, bordered by quiet, watchful windows and doors. I grasped the iron knocker on the nearest door, gave a sharp rap and pushed the door open. This is not an establishment for tourists, nor yet for gourmets. One eats at a big square kitchen table. This is where hungry fishermen come, - and routiers who are "in the know."

Buxom Madame Duttine looked back from the stove at our entrance, and smiled a surprised welcome.

'Michael – it is good to see you again!'

I introduced Jenny and Frank. She studied Jenny from head to toe and there was approval in her eyes.

Then she took in Frank's still wan appearance and her mothering instinct overflowed.

'Oh la-la! Pouvre petit! Didonc – I think he must eat plenty!'

She sat him at the table and laid a plump hand on his blond locks.

'Such beautiful curls he has. This one, I look after well!'

Chuckling, she rolled back to the stove, leaving Frank with a face like the setting sun.

Stoker had been ignored, but now he walked casually round the table, to stand at the side of Madame Duttine. She finished stirring the pot, whacked the ladle on the edge, and spoke to him in French with an easy familiarity.

He answered her in the same vein, and in what seemed to me to be fluent French, at the same time, helping himself from an open pack of Guitanes on the shelf.

I felt miffed – almost jealous. This was my oasis, my secret, and here was Stoker, obviously more at home in it than me, blowing smoke happily in all directions.

He opened a door in the corner, stepped through. There came from within, the sound of something falling, and a cheerful curse from Stoker.

Madame called a jocular remonstrance, and Stoker came back through the door, wheeling a very tall, very old, bicycle which shone brightly from years of loving care, and whose chain and wheel hubs glistened with oil.

We all watched without comment, as he tested the tyres, tested the lights, leaned the machine against a chair, and began to tuck his trousers into his socks. Then I could keep silent no longer.

'You going somewhere?'

He pushed the bicycle to the outside door and opened it. 'Yeah – I'm going home.'

I felt my mouth open and shut like a goldfish. As he pulled the door closd behind him, he looked back through the narrowing gap.

'I ain't jumping ship. I'll be back termorrer. 'Night all!'

The door latch clicked and he was gone. Jenny and Frank stared at me for an explanation, their faces reflecting amused perplexity.

Madame put bowls of steaming soup before us. I asked her where Stoker had gone.

'Stoker? Who is Stoker?'

'Er, Ronald is Stoker.'

'He has gone home. He tell you already.'

'Yes but where?'

'You don't know? I thought he was your friend?' She pushed a bottle of wine and a corkscrew across the table to Frank, with quick-fire instructions in French, then added to me:'To St.Pol de Leon and his wife, where else would he go?'

I shrugged, -- smiled at the others -- and started on my soup.

Where else indeed?

****

At eleven-thirty next morning, Jenny, Frank and I, had been sitting in the Cafe des Quatre Aigles for over an hour.

Frank took another sip at his beer and moved his head to scan the road through the sign-writing on the plate glass.

'And that's all the note said?' He asked for the third time. 'No date nor time?'

'I've told you,' I tried not to sound irritable, 'just 'Four Eagles' nothing else.'

In my halting French, I'd asked the "Patron", a tall, thin man, with protruding eyes and a spotted bow tie, if Mr. Gregory had been in lately.

The patron said he didn't know a Mr.Gregory.

Had anyone left a message for Mr. Peterson?

The patron said he did not know a Mr. Peterson.

'Non, je suis Mr. Peterson.'

'Ah! I understand. No, -- no message.'

Frank rubbed steam from the window and laid his cheek against the glass, in order to lengthen his view back up the sand-strewn road towards the town, half a kilometer distant.

Directly opposite us, undulating dunes, sprouting coarse, grass whiskers, kept back the sea and hid it from view.

I wondered morosely what else we could do except sit and wait.

Something soft caressed my ankle: Jenny's foot.

I looked at her and realised she was not just playing footsie. Her green eyes were fixed on a spot behind me.

I twisted round to find out what was so riveting, and in the dark shadow of the doorway beyond the zinc topped counter, saw the blurred smudge of a man.

Not the Patron, the smudge slid forward a pace, and became sharply defined: A seaman's peaked cap, pulled low, dark glasses and the beginnings of a Charlie Chan moustache. An untidy stubble on chin and neck disappearing into the roll-neck of a black jersey.

Frank turned from the window too and looked at the newcomer. 'Well I'll be – ' he said, if it ain't old Dave himself. Hallo Dave!'

David Gregory took a bottle and glass from beneath the counter and poured himself a generous measure.

'Well, so much for the disguise,' he said.

He removed the dark glasses and brought his drink over to our table. His smile was self-assured, but I thought it lied. He was putting on his 'devil may care' look for Jenny's benefit.

'Frank, I know, – you, I know and this lady I would very much like to know!'

'Mrs McLaine – David Gregory.'

He took Jenny's hand, and held it, repeating the 'Mrs.' with heavy mock sadness.

'It always happens to me! Why are the most beautiful women always married?'

'Dave,' I said patiently,' would you mind telling me, why you scuttled the Garland? And why you couldn't have timed it a little better? You almost put paid to the Pelican —and me.'

'*Scuttled*? God almighty! — You think *I* did that ? The Garland was all I *had*. Somebody planted gelignite under the fuel tank. I only found it by accident when I was looking for a leak.'

I remembered the stink of petrol and the rainbow streamers on the water, ‘Couldn’t you have disarmed it?’

‘No way. I could have set it off by touching it for all I knew. I just threw the inflatable overboard, jumped in, and paddled like hell.’

‘But you knew I was behind you. Why didn’t you make for the Pelican?’

He regarded me thoughtfully, waiting for me to provide the answer myself.

It was my turn to be incredulous.

‘You thought *I'd* planted the bomb? How stupid can you get? Why would I do such a thing?'

'Look mate, all I knew for sure was: somebody wanted me dead. So I decided to *be* dead so they’d stop wanting. It could as well have been you as anyone.’

‘Thanks! Well, now you’ve had time to think it out, who’s the next most likely candidate?’

He rubbed his chin, making a rasping sound. ‘Chap called Ruyter. You wouldn’t know him.’

‘Ruyter is dead. He was shot!’

The barely hidden nervousness in Dave Gregory surfaced. He drained his glass.

‘Shot? Who by?’

‘Bloke called Bennett is the number one suspect.’

I told Dave how I’d found Ruyter’s body: ‘I’d seen Bennett and another man drive away earlier and they were in a hell of a hurry. Before that, Ruyter had tried to proposition me into going after the gold with him.’

Dave Gregory’s eyes became guarded. ‘Seems there’s a lot been going on I don’t know about. How much do *you* know about the gold?’

I filled him in on events and he nearly blew a fuse when I got to the part about them searching the dockside store.

I asked him why he’d thought Ruyter might have put the bomb in the Garland. His chair legs squealed against the tiled floor as he rose.

‘Come with me: I’ll show you something!’

He led the way out through the back yard and into a small lean-to storage shed, where he started to move beer crates from against the wall.

At last he knelt and pulled out a sacking bundle, which he placed on a crate and opened carefully, exposing a barnacle encrusted box with the lid open. The box had a hole in both sides, about an inch across, and in the bottom was a congealed featureless mass, from which protruded wires which were also decorated with tiny crustaceans.

Jenny touched the box with a delicate fore finger. ‘What is it?’

Dave pulled the wire gently and a small lump dangled from the end. ‘This, my dear Mrs McLaine, is an infernal machine – a bomb. Much like the one that blew up my boat, but forty years older. --- And what about this then?'

He knelt again and brought out another sack, which he hefted up and unwrapped on top of the crate.

Frank licked his lips. ‘Is that what I think it is?’

Dave didn’t answer but instead asked me to pick it up.

I did.

‘You’ve handled the other,' Dave said, 'what do you think?’

I jigged my arms up and down. ‘This one is lighter – a lot lighter.’

‘That’s because it’s lead; – gold leafed over.’

He took it from me and turned it over, so that we could see the part he’d scratched clean. Then he wrapped it and stowed it back out of sight.

Frank’s face crumpled in disappointment.

‘Have we come all this way for a lump of painted lead?’

Jenny’s question was more to the point. ‘What is lead doing masquerading as gold at the bottom of the sea? I take it you found the lead and the bomb on the motor torpedo boat?’

‘That’s right!’ Dave poked his finger into the hole in the box’s side. ‘I reckon that was made by a cannon shot. It could have set the bomb off but instead it broke one of the wires and stopped the detonator from working. Somebody was working a gigantic fiddle and that boat was meant to go down, no matter what.'

'Any idea who was behind it?' I asked.

There’d been a drumming on the corrugated roof for several minutes, and now a stream of water found a way through and fell onto the ammo box ‘bomb’. Dave pulled the sack around it, pushed it behind the beer crates, then stacked more crates around it.

‘Come on, let’s go back inside,’ he said.

The Cafe was empty, save for two bicycles, which leaned against the wall dripping water onto the beige tiled floor. I recognised the larger one from the night before.

As the rest of us went back to the window table, Dave Gregory went behind the counter and called Stoker's name. Then he brought over bottle and glasses and poured us each a measure of three-star Martel.

Stoker came out from the back room with a cheery ‘Hallo folks!'

I hardly knew him: — blue suit — collar and tie and polished shoes. Plus two fresh nicks in his chin from a close shave.

He was followed by small neat lady with a happy face. She was dressed in dark blue, her iron-grey hair pulled back in a bun.

‘This is my missus: Josephine.’ Stoker said.

His eyes held a light of pride.

Extra chairs were brought, more drinks poured. Stoker’s comings and goings were getting beyond me.

‘But what are you doing here?’ I asked him.

He waved a hand airily. ‘I brought Jo to see her sister.’

The spotted bow-tie had put in an appearance again, and another woman: a slightly younger version of Josephine. A rapid three-cornered conversation ensued between the two French women and bow-tie.

Surprisingly, I heard Jenny join in, her French gaining fluency with her confidence. They seemed to be talking about food.

I glared accusingly at Stoker.‘You didn’t tell me Dave was staying here. In fact there’s a hell of a lot you haven’t told me.’

Stoker closed one eye. ‘I learned a long time ago not to let one hand know what the other was doing. It kept me out of trouble and it got to be a habit.’

He took a crumpled pack of Gitanes from his pocket, lit one and pushed the pack into the center of the table in invitation,

Dave and bow-tie helped themselves, and soon clouds, spirals and striations of blue and grey were eddying about us.

I sniffed gently, appreciatively, and was taken by surprise when everyone else leaped to their feet and started re-arranging the furniture.

Tables were pushed together and the chairs set around afresh.

'Early dinner time,' said Stoker, ‘You’re invited.’

The two sisters went away into the kitchen and I was introduced to bow-tie who, it turned out, was Alphonse Nedoc, Stoker's brother-in-law.

I turned to Dave Gregory, who was now seated on my right, and asked him again if he knew who had made the switch from gold to lead.

Dave's face became tight lipped and hard. "I know who all right. Trouble is, I was a few years too late!'

'I don't get it! Too late for what?'

His answer was almost a snarl. 'Too late to kill the bastard. My old man went to the bottom with that MTB.'

I heard Jenny gasp and her softly breathed 'Oh – no' was like a prayer.

I was getting confused again, Stoker hitched his chair forward and leaned on his elbows.

'You see, it's like this: I go over, and visit my old dad in Bristol now and then. Early this spring, he told me he'd seen an old oppo of mine in the Royal George — bloke named Bert Smallridge. Now this was a shock 'cos I'd last seen Bert when he passed me a drum of ammo for the Lewis gun, just before I went overboard forty years ago. The barman knew where he lived, so I went round to his house and of course we chewed the fat about that night, and it turned out that he knew almost *exactly* where the boat had gone down.

'Seems that, after I went missing, the tide lifted them off that rock and they drifted south with the current for a while, getting lower and lower in the water. A couple of the lads were already dead and P.0. Gregory, Dave's dad, was wounded. Just before dawn, the R.A.F. made a raid down the coast and the searchlights lit up a headland in silhouette. Bert said it looked just like the outline of a lion's head. He drew it for me and I knew where he meant from that bit of a drawing:--Point de Leon.

'According to Bert, that's where the boat started to spin around and go down. They launched a carley-float and tried to get Dave's dad on to it, but 'e was unconscious and it was dark and choppy.' He shrugged and pulled a face, 'Somehow they lost him. That left Bert and the captain, a Lieutenant Turner... Not a bad bloke – a bit wet behind the ears, that's all.'

Stoker twisted his neck to look at the wall clock, with it's slow, bronze pendulum. 'I ain't 'arf getting 'ungry. Has that thing stopped?'

Jenny rapped her glass sharply on the table. 'That's a bad habit of yours, Ronald: --interrupting yourself..'

'Eh? Oh – yes, right then: — well, about half way through the next morning, Bert and the captain get picked up by a German patrol boat. That was the end of the war for *them.*'

Stoker drained his glass and lit another Gitane.

'So there you are: I had the rough location of the MTB. All I had to do was pinpoint it and get the goods to the surface. Simple, except I'd never done no diving and I didn't 'ave a boat.

'I saw Bert again, in the Royal George, next day, and he 'appened to mention he thought PO Gregory's boy was fishing out of Plymouth.

'I hadn't mentioned the gold to Bert, mind; not that I'm mean, but he might blab.

'I thought "allo this might be just what I need", so I goes to Plymouth to sort out Dave, and off we go to find the gold.'

'Just like that?'

'More or less!'

The smell of cooking wafted over us as the kitchen door opened and Josephine and her sister came through.

We began bobbing and weaving, as plates and cutlery were thrust between and over us, to clatter onto the tables.

Dave Gregory took up the account.

'The water's fairly clear where she lies, but there's plenty of contrary currents and that makes diving a bit difficult.

'Still, I found her on the third day, in about five fathoms. We put a few pots over the side as a "cover", and I got cracking. She was fairly well silted over and it took a while to free the hatches.

'Once inside, I broke open the boxes and dug out what I was looking for. I sent three ingots up in the basket, then I found that little device.'

He jerked a thumb at the back door. 'That made me a bit suspicious, so we scraped the ingots, one was genuine, two weren't, and it looked obvious that somebody had been on the fiddle.

'Now, I don't mind that so much, but when you couple it with the bomb, and the fact that my old man was a victim...

'Anyway, the weather was worsening so we pulled out for a

couple of days. When we went back, we took Alphonse with us.--Alphonse is a wizard when it comes to underwater photography.'

On hearing his name, Alphonse flashed a toothy grin in our direction and waved his fork. Somehow, without me noticing it, food had appeared on the table and we had begun eating.

Dave delved into an inner pocket and pulled out an envelope which he passed over to me. Inside were half a dozen photographs of the sunken torpedo boat, taken from different angles. Three of them showed the area where the guns and ammunition were stored, a tumbled confusion of wooden and metal boxes, some intact, some with their lids removed. All were encrusted with forty years accumulation of marine life.

At least two ingots, either lead or gold, were identifiable by their shape and one photograph showed the stern of the vessel, scraped partly clean to reveal a four figure number.

'Alphonse had just finished taking those when the French Navy gun-boat showed up. Someone ashore must have been watching our antics and tipped them the wink. They cruised back and forth a few times, watching us through binoculars, so I got Alphonse to play around on deck with his camera and I casually raised the crab pots and we ambled away. I'd have liked to have got everything up in one go, but it was too risky when we were being watched like that.'

Dave pushed his plate away and gently explored a gap in his front teeth with a fingernail.

'So I stashed the evidence and we went back to England with the photographs.

'Stoker remembered that a Captain Poplar had helped stow the cargo, so it seemed reasonable that he knew most about it.'

'How did you trace him?' I wondered if he'd gone through every Poplar in the book.

'Stoker also remembered that he used to go on leave to Helston, so it wasn't difficult. You know what I found – the Captain had died and his brother is living in the house. And it's some house, believe me! Not the house itself – that is ordinary enough but what is in it. It stinks of money. Antiques — paintings — tapestries, and probably all bought with that loot!'

His face was grim, bitter. His voice cracking with the enormity of it. 'And my old man rotting at the bottom of the Channel because of it.'

Frank obviously had not seen the significance of the makeshift bomb.

'But the Germans sank him Dave!'

Dave looked at him as though such stupidity was beyond him. 'I know that, you idiot! But that was sheer chance. That MTB. Was primed to sink without trace. Captain bloody Poplar couldn't let it reach wherever it was bound for, could he? He'd have been rumbled.'

Jenny wanted to know if Captain Poplar could have had an accomplice.

Dave said he didn't see how he could have done it alone.

'The brother himself, could have been an accomplice, for all I know,' he said, 'I told him what I'd found, and he pretended not to know what I was talking about at first.

'I showed him the photographs and asked him what he thought the papers would pay for a story like that. Up till then, I wasn't *sure* that he did know anything, but when he saw the photo with the boat's number on the stern, he had a right fit of the jitters.

'He calmed down eventually and tried to feed me a load of guff. He said, his brother had only removed two ingots out of a total of ten, and why didn't I just recover the rest and be satisfied.

'He could have been speaking the truth about that, because I've so far brought up two lead ingots and one gold. What's left down there might be all genuine stuff, but I doubt it.

'I told him I wasn't pleased about my dad being sacrificed to cover up his brother's crime. Then he tried to tell me that the time bomb was only going to be set to scuttle the boat if it were captured.

'I didn't buy that one either, so he offered me ten grand for the photographs and the location of the wreck.

'I didn't answer, and he starts frantically pushing the offer up and up. Before I know it, he's begging to be allowed to put a hundred thousand pounds to my credit with a Swiss bank.'

'Whew! What did you say to that ?' Frank said.

Dave's grin was wolfish. 'What do you think?' For all I knew, the French might have been curious to see what we'd been photographing, and be diving on the wreck themselves by that time.

'So I thought I'd go for the "bird in the hand" first. I said okay,

I'd bring him the negatives and a chart with an 'X' on it and we'd do a deal.'

Something was bothering me. The arithmetic didn't seem to add up. 'If his brother pinched two bars, why would he pay so much to hide that? Two bars at to day's prices would only fetch just over fifty thousand.'

Dave shrugged. 'So, most likely, he was lying. He'd probably copped the lot except for the one I found. Anyway, he didn't intend to pay me, did he? He was going to have me killed.' He spread his hands.-- 'Cheaper! – '

'Then, shortly afterwards, this Ruyter guy appears on the scene, with a couple of bully boys. He says he'd heard I'm on to something good, and he wants in . He says he's got the right contacts for marketing dodgy merchandise.

'Well, I guess he's come from Poplar so I string him along. And next thing I know, somebody's planted gelignite aboard the Garland.'

'Most likely Bennett,' I said, 'I think Ruyter was hired to get rid of you, but he was sniffing gold. 'Bennett's different though. All his brains are in his 'bovver-boots'. Poplar probably paid him to blow you up. I expect he paid him to shoot Ruyter too.'

Stoker stirred and burped. His collar button was undone for comfort and he had ash down his smart tie and his lapels. 'You know – this speculatin' is all very well but it ain't getting us nowhere,' he said, 'When are we going after the rest of the doings?'

'Soon,' Dave raised his glass, 'Let's hope the gallant Captain Poplar *didn't* pinch it all!'

It had been a good meal. The air was thick with cigarette smoke and my head with wine fumes. I felt a great desire to fold my hands on my stomach and sleep.

Instead, I rose, thanked our hosts in wine-improved French and said I must make the Pelican ready for the great adventure. At the door, I waved my arms grandly at the rest of them.

'Vive la compagnie!'

'Steady, sailor!' Jenny put an arm about me and steered me outside where the air soothed like balm.

'Whew, – I suddenly felt squiffy,' I said.

She laughed. 'You sounded it.'

'Funny, I was fine until I stood up.'

The rain had stopped and a watery sun was playing hop-scotch in and out of the hurrying clouds. Wind rippled the puddles in the road, splashing our eyes with flashes of reflected light. I took Jenny's hand, and ran with her through the dunes, until we were looking over the sea; over the white-flecked greyness that hurled itself, roaring, at the black, glistening rocks, flinging cascades of joyous spray fifty feet into the air.

In that wild lonely place, we made love, suddenly and with abandon.

CHAPTER 14

I was checking the Pelican's rigging, when I saw the dapper figure of my friend, the 'douane', approaching along the quay in leisurely fashion.

I felt unnecessarily guilty. After all, we hadn't done anything yet.

'Good evening Michael. Are you busy?'

I suddenly remembered, we'd been going to have a drink together.

'No. As a matter of fact, I was about to come looking for you.'

'Good. I am off duty since one hour. Perhaps the young lady would care to join us?'

I called to Jenny, through the open roof light 'Coming for a drink?'

Faintly, her voice came back. "You go darling – I'm washing my hair!'

We walked across the car park and stood by a patch of beaten earth, to watch the local boule kings at play.

Small round men, with flat caps and two centimeters of Gauloise stuck to their lower lips, were hurling small cannon balls about, in a way which would not amuse the governing body of Crown Green Bowling.

Justin Duprez let out an 'Ah' of satisfaction as one steel projectile landed on top of another, sending it skittering away to the side of the rink.

'Superb marksmanship Michael. I think this is the version of the game that your Drake must have played. It is basic, like the sea itself.,

'It is a piratical game,' I said, ' – like the seamen of that time.'

We strolled across the street towards a conservative- looking cafe, with an aspidistra in the window.

'There are still seamen like that, Michael.' Justin walked slowly, his eyes on the ground ahead.

I had an uneasy feeling that he was not just being idly philosophical.

We mounted the far pavement and pushed open the cafe door, setting a cluster of wind chimes jangling somewhere in the dimness beyond the polished counter. Choosing a window table, Justin stretched out his legs and looked critically at his toe caps.

'I read about the Garland,' he said, 'Do you know yet what really happened?'

'I know what everyone else knows – that she blew up.' I looked at him keenly, while doing my best to sound off-hand. 'Was it reported in the French press?'

'Possibly – but that is not where I read it.'

He took from his wallet a folded newspaper cutting, smoothing it open on the table.

It was from the Western Evening Courier, and showed a fuzzy picture of the Garland, dressed overall, taken during that summer's regatta.

There was a brief account of the mysterious sinking — including a couple of 'quotes' from me which I could not remember uttering — and, inset, a small head and shoulders of: "Dave Gregory, popular local skipper, missing, feared dead."

'I sometimes pick up an English paper in the ferry cafeteria.' Justin returned the cutting to his wallet. At that moment, the patroness came out to take our order. I asked for a beer. Justin chose a 'Fine'. We were silent until the drinks were before us.

'Sante!'

'Cheers!'

Justin sipped, savouring the taste and put his glass down.

'I must confess, I am very curious, Michael.'

'About what?'

'About Monsieur Gregory. You see, I saw him pass through passport control, less than forty-eight hours after he was supposed to have been blown to pieces. Further: – according to your local radio post – which I listen to, to improve my English, his body is still being sought."

This was a hell of a note. To gain time, and work out what attitude to assume, I took a long pull at my beer, and in doing so, left it too late, to act surprised.

I fell back on looking enigmatic, and regarded him for long seconds, dead pan, waiting for him to continue.

'Also I am curious about your connection with Langon.'

He had me there.

'Who is Langon?'

Justin raised his eyebrows. 'Ronald Langon came ashore from your Pelican, last evening. I assume you brought him with you from England?'

He must mean Stoker. I nodded warily. 'I didn't know his surname.'

The 'douane' spoke heavily, twirling his glass on the green-tiled tabletop.

'I think that you are not being straightforward with me, Michael. We have been friends for some time – no? Oh, I know you have other friends: David Gregory for instance.

'Divided loyalties can be a heavy cross to bear. I know it well, Michael, but consider:' he rubbed his chin, fixed his eyes on the ceiling and began again: 'David Gregory, who is supposed to be dead, comes to Roscoff, and immediately goes into hiding in a local Cafe.

'Ronald Langon, a respectacle citizen of St.Pol de Leon, the proprietor of a bicycle shop, and the grandfather of many children, also returns to Roscoff, in your small ship.

'The following day, you and he visit Monsieur Gregory at his hiding place, which just happens to be owned by Langon's brother-in-law.'

'He spread his hands. 'You must see that it all looks a little bit suspicious.'

I tried a light laugh. 'Are you a policeman Justin?'

He leaned forward, and there was no levity in his face. 'I am a *douane*, Michael, and anything suspicious connected with ships and sailors interests me. What is going on?'

I wondered if his interest had been passed on up the ladder. I decided that part of the truth might suffice. I lowered my voice, confidentially.

'David Gregory has enemies who tried to kill him. It is best that they believe they have succeeded.'

'Does this concern drugs? Smuggling?'

I shook my head, I hoped convincingly,

'It concerns a salvage operation that has generated strong feelings.'

I was rather pleased with that.

He relaxed a little. 'Ah, I see: a business rivalry! But Michael, if anything should happen which affects my office, the fact that we are friends would be of no account. I do hope you understand that.'

'But of course, Justin,' I raised my glass, 'You are a man of honour. Now, drink up and have another.'

****

Our taxi driver had dropped us at Stoker's bike shop, with the helpful suggestion that: if there was no one in, they would probably be at the boulangerie of Madame Langon's sister, in the Rue Capra.

The shop was closed and no-one answered the doorbell.The sign over the shop said 'R. Langon. Velos', and the centre piece of the window display was a Raleigh racing cycle surrounded by blue velvet. It gleamed silver and gold in the concealed lighting, and looked light enough to float away on it's own.

I pressed the bell again and stepped to the pavement's edge in order to look at the darkened window above.

A gust of wind swept a fusilade of raindrops up the street, and I quickly rejoined Jenny in the doorway.

Couples, families, youths, all bent on enjoyment crowded under shop awnings, heads twisted against the shower.

It passed quickly; Jenny hooked my elbow and we joined the flow of people towards the main square.

The raucous jangle of a jukebox battered its way out of the open door of a cafe. Inside, people milled, danced, laughed and drank, shouted and sang.

So many people that it seemed the room could not possibly hold any more.

Then a gang of youngsters crossed the street and entered with only the minimum of difficulty, as if the back wall had given way.

Two doors along, another cafe: this one almost empty, the patron, bald, shirt sleeved, leaning his elbows on the dark counter and staring at the brown wallpaper. His two customers, a man and a woman, sitting like depressed waxworks.

Not even their eyes twitched as we walked by.

We had come to St. Poll de Leon on impulse, lured by a bright wall poster on the dockside, which told us, the place would be celebrating the birth of their Patron Saint.

Frank Gregory had elected to spend the evening at the Four Eagles, catching up with cousin Dave.

The rain stopped and we decided to forget looking for Stoker for a while and head to where accordion music floated above the heads of a small crowd outside a restaurant.

On the pavement, beneath the restaurant awning, two men and two girls, in old Breton garb, twirled and kicked their heels.

A gust of wind shook the pendant raindrops from the awning fringe onto the back of my neck, and I stepped back sharply, into something that said ‘Oof! Steady Captain.’

I turned to find Stoker standing behind me.

‘Sorry, Monsieur Langon,' I said, 'We looked for you at your shop....’

He grinned proudly and stuck out his chest. ‘Oh – yeah, the shop. What do you think of the window display? That’s the wife’s doing. I’m just going to-pick her up now.’

‘She’ll be at her cousin’s, in the Rue Capra,’ I told him airily, ‘Don’t be late aboard to-morrow. Busy day ahead.’

'Yeah – let’s hope it’ll be worth all the bother.'

He moved away, walking in the road, to avoid the crush on the pavement. After a few paces he turned round and called out, ‘Hey; how do you know where her cousin lives?’

I yelled back, ‘I’m clairvoyant, that’s how!’

The Breton dancers finished their number and went inside the restaurant, followed by most of their audience.

From a side street, a small brass band marched into the square: a noisy, brightly-uniformed head, followed by a strutting, laughing tail When this happy dragon reached the centre of the square, it was caught in a surprise cross-fire of hailstones, which caused it to stagger, fall mute and finally disintegrate as it’s components parts scattered for shelter.

I pulled Jenny by the hand to where steps led down to a grotto-like basement opening. Over the archway, a flashing neon sign told us that this was the "disco d'or".

Within the cave opening, an ultraviolet strip-light lit up the white shirt-front and teeth of the doorman. I pushed coins through the grill of the cash desk, and had some of them pushed back at me, together with two tickets.

The floor seemed to be sending rhythmic shock waves up my legs, and from somewhere came a faint trumpeting sound.

We checked our coats and the doorman swung open a heavy baize door, letting out a juggernaut of sound.

As we entered: the trumpeter finished on a harsh blaring note, the drummer gave a flourishing roll and crash of cymbals and the tangled mass of dancers deserted the tiny, polished dance floor, to search for their drinks in semi-darkness.

With difficulty, we wedged ourselves into the angle between bar and wall, and I ordered two dry Martinis.

The three-piece group, now relaxing on the dais, lit their cigarettes, then a girl in a long red dress squeezed between them, put a record on the music centre, and flicked a switch, sending coloured lights to drift over everything and every one, like exotic butterflies.

The girl put her hand on the drummer's shoulder as she turned, and he pulled her onto his knee, with a triumphant laugh, holding her there while she struggled unconvincingly.

Quadrophonic rhythm crashed inwards from the corners of the room, and dancers filtered back onto the floor; at first rocking several feet apart, but moving closer and closer as their numbers grew.

Jenny took a sip of her drink. 'It's odd about Stoker, isn't it?'

'There is a hell of a lot that's odd about Stoker,' I agreed, 'But what especially?'

Her face went from gold to blue, to silver. 'For one thing, why is he still here, using a false name? The war has been over for nearly forty years!'

'Well, I expect he was pretty settled by the time the war finished. He probably preferred what he was doing, to the Royal Navy.'

'Yes, but surely, he could have reported back to the Navy, got "demobbed" and then returned to Josephine and the farm. It seems to me, he's thrown away four years back-pay.'

I shrugged 'One day, when I've a week to spare, I'll get the whole story from him.'

The band was back in action. My feet began to twitch and I nodded at the press of humanity.

'Care to dance?'

Jenny's face registered mock-horror. 'In that lot?'

'Come on,' I said, 'let's live dangerously.'

I didn't know just how dangerously. We were sucked quickly into the seething mass as the insistent beat swelled and eddied about us.

Then, as I completed a turn, Jenny was gone and I was looking at the back of a blue, bulbous neck, which melted over its collar.

My eyes, searching for Jenny's red hair, hooked onto a girl with a green face, who twitched just out of phase with the rhythm, as if she heard a different rhythm inside her head.

The place was a throbbing, many-coloured drumbeat. Faces came and went before me, large eyes staring, inviting, the press of bodies challenging.

With another crash of cymbals, it was over. People sagged, looked about uncertainly, and began to drift off the dance floor.

I remained, still looking for Jenny, letting my eyes move slowly around the room.

The coloured lights drifted aimlessly and I couldn't see her.

The bar was slightly better lit. My eyes were drawn towards it and, at first, my mind refused to register what was quite plainly visible:

Bennett was watching me over the rim of his glass as he drank.

The floor was almost clear by now, and I swept another swift glance around. This time I spotted Jenny's flame red hair in the corner of the room. A tall man, wearing a light raincoat, was talking to her. He stood with his back to me, leaning with one extended hand on the wall, as if to stop her escaping.

She saw me at that instant, ducked quickly under the outstretched arm and shot to my side. I gave her a squeeze and turned her to face the bar.

'Recognise anyone?' I asked.

She gasped and her features showed disbelief when she saw Bennett.

'It's him!' Her voice was a strangled whisper.

I stepped towards him and he continued to watch me closely as we got near.

Now there was a smirk on his face. I felt my gorge rise. , my left hand stretched out and grabbed his shirt front; my right fist clenched and drew back to strike.

A sharp voice behind me said: 'Stop that Mr. Peterson We will all leave quietly.'

I held the pose and twisted round to look. The man in the raincoat stood close to Jenny, one hand holding her wrist in a seemingly casual way.

He was not only tall, but, but broad and powerful looking. His square, sallow face held eyes that were piercing, almost black. The lid of the left one sagged a little as if caught in the act of winking.

'Why should we go anywhere with you? Who are you anyway?' I said.

'You will go with me because I have a gun!' He jerked his right hand, which was in the raincoat pocket and ignored my second question.

I released Bennett's shirt with reluctance and he bridled like an offended cockerel. One or two people were beginning to notice and stare inquisitively.

'You mean, you'll shoot me if I refuse? In front of all these people?'

'No Mr. Peterson; I will shoot Mrs McLaine.'

It was said in such an ice cold way, that I thought he probably meant it.

Bennett eased round me and took hold of Jenny's other arm, and again my instincts were to lash out at him. The other man took a short pace towards me and something hard pressed into my side.

The trio on the small stage had started to play again: A loud, brassy, foot-stamping number, and people lost interest in us.

'Walk to the exit – now!'

With an effort, I moved and did as he ordered. Once through the baize door we retrieved our coats and climbed the steps into the rainy, lamp-lit night.

'Walk in front. Turn right into the first side street!' The tall man's voice had no definable accent, but he sounded educated. Jenny put her arm through mine as headed for the corner. She pitched her words low.

'We could make a bolt for it – '

'Try it – see how far you get!' Bennett said gloatingly from behind.

We reached the corner and turned into a narrow lane, little wider than an alley. Fifty meters down, wet and glistening under a dim wall light crouched an old black Citroen: two wheels up on the pavement, so that only one side could be used.

Bennett slipped ahead and unlocked it, swinging the doors wide.

'Get in the back.' He said.

We squeezed inside, and as the other two arranged themselves in the front.

Jenny said cheerfully. 'The police will spot us in no time. The fools have pinched "Inspector Maigret's" car!'

The tall man sat in the front passenger seat, twisted towards us and rested the barrel of a stubby pistol on the back of his seat.

'I'm glad you are keeping cheerful Mrs. McLaine. Believe me, this need be no more than an inconvenience to you. But of course, if Mr. Peterson tries any foolish heroics – '

He let the threat hang there like a primed grenade. We were out in the country now, and I couldn't see his face.

'Are you Dermot Poplar?' I asked.

'Who I am doesn't matter.' His voice regained its former hardness. 'All you have to think about is Mrs. McLaine's safety.'

There was silence then, save for the purr of the engine and the hissing rumble of tyres on pave.

It was time I thought of a way out of this, but my mind seemed to be setting, like drying plaster.

There were street lights now. We were back in the outskirts of Roscoff.

'Where are you taking us?' I didn't expect an answer, but I got one.

'To your boat, Mr. Peterson. Where else? Oh – and I should warn you that my assistant is also armed with a pistol.'

When Bennett had parked the Citroen on the dark side of a fish warehouse, they both got out carefully and stood back while Jenny and I climbed free. I raised my hands to shoulder height.

Jenny looked at me sideways and did the same.

Poplar; – I was fairly sure it *was* Poplar, told us patiently to lower them.

'We don't want to attract attention do we?' he added,

' Now walk towards the Pelican.'

Jenny pointed at the car. 'Aren't you going to lock it? There are some very dodgy characters about, this late at night.'

Bennett sniggered. 'I like you, Missus. You've got a great sense of humor.'

'That's nice.' Jenny said, very sweetly.

Rain began to fall more heavily as we hurried towards the Pelican.

CHAPTER 15

The dockside lights were enough for us to see our way around as Jenny and I dropped down to Pelican's deck.

I turned to watch Poplar follow us, wondering if I would get a chance to do something,— anything.

He gestured with his gun hand towards the wheelhouse and told me the start the engine.'

I took the key from my pocket and then spotted the newly splintered wood of the frame. The door slid open without help from the key.

'This isn't your first visit I take it.'I said

'Just start the engine!' He stood against the rail, holding Jenny's arm just above the elbow with his left hand, his right still held the pistol.

The big diesel fired with the minimum trouble. Bennett cast off the forrard cable, and as the Pelican's bow eased away from the wall, did the same at the stern, and dropped down onto the deck where he quickly recovered and stowed both. He seemed to know his way around the deck of a boat.

Poplar pushed Jenny towards Bennett and told him to take her up into the bow.

Bennett threw me a lecherous leer, and put an arm around her, to urge her forrard.

For my benefit, Poplar said loudly. ‘If Mr. Peterson gets out of hand, you will shoot Mrs McLaine.’

Bennett sniggered again. ‘What a waste that would be!’

'I’m fast losing my sense of humour’ Jenny told him firmly. ‘I’m very wet and very cold, and unless I’m allowed to remedy that, then you can just shoot me now, because I’m going down into the cabin.’

‘There are oilskins in the chain locker.’ I told her quickly. There’s no light down there. You’ll have to feel around in the sail chest.’

Poplar nodded at Bennett. ‘Let her get them.’ Then to me, ‘Put on your navigation lights.'

In the wan glow of the masthead light, I saw Jenny bend and fiddle with the tiny catch of the chain locker, lift it and wriggle through to drop from sight.

I was keeping bare steerage way on the Pelican, and the end of the stone pier was coming slowly nearer.

I set the wipers going and, glancing back at the friendly lights of the shore, felt a tightening inside. Would we, Jenny and I, ever be going ashore again?

The last pier light swept astern and we picked up the first of the flashing buoys, passing to starboard of it.

Pelican began pitching gently, and Poplar came into the cuddy, half closing the door.

‘Increase your speed a little — to about six knots.’ he said.

‘Where are we going?’

‘On a treasure hunt, of course. Isn’t that why you’re here?

‘Of course,’ he went on, ‘you won’t be making the profit you expected, but if you co-operate, I'll reimburse you for out-of-pocket expenses. I’ll even add a little to salve your disappointment, if I think you deserve it.’

Jenny had not reappeared, and Bennett was kneeling on the wet deck and peering down the hatchway. He looked angry. I saw his mouth working and his voice came but faintly through the thick glass. Then he stood and cupped his hands to shout at Poplar.

‘The cow won’t bloody-well come out, – she’s hiding down there!’

Poplar stuck his head out and shouted back ‘Put the hatch on you fool. She can’t go anywhere, can she?’

Bennett shouted more imprecations down into the blackness, then slammed the cover home viciously. He turned his wet collar up and leaned against the lee rail, watching the hatch morosely, as a cat watches a mouse hole.

We were well clear of the shore now, and feeling the effect of short steep waves. Pelican began to roll as she pitched, and take white spray over the weather bow, most of which seemed to land on Bennett.

At last he came aft and pushed his way into the cuddy. 'Sod that for a lark! I can watch just as well from back here.'

The chain locker would be uncomfortable, but at least, it was dry and Jenny was out of reach of Bennett, if only temporarily.

Five minutes passed in silence, save for the drumming of the engine. The rain-distorted reflections of my two guardians melted and reformed at every slow sweep of the wiper.

I wondered what the next move would be and it was as if the thought triggered Poplar's vocal cords.

'Go and bring him up.' he said to Bennett.

Bennett elbowed me aside, slipped the latch and twisted down the short companionway into the cabin. As he fumbled for the light switch, I stooped and peered down, curious to see who was to be brought up.

The light showed Stoker lying on my bunk, trussed like an oven-ready turkey, and gagged.

With a clasp knife, Bennett cut through the bindings on Stoker's ankles, jerked him roughly from the bunk, and pushed him halfway up the steps.

When Stoker's head and shoulders came level with the wheelhouse, I saw that the gag was red with blood, and there was an ugly cut across his bald patch. His legs folded, he fell from view, and I heard his head strike a step.'

Bennett swore, 'On your feet, you useless git; or do you want some more?'

Poplar said sharply, 'Stop that and untie his arms, he's not going to hurt you!'

I thought, 'Hallo, a little compassion perhaps, and just a faint needle job?,' I wondered if there was enough to-be useful. Stoker's head and shoulders came up through the opening again. Without the gag, I could see the dried blood around his mouth. His face was a sickly yellow-white, and when he tried to grin, the effect was close to horrific.

He licked his lips, carefully, and lisped, 'Anybody got a fag?'

I hadn't, and Poplar ignored him. He sank weakly onto the slatted seat rubbing his wrists which were white from the rope's pressure.

I looked at him carefully. 'You're in a hell of a state, mister. Did pig-face here do that?'

Bennett was coming up from the cabin and his porcine features reddened at the jibe, but the curse welling in his throat was forestalled by Poplar ordering him to take the wheel.

To me Poplar said. '

'You will go below, Mr. Peterson.'

Just before the latch clicked behind me, I heard him tell Stoker to direct Bennett on a course for 'Point de Leon'. I stretched out on my bunk and glumly speculated: 'What now'? Poplar had mentioned reimbursement, so maybe he didn't intend doing away with us.

On the other hand, that could be a way to prevent too much trouble until our usefulness was at an end.

Pelican seemed now to be rolling more than she pitched. I looked out of the starboard lantern light. Through the driving rain, the occasional silver-bright pinpoint from the shore confirmed my impression that we were sailing almost due East. I did a rough calculation in my head. Point de Leon was thirty miles distant. At our present speed, we would be there in four or five hours. My wrist-watch told me it wanted a few minutes to midnight.

I thought about Jenny and hoped she was not too uncomfortable. If she propped open the lid of the sail chest, she could make herself a pretty cosy nest in there. I pictured her asleep, curled up snug, and hoped that my projected thoughts could reach her, tell her what to do.

Then I wondered about Stoker. Had they abducted him in the street? Or had they taken him from the midst of his family?

Did anyone ashore know what was happening? I think I dozed then, because, suddenly I was disturbed by the sound of a drawer opening. Bennett was leafing through charts. He selected one, left the rest in a mess, and went back up into the wheelhouse, slamming the door behind him.

My watch showed a quarter past three and we were barely

moving.

I could no longer hear rain on the deck head, but I could smell fog. It was time I started to assert myself. The opposition had two pistols, and a proven record of violence!

I decided to make coffee, put water on to boil and opened the roof vent, letting in the regular double clang of a fog bell from fairly close at hand.

When the coffee was made, it's aroma filtered into the wheelhouse, and in no time at all, the door was pushed open and Bennett was peering down.

'You can pass up some of that for me and the 'admiral.' I assumed he meant Poplar and not Stoker.

'Make your own!' I said and raised the steaming mug to my lips. I was rewarded once more by the flush of anger on his face as he dropped down into the cabin and put out a hand.

'Gimme that!'

'Catch !' I said, and threw the almost boiling contents full into his face. He gave a squeal of rage and pain, and twisted his head aside, clawing at his eyes.

Without giving him time to recover, I gave him a clout above the ear with the mug. He seemed to crumple in slow motion, and before he hit the deck, I was on him, tugging at the zip of his wind cheater.

Poplar shouted my name. I had my hand on the butt of Bennett's pistol now, and was pulling it free.

I looked up through the hatch. Poplar's gun was leveled at me from a few feet away.

He saw the gun in my hand and I knew by his eyes that he would fire but before he could, Stoker grabbed his wrist and twisted.

Poplar's gun roared deafeningly in the confined space, and the bullet tore out through glass. Before he could take fresh aim, I pointed Bennett's pistol directly at his chest, and pulled the trigger.

There wasn't even a click and I wasted precious seconds, staring stupidly at the thing, before I worked out that it needed cocking.

Poplar shouted my name again, his voice shaking with fury. I dragged my eyes from the gun in my hand, to see that he was holding Stoker between us, as a shield. 'Throw the gun up here or I will shoot him.'

Stoker kicked violently backwards, with his heel, and Poplar grunted with pain, this was followed by a similar grunt from Stoker, as his arm was twisted up behind him. I was reluctant to give up the pistol, so easily, and I scrambled up onto my bunk and crouched in the corner out of Poplar's sight.

Before I answered, I cocked the pistol, and made sure the safety catch was off.

Bennett meanwhile, was curled in a ball, groaning and rubbing his eyes.

'You shoot Stoker – I shoot Bennett !' I put as much confidence as I could into my tone.

I don't need that useless – moron'

I reached out a foot and prodded Bennett.

'Did you hear that?' I asked him. 'It seems that you are surplus to requirements.'

He was breathing noisily through his mouth and didn't answer.

'O.K.' I called out, still careful to keep out of sight. 'You shoot Stoker and you've lost your shield so then it's *your* turn. How does that grab you?'

I strained to hear his reply, and was aware of the loud thumping of my own heartbeats. Then there was the sound of the cuddy door sliding open.

From out on deck, Poplar could shoot me easily through a fanlight or vent.

I flicked the cabin light off quickly, but too much light was spilling in from the wheelhouse.

I slammed the two halves of the hatch closed, and felt the immediate comfort of concealing darkness.

Shoe leather rasped on the deck and I followed the progress of the scuffling footsteps forrard. When I could no longer hear them, I flapped open a half door and risked a quick look up into the wheelhouse. It was empty.

On hands and knees, I crawled as fast as I could from the cabin and up through the hatch, switching off the cuddy light as I stood slowly upright, and peered towards the bow.

Prodded by Poplar's handgun, Stoker's top half was just going from view, down into the chain locker.

Then Poplar knelt and pointed his pistol down the open hatchway. He looked aft, at the darkened wheelhouse. He couldn't see me but he knew I was there.

'Peterson, You have ten seconds to slide the gun along the deck towards me. If you do not, or if you step from the wheelhouse, I shall fire my pistol repeatedly into this open hatchway. Mrs McLaine and Figgin will almost certainly be injured if not killed.'

Salt-laden fog wreathed in through the open door, and out of the bullet-shattered glass in front of me.

Poplar's shape was partly obscured by the mast, and I knew that to attempt to hit him from here would be useless.

'Five seconds Peterson!'

'All right!' I yelled desperately.'

I dropped to my knees, and feverishly pulled the magazine from the butt of the pistol, thumbed the cartridges into my palm, changed my mind, and replaced one round, clicked the magazine home and put my head out of the door.

'Here it is!' With a flick of my wrist, I sent it spinning along the smooth deck planking.

The rise of Pelican's bow, caused it to stop half way between us, and it lay glinting, blue-black in the faint glow of the masthead light.

Poplar rose to his feet. With one hand he wrestled the hatch cover into place then walked over and picked up the gun.

Back in the wheelhouse he ordered me to put on the light and bring us back on course.

He pocketed Bennett's pistol and kept the other pointed at my middle.

I tipped the light switch.'What course would that be?'

I tried to sound off hand, but my throat was so dry, the words came out in a croak.

'Six degrees north of east!' He pushed at the cabin hatch with his foot, and peered down, while keeping as far away from me as he could. He called down to Bennett, and a muffled curse came up in reply. I swung the wheel to bring the Pelican back on her required bearing, and tried to gauge the direction of the fog bell, which was still loud but becoming less so.

It seemed to come from astern. I looked around for the chart Bennett had taken from the cabin, and saw that it lay scuffed and torn in the corner, a victim of Stoker's scuffle with Poplar.

I nodded towards it.'Where are we? And where are we headed?'

The answer to the second question could only be Point de Leon, but I wondered if he really knew.

'Just steer,' he said shortly.

There was a scrabbling on the cabin steps, and Bennett came slowly into the cuddy. One hand was pressed to his head, above the ear, and he fixed me with a malign stare.

'You bastard,' he said, 'I ought to tear your guts out.'

I shrugged. 'If you want to be a "tearaway", you'll have to learn to take the rough with the rough.'

Before he could frame another threat, Poplar handed him back his gun.

'Take this, and try to hang on to it this time!'

Bennett started to put the gun back inside his wind cheater, changed his mind and removed the magazine from the butt.

He looked at it suspiciously, saw the single round on top and, to my relief, didn't check further, but replaced it and put the gun away.

A slow hour passed while the fog gradually changed from a cloying blanket to a tenuous film.

Then a single star, shone directly through the jagged hole made by Poplar's bullet.

Two stars--three, and suddenly there was no more fog, and a whole heaven full of stars glittered down at us as the Pelican undulated over the gentle waves.

I checked my watch: four-fifteen. It would be light in a little over an hour.

A brittle coldness filled the cuddy, and clawed at my ribs. Bennett had on my anorak, and I wasn't going to ask him for it back.

Without saying a word, and moving casually, I put the thong over a wheel spoke, and dropped back down into the cabin.

There were four seconds of 'no reaction' from my two captors, then Bennett exploded with a torrent of blasphemous invective which, broadly translated, invited me to rejoin them in the wheelhouse.

I ignored him, and rummaged in my locker for a thick jersey.

Bennett kept on raving, but Poplar told him to shut up and take the wheel himself. Then more loudly, for my benefit, he said.

'When the time comes that I need him, he will co-operate.'

I thought of Jenny, in the chain locker and had to admit to myself that he was right. There was no bread, but plenty of dry biscuits, and no end of tinned food. I made a pig of myself, for ten minutes, while I watched the lights of a string of mackerel boats heading for shore and the early market.

I'd have given a lot right then to be a part of such traffic.

I tried to think back and work out how I'd got myself involved in this lot. I put my feet up on my bunk, to help my thought processes, and found myself dozing again. I fought the drowsiness and next, decided 'the hell with it!'

When I woke, the stars were pale and were being swallowed by the dawn.

With daylight came cloud and a rising wind that moaned in the rigging and set the once-gentle waves cavorting and throwing up their heads, like nervous horses.

Through a side-light I could see, fine off the starboard bow, the silhouette of a headland. It was shaped like the head of a lion, its flowing main formed by dark woods.

I twisted my head back to look up into the cuddy. Bennett was slumped on the bench, eyes closed and collar up. His face, even in sleep, still bore the tense stamp of violence.

Poplar, slack jawed and red eyed, had the wheel. I swung my feet to the floor. Now I could only see Poplar's legs. His weight shifted from one to the other, and he called down with a hoarse, early morning voice.

'Come up here, carefully – and keep your hands in sight.'

At the sound of his voice, Bennett stirred, blinked and scratched. Before he was properly awake, I'd gone through the wheelhouse, and was leaning over the stern, watching the flattened water surge and break.

I heard Poplar say 'watch him', and Bennett came out to stand yawning and shivering, one hand inside his jacket holding the gun.

I thought about Dave Gregory and the rest of them in Roscoff. When they found the Pelican gone — and Stoker — would they imagine we were double-crossing them by going after the gold ourselves?

Pelican had little way on her now, and was rolling and pitching uncomfortably in the confused sea. Poplar ordered Bennett to go and fetch Stoker, then told me to bring up my two sets of diving gear from below.

I decided to try a spot of civil disobedience, crossed my arms, and leaned back on the stern rail.

Poplar came half way out of the cuddy and, keeping one hand on the wheel, he pointed the gun at my feet and fired.

The bullet gouged the planking between my feet. Beyond Poplar, Bennett whirled at the sound of the shot and crouched, his pistol ready.

'That was meant to go through your foot!' Poplar said, 'Now do as I say!'

I went amidships and lifted the hinged hatch cover from the main hold.

A sudden fierce flurry of ice-cold raindrops swept the deck as I went down the vertical ladder and opened the chest which contained the neoprene wet-suits.

Stepping quickly to the bulkhead separating the hold from the chain locker, I rapped hard with my knuckles. 'Bump, didi-bump-bump'.

I put my ear to the paneling and listened intently. A few heartbeats later, Jenny's reply came, muffled but distinct: 'bump-bump!'

Until I heard that faint sound, I hadn't realised how far my spirits had sunk. Suddenly, by comparison, I felt as light as air.

I picked up an armful of gear, and turned back towards the ladder. Bennett's bulk blotted out the daylight.

'Hurry it up!' he growled.

I went up three rungs, and heaved the load up onto the deck, then went back for the cylinders, flippers, goggles, weights.

With a rush of excitement I ran my hand through the remaining odds and ends in the bottom of the chest, feeling for the sheath knives.

They were gone.

Ah well, they would be, wouldn't they.?

When I clambered back onto the deck, Stoker was at the rail, braced against the deck's heave and lift, and had my binoculars focused on the shoreline, about a mile and a half away.

'Now!' he said, 'This is about right.'

Poplar cut the engine and signaled to Bennett, who was standing by the anchor winch in the bow.

He dropped the hook, and Pelican swung and wallowed at the end of the cable.

Stoker pulled a wry face as he turned to me.

'Sorry skipper, – not the way we meant it to go eh?' His face was grey and his lips blue. 'What ever happens. I 'm going to get that bastard before this lot's finished.' His voice was low, and he was staring hard at Bennett's back.'He knocked my missus about!'

Poplar told me to get into one of the suits, and while I changed, he sent Bennett below for a fish basket and sufficient line to reach bottom.

By the time he'd lowered the basket over the side, weighted with a lump of scrap iron, Stoker was helping me strap on my air bottle. I'd assumed Bennett would be using the other suit, but Poplar started peeling off his outer clothes, while his accomplice stood off to one side watching Stoker and me, both guns in evidence. Poplar handled the gear as though used to it.

'While you and I are down, Mr. Peterson, Mrs. McLaine and Figgin will be surety for your good behavior. Bennett knows what to do, should anything happen to me. Is that clear?'

It was clear as crystal.

I nodded briefly without looking at him, adjusted my face-mask and checked the operation of my air bottle.

Poplar did the same. 'You go first!' He said.

Stoker hooked the ladder over the lee rail, and I splayfooted it across the rain-wet deck and clambered awkwardly over the side.

Pelican was rising and falling several feet. I waited till the sea came up to meet me and dropped backwards off the bottom rung.

All the while I'd been getting into my suit, I'd felt a rising excitement within me. Now, despite what was happening aboard Pelican, I let the feeling well up and take over.

Whatever the circumstances, this was still a treasure hunt, and I was eager to see what was down on the bottom.

Head down, I flippered almost vertically, following the rope, which was attached to the basket. The light on the seabed was none too good, and I could see clearly for no more then about ten feet in any direction. The bottom was sandy with a ridge of weed-covered rock running away into the murk.

Looking upwards towards the opaque surface, I saw my air bubbles rise and expand. From the dark shadowy bulk of the Pelican, a smaller shadow detached itself and descended towards me.

When he reached me, he took a thin line from his belt, attached one end to the weighted basket and swam off with the other towards the Pelican's anchor cable, after first giving me 'stay put' signals.

He went from sight and soon the line tautened, then began to move in a slow clockwise circle. The basket slid away from me, over the sandy bottom, disturbing a couple of crabs, which quickly re-buried themselves.

I sat on it and waited. Two, three small striped fish appeared from nowhere and stared into my face mask from eighteen inches away. Then one flickered off to return in a flash with two more. There was no doubt about it: I was an object of interest.

The thin line moved through about three hundred degrees, then stopped, and jerked several times.

I rolled from my perch and my striped audience scattered as the basket moved away over the sandy bottom. I followed it until I came up with Poplar. He pointed to an indistinct mound of weed-covered silt.

We swam towards it and over it, and on the far side turned and hovered side by side, to view the forty- year old relic.

The MTB lay over on her side, with her deck clear of silt but encrusted with barnacles, as were the twisted rails and every unrecognizable bump and hump.

Poplar moved towards the square hole in the deck, and pulled himself through. I followed, added the beam of my forehead lamp to his, and lit up scattered metal and wooden boxes of different shapes and sizes.

Some were open, and hundred upon hundreds of encrusted cartridges lay in and among them.

Poplar took a small crowbar from his belt and prized open the catches of a long wooden box.

When he turned back the lid, the hinges disintegrated and the lid floated up to be trapped against the deck head. Two Lee-Enfield rifles lay on a bed of cotton waste.

Poplar removed them hurriedly, exposing the dull glint of what we had come to find: Gold.

My heart started to beat more quickly at the sight, despite the fact that I wasn't to reap the benefit of it.

There were three ingots in the box. Poplar scratched deeply into the soft metal of each one with the crowbar, examining the results closely with his light.

He pointed to the end of another box, which protruded from the silt, and I started to clear the sand from it with my hands.

Poplar swam up through the hole, and returned with the fish basket. He put the three ingots into the basket, found he couldn't lift it, removed one and tried again.

In the end, he pushed the empty basket back out of the hold, and carried the bricks out singly. I floated to the opening, and watched him put one only into the basket, and give two pulls on the rope.

The slack was taken in, and the basket ascended vertically through the foggy water. With my eyes, I followed its progress and saw that the Pelican had been maneuvered into position directly above the MTB.

Poplar came back into the hold, and together we pulled the other box free. He prized it open as before and again uncovered three ingots beneath the rifles and cotton waste.

We moved these out and placed them alongside the first lot as the basket settled beside us. Poplar put another one in the basket and jerked the rope, while my mind was tripping over its feet, trying to work out the value of our haul.

Six — no, seven, gold bricks, with the one under the coal.

From what I'd read, that must amount to something approaching two hundred thousand pounds.

What was I doing out here? I flipped over and started to enter the hold again.

Something caught my ankle in a vise like grip and panic welled up in my throat.

I twisted violently, to ward off Poplar's attack and felt foolish when he loosed his hold and pointed to the hold with one hand, while giving the thumbs down signal with the other.

He was clearly telling me that there was no more. We'd been down for seventeen minutes. Plenty of air left yet.

The basket came down again and again was sent on its way. I wondered if Bennett would just up-anchor and sail off without us when he'd got the last one aboard.

But then, he probably wouldn’t know which *was* the last one.

The last ingot started up and Poplar signalled me to follow.

I didn’t much fancy having him behind me and I rose, warily keeping one hand on the rope, and one eye on Poplar.

The basket was ten feet from the surface when it stopped.

I stopped too, uncertainly, but Poplar didn’t.

He went past me like a bullet, heading for the light. I started to follow, looking upwards, and at that instance there was a black disturbance on the surface, and a formless mass sank swiftly towards me.

A mass that grew thrashing arms and legs as it came. It landed squarely on top of me and the limbs stopped thrashing and hooked themselves tightly around me.

Then Bennett’s face was inches from mine: eyes and mouth open in nameless horror, blood and air bubbles welling, mixing. The fingers tightened in panic around my air pipe and the mask was twisted from my face. I loosed my hold on the rope,- tried to fight him off - and together we sank rapidly to the seabed.

Bringing my knees up as high as I could, I forced my arms inside his, and exerted as much outward pressure as possible.

It wasn’t a lot, as I’d been exhaling when he robbed me of my oxygen, and there was not much air in my lungs. I got a hand beneath his chin, and desperately strove to force his head back, and all the time the eyes stared, and the mouth grimaced.

Suddenly, there was no resistance. The arms and legs lost their grip and Bennett started to float away, like an ungainly starfish.

Even in death though, he was not finished with me. The fingers of one hand were still locked tightly around my air hose.

It was several fear-packed seconds later, that I managed to prise them loose, and thankfully push the mask to my face.

Forcing myself to take controlled breaths, I knelt on the seabed, listening to the loud thumping of my heart and watching Bennett’s body, caught by an underwater current, roll gently away.

From his chest protruded the shaft of a fish-spear and five fathoms of nylon line.

As he went from view beyond the MTB, one arm seemed to beckon. There was a tug at my elbow... One end of the nylon line had arranged itself in a neat half-hitch around my arm.

With a shudder, I pulled it free, and kicked for the surface.

Even in the short time that I'd been down, conditions up top had worsened. The wind had risen, whipping gouts of spray from the steep breakers, and sending the ragged, grey clouds racing.

But however rough the waters, I felt my situation to be idyllic when compared to the panic filled minute and a half I'd just spent. For a long moment I allowed myself to float on my back and watch the gyrations of the Pelican at the end of her anchor chain.

I'd come up, about forty yards off the starboard quarter, and when my pulse rate had slowed somewhat, and the strength had returned to my muscles, I started to swim slowly round to the boarding ladder.

There was a cry from above, almost lost in the noise of the rising wind.

I looked up, and saw Jenny leaning far out over the rail, her hair blowing red and wild. She was pointing at me and calling over her shoulder.

Stoker joined her at the rail. I waved at them both, then carefully approached the boarding ladder.

Judging, as best I could, the movements of boat and wave, I lunged for the bottom rung, caught it, and almost lost my grip as I swung heavily against the hull.

It seemed a long climb before willing hands hooked themselves beneath my armpits and dragged me over the rail, to flop onto the pitching deck. Then I was sitting on my bunk, my rubber suit was being peeled off, and Jenny was rubbing my back with a rough towel.

'Better get the hook up,' I said to Stoker. 'If it drags, we'll pile up on shore.'

'Aye-aye Sir' Stoker gave me his broken toothed grin and went up into the wheelhouse to start the engine.

I hugged Jenny tight to me. 'What have you done with Poplar ?'

It was Jenny's turn to grin. 'We stuck him in the chain locker, and I hope he enjoys it as little as I did!'

After dresseing quickly followed the others up into the wheelhouse, taking the wheel while Stoker went forward to secure the anchor.

I eased Pelican slowly ahead, through the worrying maelstrom, waiting for the moment when I could open her out and get away from the lee shore. My mind seethed with questions but they could wait until we were on our way home.

Then Jenny shook my arm urgently and pointed. Barely visible, off the starboard bow, a grey vessel was emerging through the driving rain, a light flashing from her bridge.

My heart sank as I recognised the lines of the French customs boat based at Roscoff.

Half an hour ago, I'd have welcomed their intervention, but now, with Pelican back in my possession, and God knows what value of gold aboard, they were going to be an embarrassment.

The Frenchman passed by, a cable's length to starboard, and for a while we lost sight of her, as another squall hurled it's fury across the violent waters.

The germ of an idea was beginning.to take shape in my mind.

'Jenny, take the wheel – keep her quartering the waves,okay?' I closed her small hands on the spokes with mine and kissed her hair.

She didn't ask questions – just nodded and braced herself against the kick and twist of the rudder.

Stepping out from the shelter of the wheelhouse, the wind took hold of me as it would a paper bag, causing me to grab the rail and use it to pull myself along to where Stoker was crouched by the anchor winch.

He jerked a thumb in the direction of the Frenchman and cupped his hands to shout.

'She'll go-about and come after us. Looks as though we're going to lose the lot!' His face was glum.

'Maybe not!' I shouted back. 'Give me Poplar's gun.'He looked startled. 'You're not going to shoot at them, are you? They've got a bloody Oerliken. They'll blow us out of the water!'

'Of course I'm not; give it here, quickly.'

He dragged it from his pocket, handing it over reluctantly, still doubting my intentions.

I emptied the magazine, checked the chamber then lifted the hinged lid of the chain locker.

Poplar, was sitting on the sail chest, his head in his hands, his shoulders slumped. He showed no signs of stirring.

'You can sulk later.' I told him. 'Right now you've got a choice to make. French gaol or English gaol

He looked up. In the grey light from above, his face was haggard, his eyes dead. I pushed the gun towards him, butt first, and he looked at it, puzzled.

'You're back in charge of things,' I explained and told him about the custom's boat. 'You'll have to persuade them that you'll shoot us all if they don't clear off. Do you understand? --- If you put up a good performance, we may get clear.'

He nodded, took the pistol and licked his lips.

I guessed he was already wondering how he could twist this turn of events to his advantage.

'By the way, that gun's empty and I've got Bennett's,' I said, 'Right then – up you come, and keep close behind me – we don't want them picking you off with a rifle, do we?'

'They're running parallel,' Stoker shouted, 'Their Aldis is going nineteen to the dozen.'

'Can you read it?'

He shook his head. 'It's been too long. ---I can make a guess though. It's probably saying: 'you're nicked!'

'Right, let's all get back to the wheelhouse!' Poplar clambered out of the chain locker, and with the wind behind us, we slithered quickly aft and piled into the comparative comfort of the cuddy, slamming the sliding door shut.

Stoker wiped the condensation from the glass and we looked across the turmoil at the custom's boat.

She was close, too close for safety in these conditions, like a television news-shot from the Icelandic cod-war.

A muffled figure was wedged abaft her wheelhouse and I recognised the general shape of Justin Duprez. He raised a loud-hailer to his lips.

'Ahoy Pelican! You are under arrest! You will accompany us to Roscoff. Do you understand?'

I unclipped our own tannoy, and handed it to Poplar.

'You're on kiddo'. It all depends on you.'

'I'll do my best.'

No sense of humor at all.

He slid back the door a crack and spoke through the instrument, hesitantly at first but gaining strength with every word, as if he were coming to believe it himself.

'I – have – I have three hostages. I am taking Pelican out to sea. If you attempt to interfere, I will shoot the hostages one at a time. Is that clear?'

Over Poplar's shoulder I could see Justin raise his trumpet. His voice came over clear and clipped. "Are you alright Michael?"

I showed my arm out, through the hole in the glass and waved it.

Justin again: 'And Mrs McLaine – and Langon?'

I waved my arm again and gave him the thumbs up. For a while, the two craft continued running parallel, pitching and rolling. Then they started to converge

Were they going to try something: a boarding party—a sudden rush over the rail? The sea was far too rough for such Corsair tactics.

I took the wheel from Jenny and steered a fraction more to starboard, to open up the gap again. Pelican was slamming hard into the breakers, green water poured the length of the deck, and spray splattered against the wheel house glass, and through the hole, into my face.

'Hallo Pelican!' Justin's amplified voice volleyed at us again.

Poplar looked-at me enquiringly.

'Ask what they want.' I said.

He slid back the door to comply, but before he could speak, the custom's man shouted again.

'You will be arrested wherever you make landfall. Surrender now, and save yourself much inconvenience.'

Poplar shut the door.

'That means they've put the word out,' Stoker said glumly, 'The navy will be looking for us and all.'

'But what are they doing here?' Jenny said, 'Who told them where to find us? And why?'

'I reckon they must have picked up Dave Gregory after all,' I said, 'They knew there was *something* fishy going on.

The side window was steamed up again. I leaned across and cleaned a small circle. Through it, I could see that we were being closely observed through binoculars.

Stoker cleaned a circle the size of a penny, and put an eye to it.

'How are we going to get rid of 'em?' he said, 'They could follow us to kingdom-come at this rate.'

I concentrated on getting Pelican through the waves as gently as I could, while I thought about it.

Ahead, the clouds were suddenly cleft by a band of light blue, through which the sun poured vaporous white rays onto a rolling black tanker which was about to cross our path a half-mile ahead.

Beyond her, sky and sea were a solid wall of blackness, bearing down at a terrific speed.

A drum roll of heavy raindrops reinforced the spray's assault on the wheelhouse glass. A sweep of the wiper's arm, and the black coaster showed us her deck entire, as she was pushed over by wind and wave, seconds before the squall obscured her.

I braced myself to meet the onslaught and warned the others to hold tight. Pelican was poised on a wave crest when it came.

She flinched and fell awkwardly into the trough, riding up the next slope at a bad angle. Then we were engulfed in black noise, and I was sure she was going to broach.

Straining hard at the spokes to bring Pelican's head up, I heard myself shouting and was conscious of other hands on the wheel, heaving and straining.

Huge seas threw themselves aboard and swept the length of the deck, to slamming solidly against the wheelhouse before pouring into the scuppers.

Gradually we got the better of it, and the next three waves were taken in a generally controlled manner; though the force of rain and hail were so great we were sailing virtually blind.

We could see no further than twice the boat's length but I felt we had the measure of things and the worst was over.

Then, as we teetered on the ridge of another mountain, the bows of the black tanker appeared, two waves ahead.

She was coming straight for us, practically surfing along. With sick horror gripping my stomach, I spun the wheel to starboard, but by this time, Pelican was nose-diving, and her rudder was out of the water.

She settled for two seconds in the trough, crabbed drunkenly up the next rise, and, as we sea-sawed over the top, the tanker rose to meet us; --- a monstrous iron boot, intent on crushing Pelican like a beetle.

The impact was bone jarring, and the scraping seemed to go on forever as the Pelican was thrown on her beam-ends, and the four of us became a tangled mess of bodies.

The side doors slid open and water filled the wheelhouse.

Finally managing to get my feet beneath me, I came up coughing and spitting as the sea ran out again.

Jenny was kneeling and holding onto the wheel-spokes for dear life.

Poplar came up wild and panicky.

Stoker was gone.

Chapter 16

Pelican's engine had stopped and like an old, crippled horse, she struggled to come upright.

I felt sick at losing Stoker, and glared malevolently at Poplar.

He was wedged, half-upright, in the corner, pale faced and nursing his left hand carefully with his right.

‘It should have been you,’ I snarled at him, 'Why the hell wasn’t it you?'

It was imperative to get steerage way on Pelican if we were to avoid being carried back to the French coast and wrecked on the ashore.

As a gesture, I tried to re-start the engine, knowing full well, it would be useless.

Jenny took Pelican's wheel again, struggling once more to keep her pointing into the wind, and I dragged Poplar by the arm out onto the tilting deck.

We unfurled the jib just enough, released the ties on the mainsail and raised about a third of it. Then we gathered-in the billowing canvas and reefed down.

Poplar worked awkwardly, favouring his left hand and appearing to be in some pain. At last, the sails were set and Pelican rode more easily, broad reaching, taking the waves under her port quarter.

I looked around at the boiling sea, hoping to see Stoker’s waving arms.

Mixed hail and rain still lashed viciously across dark, confused water, and the radius of clear vision was barely fifty yards. Within that circle there was no sign of Stoker.

Neither was there any sign of the French custom’s craft nor the tanker.

I cupped my hand and shouted to Poplar to slacken off the main-sheet.

Without waiting for an answer, I ducked back into the wheelhouse and leaned my weight with Jenny's on the wheel.

Sluggishly, Pelican's bow came about until she was sailing a reciprocal course, her boom well out.

Poplar was slow at his task, and I held my breath until he had two or three turns round the cleat, Once more I went forward, collected my new deckhand on the way, and sent him down into the chain locker.

As he lowered himself into the hatch, I could see that two fingers of his left hand twisted brokenly.

Several feet of water sloshed about down there, and it came over Poplar's knees.

'You stay down there.'I told him.

'Is this necessary? I give you my word, not to cause you any trouble—I've broken my hand.'

I didn't bother to answer but flipped the hatch cover over with my foot and closed it.

Leaning over the port bow for a look at the damage I could see there was a jagged, splintered rent in Pelican's hull, four feet long and a good two feet at it's widest. It was above the waterline, but every time we dipped, a large amount of water surged inboard.

We back-tracked for half an hour, looking for Stoker without success.

Fine reaching and back on course for England's south coast, we zig-zagged Pelican through the waves for another spell, hoping some miracle would deliver a living Stoker into our path.

I wondered how long Poplar would survive in the chain locker in those conditions. I had no sympathy for him, but dead he would be an embarrassment.

Before rejoining Jenny, I reluctantly transferred him to the relative comfort of the main hold. He was shivering, mainly from cold and being wet for so long, but also from the pain of his injury.

When I got back into the wheelhouse Jenny too, was clenching her teeth to stop them chattering.

One glance into the cabin showed me that it offered no refuge.

The water was up to the level of my bunk and every blanket, every scrap of clothing, was saturated. I drew her into the crook of my arm, kissed the top of her wet head and asked her what she wanted to do.

'Do?'

‘Roscoff is nearer’ I said carefully. ‘Warm dry clothes in two hours at most.’

‘Or?’

‘Or straight on for home. A hundred miles or more; a hundred and fifty, the way we’ll have to sail it. At this speed it could take us two days.’

‘Is there any chance of getting the engine going?’

I shook my head. ‘I doubt it. I’ll have a look later, but there will be too much sea down there.’

The batteries would be fully discharged too, with all that salt-water treatment. I flicked on the wheelhouse light. The bulb gave a faint glimmer and died.

I wondered about the donkey engine: If I could get that working and charge up the batteries it would be a start.

Down in the cabin, groping beneath the scummy surface for my toolbox, my fingers closed on a food can—then two more: all with their labels washed off.

Next I salvaged a can opener and two spoons and passed the whole lot up to Jenny.

‘How would you like a surprise lunch?’

She opened two tins, one pork and veg., the other spaghetti. We ate them cold, then I ‘went back out into the wind and rain to look at the donkey engine.

Before I started, I lifted the main engine cover and made a brief check. The top surface of the diesel held water in every crevice, but the bulk of it had drained into the bilges.

Maybe, she wouldn’t be too difficult to start, once the batteries were up.

I unbolted the carburetor from the donkey engine, took out the plug and went back into the wheel-house, where I dismantled and dried them out.

An hour later, the fingers of both hands bleeding, I was rewarded by the slave firing for almost ten seconds before stalling.

I fitted the starting handle for the fiftieth time, time, said “Please

God!", and gave it another twirl.

Ten seconds of splutter, --a cough, -- ten more, and I carefully adjusted the throttle and got to my feet as the little motor settled down to run sweetly.

I stretched my back with a sigh of relief, looked into eternity and breathed out a delicate: 'Thank you God!'

It had stopped raining too, and there was a slit in the clouds ahead. This time, the light that came through was strong and yellow and there was no solid black wall beyond it.

In the wheel-house, I cut-in the slave-operated bilge pump then lifted the trap in the deck which hid the main batteries.

In the near-capsize, they'd both been thrown from their cradles, and the terminals of one had shorted out on metalwork.

I righted them and checked the acid level. It was okay, and with another jubilant whisper of thanks I flipped the charger switch and watched the ammeter needle fly over to full charging rate.

I spent the next hour with a bucket and plastic bowl, baling out the cabin, and all the time I was working, passing up the containers for Jenny to tip out of the lee door, the weather was improving, and I was thinking about Stoker.

Poor old Stoker! His luck had run out with a vengeance. I found my old spear gun lying between the bunks and held it up.

'You haven't told me what happened to Bennett.'

Jenny shuddered as her memory conjured up the gruesome picture.

'Stoker found that old spear gun in the sail chest and stuck it inside the leg of his trousers. It gave him a bit of a limp, but Bennett didn't notice.'

She concentrated on steering, while I blew the water from the gas burner and lit it. I looked up at her, waiting for the rest.

'I think, Stoker intended to wait until you were back aboard before starting anything, but Bennett began pushing him around again.

'Stoker tried to get the spear gun out on the quiet, but Bennett saw, and shot at him. The boat dropped into a trough, and he missed.

'But Stoker didn't miss. It was horrible, Bennett hung over the rail screaming, and Stoker caught hold of his legs and tipped him overboard.'

'It couldn't have happened to a nicer bloke,' I said with attempted flippancy.

I tried to blot out the memory of my final encounter with Bennett, on the seabed. Then another thought struck me.

'By the way, where is the loot stashed?'

'In the hold, with Poplar,' Jenny said.

'Almost poetic,' I laughed, 'I suppose I'd better feed him.'

'He doesn't deserve it!'

I opened the main hatch, dropped a label-less tin and an opener through and waited until Poplar emerged from the shadows. He picked them up, then his drawn white face squinted up at he light.

'What do you intend to do?'

I squatted by the coaming. The sun was warming my back and my shadow blocked him out.

'Me? I intend to go home and enjoy my share of the salvage money. How about you?'

'But you can't! The Navy will be looking for this boat now. You'll be arrested!'

'Why should they arrest me? After all, I'm bringing them back six bars of gold, which they'd thought they'd lost forever. They might arrest me for a little while, but they'll be too grateful to keep me.'

'Three bars. The other three are lead,' Poplar said.

'Ah well, you'd know all about that little fiddle, wouldn't you?'

I felt a little deflated. Poplar had just cut my reward money in half. Still, there were always the Sunday newspapers. They'd pay well for a story like this.

I fetched Poplar's clothes from the cabin and dropped the wet bundle down the hatch to him.

'I'll leave the lid open,' I told him, 'The sun might dry them out a bit.' I turned away again, and then, as an afterthought added: 'Don't stick your head out though, -- I've still got Bennet's pistol.'

The ammeter needle had dropped back to a trickle.

'Well, here goes,' I put on a confident smile as Jenny threw me a one fingered kiss, I pressed the, starter and began to count off the seconds, as the engine turned over.

At six, the revs slowed perceptibly. At ten, the batteries were straining and at twelve, there was a release of tension as seventy horsepower rumbled into life beneath our feet.

I took a deep, satisfied breath.and hugged Jenny tight.

After furling the sails I checked on Poplar and went back to the wheelhouse to consider my options.

The priority was to clear French waters as quickly as possible. If another challenge was due it would be better coming from the British authorities than the French.

With this in mind I headed due north.

In the wheelhouse, the sun through the glass made our clothing steam and we felt sleepy. Jenny needed no urging to stretch out behind me on the seat while I steered.

After a while, my vision began to blur and my eyes would close for seconds at a time, jerking open when the bows dropped into a trough instead of sliding in gently.

Suddenly, Poplar's head popped up above the coaming and his right arm waved. I picked up the spear gun from the corner and shoved it through the broken glass. There was no spear in the barrel. It was just a gesture.

'I told you to stay put!' I yelled.

Jenny had been asleep and sat up with a start. 'What happened?'

'Oh sorry,—it's Poplar, --trying it on.'

Poplar called out. 'I want to talk to you.'

'I'll bet! Can you see any green in my eye?'

'It's not a trick. I have a proposition to make!'

'Then make it quickly.'

My voice sounded arrogant, even to myself. After all the grief this man had caused, I was reveling in the sensation of being top-dog.

Poplar was shouting again. 'If you take me home, to Windbeck, I could make it very much worth your while.'

I didn't answer, and he was silent for almost half a minute before continuing:

'My word on it. You already have this gold. Add to it what I am prepared to give you, and you'll be made for life.'

'In return for letting you go?'

'That, and something else.'

I waited for the 'something else', but his head went down below the coaming and didn't reappear.

'I wonder what he's got in mind,' Jenny murmured.

I shrugged. 'He probably wants Pelican. But whatever it is, he’s not having it.'

‘Why on earth would he want the Pelican?'

‘To escape in ... You know: —a promise to reform and a week’s start! He could lose himself in the Med.’

While we'd been speaking I was watching the approach of another supertanker from up Channel.

With recent memories in mind, I opened the throttle and studied the changing angle of her bow until I was sure she'd pass astern of us.

I wondered aloud what else Poplar was thinking of offering.

‘Go and ask him,' Jenny said, 'what have you got to lose?’

I was doubtful. ‘I don’t know... it doesn’t seem right somehow, doing deals with him. I haven’t thumped him for kidnapping you yet—Then there’s Sam Wilkins – and Stoker.’

‘Stoker’s widow will need help,' Jenny said, 'and I could use some compensation... It's up to you to screw what you can out of him!’

I went to the main hatch and called his name.

He came into the light and looked up, shading his eyes.

‘What else do you want in exchange?' I asked.

‘Two things: Your silence and the Pelican!’

‘Why don’t I just drop you over the side and have done with it? You’ve hurt a hell of a lot of people.’

‘Not me,—Bennett. He always went too far. He was a psychopath.’

‘What does that make you? You employed him!'

His voice became bitter. ‘He was my albatross! I’m glad that he’s dead.’

‘You mean, now that you have no further use for him?'

He stepped back into the shadows. 'There are reasons, -- good reasons, -- for my actions.-- You wouldn’t understand!’

‘Gold is always a good reason. I grant you that.’

‘I never wanted the gold.'

He came back into the light and his tone was intense.

'It was a terrible thing that my brother did, all those years ago. An unforgivable thing! And it would all have been made known. -- I had to do what I could to stop that. *Had* to!’

'Your brother is dead. It can’t hurt or harm him now. Are you afraid that his disgrace would reflect on you?'

He looked at me without speaking for a while, then: --'I meant what I said. Take me to Windbeck and I will willingly pay you any sum you name.'All I ask is that you and Mrs McLaine keep this whole affair quiet.'

'Quiet? There are cracked skulls and dead bodies all over the place; and the police of two countries are already involved. It's as noisy as hell!

'And then there's Dave Gregory. He knows as much as I do, and he's got more reason to hate your guts. His father — '

'Mr. Gregory and I already have an arrangement.'

That pulled me up short.

'You mean you've done a deal? Well, of all the... When did this happen?'

'Yesterday evening, at the Four Eagles. I bought some photographs from him – and negatives. For a considerable sum in cash.'

I went back to the wheelhouse to mull this over.

Jenny and I spent a long time talking over Poplar's proposition while the indifferent sun lowered itself towards the sea.

A soft smudge on the northern skyline hardened, and became England's south coast.

Soon, I would have to decide whether to go for the salvage option or take up Poplar's offer.

******

Later, with the Eddytone behind us and the breakwater less than a mile ahead, I made up my mind and, with many misgivings, turned Pelican's bow for Helford Passage.

Jenny's hand covered mine on the wheel. Her face was lit pink by the last of the light.

'What decided you?' She asked.

'Greed', I said, 'and curiosity!'

Chapter 17

Helford River at midnight was a shimmering, starlit pathway between its closely wooded banks.

Pelican, her engine throttled down to a murmur, was barely making headway against the falling tide.

From the right, sudden, bright car headlights cut the night, blinding us before traversing to briefly light-up sleeping stone cottages then flickering away between the trees.

For a while afterwards the darkness was more intense.

Poplar, a shadowy bulk beside me, had the wheel and seemed perfectly at home in this narrow waterway.

I'd been hesitant to hand over to him, but it was easier than having him con me through.

The banks started to close in on either side and I was getting edgy.

'How much further?' I asked.

Poplar's tone was almost light as he replied.'Not far now, -- about three hundred yards. You'll see the break in the trees soon.'

Jenny stirred. 'I think I see it, — look, where they dip against the stars.' She sounded very sleepy.

I wasn't happy being this far up an un-familiar river on the ebb.

'Are you sure there'll be enough water? The tide's been falling for an hour.'

'I've told you – I've been up and down this stretch a thousand times.'

He gave the wheel a gentle twist and Pelican moved trustingly, towards a barely discernible opening in the left bank.

Something had changed Poplar. He was whistling softly between his teeth.

I wondered, if it was because he was coming home. Or maybe because he'd lost out and didn't have to try any more. He cut the engine and we drifted towards the bank

'She'll be tide-bound till the next flood,' he said,' but she'll float upright against the jetty.--- Would you mind tying up?'

It was a bizarre situation: Formal politeness, when only hours before he'd been ordering us about at gunpoint.

As I stepped onto the wooden jetty with the mooring line, I wondered what our present situation would be if Stoker had not turned the tables and Bennett were still waving a pistol about.

It would not do to allow Poplar too much latitude.

Pelican's lights, wearing haloes of mist, lit weather-worn planking beneath the feet, and rusty iron stair- treads sloping upwards against an overgrown earth bank.

Then the lights went out, and Poplar and Jenny were ashore too.

Poplar said. 'This way!' and the metal treads rang dully under his feet.

Jenny hung back and whispered: 'What about the loot?'

'You can stand and guard it, if you like,' I whispered back, 'or we can fill our pockets.'

She pushed me towards the steps. 'Fun – ee!'

Poplar stood clear at the top, then led the way along a rising track towards the dark bulk of a house which loomed against the jewelled sky.

As we drew nearer the house, a dog's barking came to us faintly, and a square of yellow light appeared high under the eaves.

We followed Poplar to the front of the house, the sound of our footsteps changing as we went from beaten earth to gravel, then to flagstones.

A porch lantern came on and Poplar reached for a brass knob on the door frame. An old fashioned jangling sounded beyond the heavy door, followed after an interval by the dry rasp of withdrawing bolts and the softer sound of a turning key. The door opened, exposing an inner porch, tiled, with a fringe of wind-blown dead leaves against the skirting, and a coconut mat.

The woman, who held open the door appeared to be in her mid-sixties. She was well above middle height with braided hair and wearing a dark dressing gown.

Her eyes were anxious, and she held a mean looking Boxer dog by the collar.

'Oh, -- Mr. Poplar! --I am sorry, I was not expecting you!'

My ears caught the barest hint of a foreign accent.

She stepped aside, dragging the dog bodily with her, and we followed Poplar through into a spacious rectangular hall, dominated by a large glass case standing on a table near the foot of the stairs.

The case contained a model of a full rigged warship of the Napoleonic period. Round the walls, gold frames enclosed portraits of be-wigged and uniformed naval officers, and between them, hung swords and pistols.

'Good evening Mrs Martin. I'm sorry to waken you at this hour,' Poplar said, 'I don't suppose there's a fire in the library?'

'It is laid sir. I'll just put a match to it.'

‘I’ll do that, if you will kindly find us some food, and run me a bat?.’

‘Yes sir.’ She loosed the dog and walked towards the back of the house.

The dog wrinkled his nose at us a few times before following her.

Poplar neither spoke to the animal, nor made any move to pat it.

The library, a well proportioned, high ceilinged room with a wide deep fireplace, also spoke of the sea and seamen.

Poplar picked, up a table-lighter and applied its flame to the sticks and coal in the wrought iron basket. Smoke billowed up the cavernous flue, then a slight down draught caused some to spill and drift up over the mantle piece, where it mingled with the gun-smoke of the Fighting Temeraire, locked in eternal combat with the French.

Poplar saw the direction of my gaze and stood aside from the painting.

‘A copy, by Giles Ashburn.’ He gestured with his right hand. ‘He painted most of what you see in this room.’

I let my eyes roam slowly. Old forgotten ships, fighting old forgotten enemies, in old forgotten wars.

More portraits showed jovial men in full-bottomed wigs, aloof men in ribboned perukes, and stern men with close- cropped hair.

‘All Poplars,' he said,'There have always been Poplars in the navy.’

His voice was vibrant with pride, and his eyes shone with it. He indicated the bookshelves, which took up the whole of one wall. His manner became more intense.

‘The complete history of the Royal Navy is here, from the time of Alfred the Great. ---And Poplars have always served: often with distinction. ---'But even those who were merely competent were *honourable men'*

He broke off and seemed to shrink a little as his eyes went to a spot on the wall, which showed a rectangular patch of paler wallpaper but no portrait.

He turned away, and walked to the drink tray on a side table.

‘I’m sorry. What will you drink?’

I asked for brandy. Jenny chose soda water and we watched, as he fumblingly poured.

At some time during his stay in the hold, he had splinted his broken fingers with pieces from an old fish box, bound with twine.

I sipped my drink and nodded towards the pale-patch of wallpaper.

'Until?' I prompted.

Before he could answer, Mrs. Martin came in bearing a tray with sandwiches, and coffee in an insulated jug.

She set down and spoke to Poplar. 'Your bath is ready sir.' She hovered. 'Your hand, ... I could telephone Doctor Tregorren.'

Poplar shook his head. 'Thank you – no. It's nothing.I will have it attended to in the morning. Please bring warm towels to me when I ring.'

She gave us all a searching look before leaving the room without answering.

When she'd gone, Poplar crossed to the two tall windows and closed the curtains smoothly with a tasseled rope, shutting out the night.

Then he went for his bath, during which time I loitered within sight of the bathroom door; just in case he tried to pull a fast one.

The tall figure of Mrs. Martin passed me twice while I waited, bearing towels and clean clothing for Poplar. As she went by, I feigned a close interest in a model schooner, and in fifteen minutes Poplar came out of the bathroom, spruce and smiling.

Back in the library, Jenny had made a start on the sandwiches and was sitting in a small fireside armchair. I bit thankfully into a beef sandwich and sat on a fragile-looking upright chair, feeling the comforting presence of the pistol digging into my midriff.

Dermot Poplar dropped into a big wing-back and began his story quietly.

'My brother, Desmond, joined the Royal Navy in nineteen twenty-seven, straight from school. He served at sea until 'thirty-eight, then transferred to Naval Intelligence.

'Early that year, Desmond was on the staff of the British Naval Attache in Berlin. He met a young German woman there, at one of those unending social functions, and fell for her, hook line and sinker.

'He came back to this country at the end of thirty-eight, and was at the Admiralty until the war started. At that time I was reading History at Cambridge.' He swept a fond glance over the ranked books. 'My speciality was sea power.'

He paused, opened a carved box on a side table next to his chair and selected a cigar. With a gesture, and a raised eyebrow, he invited me to join him. I declined.

He picked up the lighter. 'Do you mind Mrs McLaine?'

Jenny shook her head, smiling.

Ludicrous wasn't the word: Not long before, Poplar had been threatening to have her shot. Now, he was politeness itself.

Wondering which was the real Poplar, I poured coffee, and its rich aroma blended with that of burning Java leaf.

'I volunteered when the war started, of course,' he went on, 'but the need for colour-blind sailors is limited – even in war time.

'However, I pestered the powers that be and eventually found a useful niche at the Admiralty, – as a civilian.

'About the middle of nineteen forty I, too, became involved in intelligence work, and it was just after that, that this whole wretched affair began.'

He stared into the fire. I took my brandy and coffee and moved my chair closer to the flames. Poplar sat forward and held his damaged hand out to the comfort of the glowing coal, gently kneading the tendons of the wrist with the fingers of his other hand.

'Word came out of Berlin that a particularly high- ranking German was anxious to defect. He was a Naval man and reputedly very close to Doenitz himself. The amount of fine detail which he offered to bring with him would have been of inestimable value. He was privy to all the enemy's technical advances: – their long term 'U' boat strategy, – even plans of 'Operation Sea-Lion'.'

'Why would any German in his right mind have wanted to defect to us at that time?' I said, We were losing hands down!'

Poplar smiled. His cigar had gone out and he tossed the remains into the fire.

'Probably he, too, was a student of history. Apart from the things I've mentioned, this man was also aware of the German High Command's intentions regarding Russia, and it was perhaps this that persuaded him it would be prudent to get out. ---He probably remembered what had happened to that other 'little corporal'.'

'And the gold was to be his price?'

Poplar nodded slowly, 'Fifteen bars was the price of his treachery

– to be landed on the French coast.'

Jenny moved back from the fire, her brows drew down a little.

'But why did he want the gold over there, if he was coming over here?'

'Because he first wanted to see the stuff safely into a Swiss bank.. A man of his rank would have had little difficulty in handling that part of it. He would undoubtedly have got himself over the Swiss border, along with the gold, and once it was deposited, flown out via Spain – or Portugal.'

I drained my cup and felt the grit of real coffee on my tongue.

'Seems to me our side were taking a lot on trust,' I said.

Poplar smiled thinly. 'Trust? No! We had someone watching him the whole time. --- Anyway, he was considered valuable enough to be worth *some* risk.'

'And your brother was involved in this as well as you? That seems a bit too co-incidental – '

'It was no co-incidence,' Poplar broke in, 'by then he was stationed up at Lossiemouth, and I suggested to my superiors that he be brought down to Devonport and put in overall charge of the operation.'

I thought I'd prod him a little.

'Brilliant! So, brother Desmond changes most of the gold for painted lead, and when the war finished you'd both be rich! You know, I could admire a stroke like that if it wasn't for the bomb in the MTB: That makes it dirty.'

Poplar stiffened - resentful. 'Neither of us had any part in that. My brother's guilt, as far as it went, was the guilt of any commander when things go wrong.'

'Let me get this straight,' I said, 'Are you saying that Desmond was a thief, but not a saboteur?'

Poplar shook his head impatiently. 'You must let me tell it my way.'

There was a moan in the chimney as a cold pre-dawn wind passed over the house. Red sparks, drawn from the glowing coals, clung to the soot of the fire-back and ran like miniature powder fuses.

Poplar shivered and leaned forward. 'I must go back to before the war: Nineteen thirty-eight...'

'I spent part of my summer vacation in Berlin that year. It was –

an unforgettable time – the atmosphere – parades -- noise – uniforms and loudspeakers. The whole nation seemed to tremble with a terrible lust for self–destruction.

'On the last evening, I was invited to go, with my brother, to a rather special celebration. A group of storm-troopers had just completed their training and this was to be a ritual letting off steam. I've never been to a stranger affair ... *weird* almost.

'Oh, the beer flowed and the songs rang out,—but it was all so *intense,* and so *ordered*! The steam only allowed to escape in controlled amounts. And the young men themselves,—fit, taut with pride, swinging their steins manfully as they sang marching songs --- but you could look through the windows of their eyes into empty skulls.'

Poplar took a poker from the stand and rattled it through the bars of the grate before going on in a quieter tone:

'Halfway through the evening, my brother introduced me to a girl, she was tall, blonde, and exceedingly beautiful. Her name was Helga Oogman and it was obvious to me that Desmond was besotted with her. You could see it in every look he gave her; ---every gesture.

'Some little time after the war started, he received a letter from her. By this time she was working at the German Embassy in Lisbon – and he foolishly wrote back.'

'To the German Embassy?' I scoffed, 'In wartime?'

'Of course not,' Poplar said, 'They used an accommodation address.

'They exchanged half a dozen letters in this way, love letters at first, and then hers began to contain broad hints that he should pass information to her. Desmond, of course, saw the light, and stopped writing.' He paused, considering. 'It was my belief that she had been 'planted' on him, in Berlin, with just this object in view but Desmond would never admit the possibility.'

'What happened to her?' Jenny's eyes, in the fire glow were bright with thoughts of romantic intrigue.

'Her last letter said that she was being recalled to Germany,' My brother heard no more of her until... but I'm getting ahead of my story.

'The planning of "operation defector" got under way in Plymouth, and then, one morning, my brother received an envelope with a

London postmark. It contained a photo-copy of a letter to the German woman, detailing convoy movements, and the likeness to his handwriting was impressive.

'There was a photograph with the letter. It was of Helga Oogman and a baby about two years of age. The inscription on the back said "Helga und kleine Desmond".

'You can perhaps imagine his feelings. That same night, there was a phone call. The caller said that unless he passed on information as requested, copies of the letter and photo would go to the Admiralty.

'On my advice, Desmond laid the whole thing before our immediate chief, and it was arranged to feed the black-mailer false information.'

'Was this to be in letters to Helga?' Jenny asked.

'We thought that would be the case, but in the event, my brother began receiving irregular telephone calls. Always short ones and from public boxes,—no chance to trace calls.

'Then, one night, there was a call with distinctive back- ground noises, suggesting a public bar. And by a stroke of luck, he heard the landlady calling 'time'.

Poplar pressed his lips together in a grim smile, and stared into the red caverns of the fire, savoring the memory.

'How could that help?' I prompted, 'Landladies are fairly plentiful.'

'That wasn't all, you see: She shouted 'time', then there was another voice. It said, "come on Auntie, your clock's fast again!" Poplar's eyes swiveled between us, small triumph lighting them.

'It could only be 'The Unicorn' in Gate Street. All the regulars called the landlady 'Auntie', and there was a pay phone in the passage.'

He relaxed again. 'So, my brother waited five minutes and then rang 'The Unicorn' and asked Auntie if she'd noticed who'd used her phone. His luck was in, she didn't know the man's name, but he was in there most evenings for half an hour or so.

'Desmond swore 'Auntie' to secrecy and asked her to ring him when the man next appeared.

'The very next night, 'Auntie' rang to say the man was in the bar. Desmond's flat was above his office in the dock yard, and only five minutes from Gate Street.

'In no time, he was in Auntie's sitting room and she was pointing out the man through the 'squint'. My brother knew him slightly, his name was Granger and he was a civilian employee in the 'yard'.

'His lodgings were searched quietly and thoroughly for a transmitter, and all his associates vetted. Nothing!

'Desmond took to donning workman's clothing and following the man at his work, which involved moving stuff around on a forklift truck.

'Then the MTB went off on its mission: – "arms for the resistance" – and didn't come back.'

In the silence that followed, I pictured the scene as Stoker had told it to me. The dark seas and flying tracers and men thrashing out the last moments of their lives in the cold Channel waters.

Jenny rose and went to the window. She drew the curtain aside a little and looked out.

'The moon's rising.' She let the drapes fall, to come and stand behind my chair, her hands sliding onto my shoulders, fingers just touching my neck. 'I hope they had a moon. It must be a lonely thing to die in the dark.'

'We tried to find out if there were any survivors of course,' Polar went on,' Both sides were obliged to record names of prisoners; but there was nothing.

'But we all know now that only *some* of the gold was aboard the MTB,' I said, 'Where was the rest?'

Dermot Poplar ignored the direct question and went on in his own way:

'Desmond continued to receive telephone calls from Granger, and feed him with false information, laced with a certain amount of irrelevant fact which was easily verifiable.

'One day, when he was following Granger about the yard, at a discreet distance, the man unfastened the padlock of a large storage shed which was built against steeply rising ground.

'He went inside and Desmond, watching through a window saw him walk the length of it and go from sight among stacked boxes at the rear.

'It was half an hour before he reappeared and went about his work.

'Desmond straight away obtained a key and investigated – alone.

'On that occasion, he made just a brief search and found nothing suspicious. Before he left however, he un-hooked the catch of the rear-most window so that he could enter again without disturbing the padlock on the main doors.

Next day, after making sure that Granger was working some distance away, he climbed into the shed through the window.

It took him some time to find the loose planks in the end wall and discover the cunning way they had been removed and replaced. Behind them he found, cut into the solid rock, a cave which was part of a bomb store from the first war.

'The lights had been tapped in the main shed, and the interior of the cave made comfortable with a bunk and ventilation.

'And under an upturned tea-chest, was a wireless transmitter.

'There was evidence in plenty of espionage: the wireless,— notes, — scribbled messages, and most useful of all, the man's code-book

Poplar gave a short bark of a laugh. 'Can you imagine, the audacity of it? He was actually sending his messages from within the dockyard!

'Naturally, Desmond made a very thorough search while he was there, but he had to be extremely careful not to mark his presence.

'If he could allow the man enough rope, there was a good chance that it would ensnare any accomplices he had.

'Desmond left everything untouched and replaced the planking.

'He was about to leave, when he heard the rattle of the padlock being removed.

'There was a recess behind a pile of junk and he barely had time to put out the light and freeze into hiding, before Granger was moving towards him, lighting his way with a torch.

'The recess was very dark and, although Granger had the torch, somehow he passed inches from my brother without seeing him.

'He went to the rear, lifted a tarpaulin and shone his torch onto the floorboards. Then something must have put him on his guard for he turned the torch full upon Desmond.

'A split-second later Granger made a rush for the door; my brother managed to trip him. There was a rough and tumble; the torch was dropped and Granger was shouting "Let go, or I'll shoot!"

'Then they fell; the gun went off --- and Granger stopped shouting and lay still.

'The torch was on the ground, it's beam shining directly into Granger's eyes, but the eyes didn't blink.

'The body was removed at night and we put a man of our own in Granger's place; two in fact. They took turn and turn about to monitor the radio, hoping for a call from Granger's contacts.

'Another of our intelligence team took Granger's old lodgings to intercept his mail but, as far as we could tell, no one at all tried to reach him from the day he died.'

Poplar lapsed once more into silence. He slumped in his chair with lowered eyes, and I could not tell if he slept or merely brooded.

I wanted to press him, about the gold but Jenny warned me with her eyes to stay silent.

The fire had dwindled to a grey ash and the room was turning chilly. I put on another log.

Poplar began to speak again, so quietly at first that I had to lean forward to catch his words.

'Three years ago, I was in Spain – Cadiz, engaged in research.'

His eyes lifted, as if drawn by a magnet, to one of the older portraits, dark brown and cracked, with the weight of its years. It showed a seaman of the first Elizabeth's time; a seaman with a pointed beard and a ruff at the neck.

'I was called home by telegram.' He gestured with his good hand. 'This has always been my home too.

'Desmond was ill: In fact, he survived for only a few hours after I got home: Long enough though, to make a confession that set the recent unfortunate events in train.

'You remember I said that just before Granger was shot he'd lifted a tarpaulin?'

I nodded.

'Desmond didn't recall that until about a week later. He was alone when he checked on that, and he found faint signs that floor-boards had been recently removed and replaced. He took a couple up and found that beneath them were concealed most of the gold bars that had been intended for "operation defector"

'Also down there was a quantity of scrap lead, a mould and a tin of gold paint. It was apparent that Granger, either alone or with help, had side-tracked most of the ransom and substituted fake bars.'

He looked again at the portraits on the wall.

'Among our forebears are some who sailed under "letters of marque and reprise" ... privateers... And the bullion had, after all, been officially written off ... .

'Before raising the alarm, Desmond moved the genuine gold bars here, to Windbeck.

'It did occur to him that the MTB. might have been sabotaged to cover the substitution, but even if that were so, the culprit was dead anyway.

'What Desmond did was illegal and immoral, but was anyone going to suffer in any way, or be deprived?'

Poplar spread his hands, and winced as his fingers hurt. His eyes were asking me to agree with him.

'What about all the mayhem you have caused since? Three people are dead. Mrs McLaine has been kidnapped – twice.' I began to get angry with him again. 'And you say no one has suffered? What do you call— ?'

'My fault, all my fault.' He interrupted quickly. 'My panic-driven attempt to cover up after Gregory first came to me with the photographs.'

'But why bother? Surely no one would suspect your brother?'

'David Gregory did, and he had the sabotage device, the remains of the time-bomb, plus at least one fake ingot, as evidence'

'Even so, you say your brother knew nothing of that.'

'Mud sticks, Mr. Peterson. If it had just been the... taking of the gold—' (he carefully avoided the word theft) — 'I could have risked the story being made public. But to have Desmond suspected of treason? After all these generations of service?'

The varnished eyes around the walls held themselves aloof.

'Why didn't you do a deal with Gregory at that time?' I asked.

'I offered him half a million but he said it wasn't enough. In fact he said that no amount of money would suffice.

'But you have the photographs now. What *did* you give him in exchange?'

Poplar looked at me levelly. 'His life, and that of his brother. Bennett and I surprised him at the Four Eagles and gained the upper hand?'

'And then you picked up Stoker, ---and then us!'

'Yes.'

I switched. ‘Why did you kill Ruyter?’

Poplar took it without blinking. ‘He was supposed to dispose of Gregory for me. Instead, he planned to go after the gold himself. I paid Bennett to shoot him, just as I’d paid him to blow up the Garland. Gregory was supposed to go up with it.’

‘But Bennett was working with Ruyter. As I remember it, Bennett was just as keen to find the stuff.’ I rubbed my nose, remembering the treatment it had had at Bennett’s hands when we'd met at Highfields.

Poplar snapped. ‘Bennett’s greed was immediate; five hundred pounds and he put the bomb aboard Garland. Another five and he disposed of Ruyter.’

‘You must have realised, that wouldn’t be enough; that Dave Gregory had got his information from someone.’

Poplar nodded and sighed. ‘I could only play the hand as I saw it. I thought Figgin was just a "gofer".I never dreamed he was the source of the information.

I kept quiet about the other survivor, Smallridge. If I decided to do a deal with Poplar, and he went free, then I didn’t want to read about Smallridge's violent death with my breakfast.

‘Okay, so the family name means a lot to you! What do you think your performance is going to do to it?’

Poplar ignored the question, and continued with his story.

‘When the war ended, Desmond desperately wanted to get back to Germany, to find Helga. He pulled a few strings and got himself attached to the Control Commission over there.

'Conditions were unbelievably chaotic. Hundreds of thousands of displaced people, speaking twenty different tongues, and half the country inaccessible because of the Russians.

' After a year, he had managed to trace Helga’s parents, to a village near the Danish border. They were working on a farm, and they had their seven year old grandson living with them: Helga’s son.

'It was the boy in the photograph, and Desmond was convinced that he himself was the father.

'Some months later, when he was visiting the parents, a cousin of Helga’s called. He had seen her and talked with her briefly only a week before. He was a seaman, and Helga had come aboard his ship when it had docked in Riga. She had been in some official capacity, —either political or security.'

'She was a communist?' Jenny said.

Poplar shrugged. 'She was whatever it took to stay alive. An opportunist! Through the cousin, Desmond managed to pass a message to her, and then he bent his efforts towards getting her out of Russia.

'It took more than a year, and a great deal of money. Without some of the gold, he could not have done it.

'Finally, they were reunited, and it seemed that there was nothing to prevent them marrying and settling here. Trouble was, her record got in the way. The fact that she'd been in the German diplomatic service, *and* worked for the Russians, rather blotted her copybook.

'Still, Desmond was very determined, and eventually, Helga and the boy arrived here, via Stockholm, with a set of beautifully forged documents, proving them to be natives of that city.

'They were married quietly in Helston. Desmond retired from the Navy and from then on spared nothing to give the boy a good upbringing.

'There was still a fairly substantial amount of gold left, stored beneath this house, and with that to back him, Desmond made inroads into the jewelry market. He was even granted a license to deal in pure gold.'

He chuckled silently at the thought of it.

'Imagine that!' He looked at me from under his brows. 'Have you heard of 'Cascade', Mr. Peterson?'

'I have,' Jenny said, 'They must be the poshest, costliest jewelers in the country.'

Dermot Poplar nodded. 'It rivals Cartier, it rivals Tiffany's and now it's owned exclusively by my late brother's son.'

'And, this is a second boat that must not be rocked,' I suggested, 'Quite apart from the family name.'

'Exactly – and there is yet a third. Do you know anything of politics, Mr. Peterson? Or politicians?'

A little flag waved in the corner of my mind. Poplar saw the light dawn on my face, and continued.

'Yes, he is *that* Henry Poplar: at the moment, just a fairly humdrum backbencher. But in inner circles it is accepted that he is on the way up. In fact it is suggested that he is headed for the Foreign Office. And I can tell you that he has his sights set beyond that post. He fully intends to be a very young Prime Minister. His background must *not* be made public!

'So why are you telling us? What exactly are you offering? --- Half of a jewelry empire?'

Poplar picked up his empty glass from the hearth, rose, and walked to the drinks table.

Crystal clinked expensively on crystal, and when he turned to face us, he held a double brandy, carefully, in his injured hand, and a small automatic in his good one.

'Not exactly Mr. Peterson. In fact, I can't offer you anything at all now – not even hope.'

Chapter 18

I felt sickened by my own stupidity and carelessness --- my arrogance in thinking that I was in control.

'So it was all eyewash then? The offer of "riches beyond the dreams of avarice" bit?'

He nodded without smiling. 'I simply played on *your* avarice.'

Jenny reached for my hand and gripped it. Her voice trembled a little as she asked. 'What do you intend to do with us?'

Poplar sipped his drink then put his tumbler down. 'Another boat trip I'm afraid. —Believe me, Mrs McLaine, if there was any way that I could spare you ...'

He crossed to the door, without taking his eyes from us, opened it, and raised his voice. 'Helga!'

Jenny and I exchanged looks. Jenny mouthed 'Helga?' Surprised, we watched the door in silence.

Seconds later, Poplar stepped aside and "Mrs. Martin" came into the room. She was dressed for outdoors, her step was purposeful, and she was pointing a double-barreled shotgun at us.

Poplar told me to put the gun I had in my waistband, very carefully on the table, using two fingers only.

He watched my hands intently while I did so.

If there had been only his pistol to contend with I'd have been tempted to try something desperate, but my stomach cringed at the thought of the twelve-bore.

Poplar spoke again. 'You and Mrs. McLaine will now return to your boat.'

I felt sicker than ever.

In the entrance hall, Poplar reached into a cloakroom and put on a reefer jacket and cap, before ushering us through the kitchen and out of the back door.

It still wanted three hours to daylight, and a thin, mournful wind cut through our still-damp clothes, making us shiver.

With the beam of Poplar's hand-lamp guiding us, and Helga following with the shotgun, Jenny and I returned to the jetty and dropped to the Pelican's deck.

Once there, Poplar ordered me to open the main hatch and told us both to climb down.

The lamp's beam swung away as the hatch cover banged down, and for long seconds my eyes retained the after-image of an elongated Helga peering down at us, with shot-gun at the ready.

Voices filtered indistinctly through the deck head, then came the sound of footsteps: hollow on the staging, flat on the metal rungs--
And silence.

I took Jenny close, in the pitch-blackness and felt her breath, warm on my face, as she spoke:

'What now Superman?'

'We escape of course!' I said.

'Oh? How?'

I left her side and groped for the chest, bolted against the hull.

In the bottom of it, lay the bits and pieces that, over the years, I'd thought "might come in useful".

My searching fingers found a claw hammer with only one claw, a screw-driver and a broken hacksaw blade.

Last winter, I'd found that part of the plywood partition separating the main hold from the chain-locker had gone spongy, and Sam Wilkins had replaced a piece of rotten timber, about twenty inches square for me.

I was hoping I'd be able to take out this patch. Running my fingertips over his work, I wished he'd botched it just a little, so that I could find somewhere to start.

Deck planks creaked overhead, as someone moved about lightly. Helga, I thought, and pictured her with the gun in the crook of her elbow. Jenny said in a low voice.

'I wonder why he called her Mrs. Martin when she opened the door to us?'

'Dunno. Perhaps it was a signal, --- a warning that we were trouble.'

I felt a faint dip in the wood's surface; picked at it with a finger nail and found it crumbly.

'He's coming back!' Jenny said.

The sound of feet on iron again. Then something heavy thumped onto the jetty. Silence, then another thump. I was holding my breath, trying to decipher the sounds. Two more thumps, directly overhead on deck this time, and low voices. I scratched hard at the stopping with the broken piece of saw blade.

'What are you up to?' Jenny asked.

'Digging us out!'

'Stop!'

I barely had time to sit on the chest and hide the screwdriver, when the hatch was thrown back and the small hand-searchlight blinded me. No one spoke and in the five seconds the top was closed again and I heard the bolt slide home.

In that five seconds something else had come down through the opening with the swirling down-draft, and in the intensified darkness I sniffed the unmistakable smell of petrol. That's what the two 'thumps' had been:- full jerri-cans. My mind flipped back to the smell of petrol mixed with fog just before Dave Gregory's Garland blew up.

Realising now that Poplar intended a similar fate for the Pelican, with Jenny and me aboard, I started again on the screw heads with greater urgency. One slot was fairly clear of paint, and I pushed the screwdriver well in, gripped hard and twisted. The blade was worn and turned out of the slot.

I swore and wished I could risk using the hammer. Well, why not? There was a wrench in the chest; I found it and thrust it at Jenny.

'Make a racket with this – hang on – wait till I'm ready, then bang away at the hatch cover, right?'

'Right! What shall I shout.'

'Try "help". Get ready!'

I felt for the screw-head once more, put the screwdriver blade back in the slot and poised the hammer with it's head sideways to give my fingers more of a chance.

'Now!'

Jenny unleashed a racket: beating on the deck-head and hatch-cover with the wrench and adding yells.

Under cover of the noise, I banged the screwdriver in as hard as I could, then with both hands tried another twist. To my joy, I felt movement. It was no more than a fraction, but I knew that that one would come out anyway. Jenny was still shouting and banging.

'Okay, — save some for the others.' I'd forgotten she couldn't see what I was doing. 'The other screws I mean. I think there are eight. Maybe more'

'Oh my!'

There came a sudden, roaring rumble, which steadied, to a regular vibration, and I felt Pelican heel slightly as she turned away from the jetty.

We were off, and I hoped that I was going to have time to get the rest of the screws out before Polar got much further with his intentions.

The others were easier to find, because I remembered, they were about a hands-breadth apart, and the next two came out fairly easily.

I started on number four and told Jenny that the gold was gone.

'Gone? How do you know?'

'It was in the sail chest with the tools. It's not there now.'

'But Poplar didn't leave the house. Our Helga must have moved it ashore when you were supervising Poplar's ablutions.'

Screw number four was being difficult. Jenny went into her act again, and I plied the hammer twice: once against the screwdriver and once against my knuckles.

Jenny stopped shouting, and asked me, what I thought they'd planned for us.

'Something spectacular. Poplar brought two cans of petrol aboard.'

'Are we going to get out Mike?' Her voice was deep with the effort of keeping it steady.

'Too right we are.' I said, with more confidence than I felt.

Pelican had started to pitch gently, and I guessed we were back at the mouth of the river. The diesel's revs increased, and the pitching rose in frequency. It all depended on how far out to sea Poplar intended taking us before the 'accident'. Four out, four to go.

The screwdriver slipped for the hundredth time.

'Bang on the cabin bulkhead for a change!' I said.

While she tattooed, I got the next one on the move, and tried to ignore the fact that the smell of petrol was setting stronger. Somebody up there must have been sloshing it about regardless. It couldn't be long now.

Careless of the noise, I hammered the screwdriver into where I thought the joint would be, and levered. To my utter relief, the whole panel moved enough for me to locate the joint with my fingers. I positioned the tool, pushed again, holding it down while I worked the single claw of the hammer into the small gap. Another wrench, and I was able to get my fingers through and pull.

This was better. I braced a foot against the bulkhead, gave an all out heave, and the patch hinged open, like a cupboard door.

'Got it!' I almost crowed. Two more wriggles and the patch came free. I pushed one arm and my head through and grabbed the bitts.

A thrust with my feet and I tumbled into the confined space of the chain-locker and felt the welcome cold wind coming in through the hole in the bow.

Behind me, Jenny was struggling audibly.

'Give me a hand, I'm stuck!'

I reached up and grasped her waving arms. 'Come on, it's not difficult!'

'I'm a different shape to you!' She puffed indignantly.

'Vive la difference!' She came through with a rush, and we landed in a tangled bundle of arms and legs.

'Charmed, but we haven't got time,' I told her.

Pale moonlight outlined the jagged hole in the bow, and washed the sea beyond.

I wondered if Helga was keeping a deck watch, or if Poplar had left her behind.

'We'll go out fast,' I said. 'I'm hoping they're towing the dinghy. If you can grab hold, do so, but if you miss, keep swimming for the shore. The tide will be helping you ... hang on a sec—'

I'd just realised I was kneeling on something soft and I dragged it from under my knee. It was an old, forgotten, plastic fender just over a foot long: a piece of recovered flotsam.

There was a yard of cord still attached which I quickly tied round Jenny's wrist.

We shared a quick hug and a kiss, then she was half way out and taking a deep breath.

As she dropped I wormed through the hole and let myself plop into the water, with a prayer that we wouldn't be seen.

Pelican's bow wave pushed me away from her hull and I gave a couple of hurried strokes to intercept the inflatable dinghy which thankfully, was bobbing astern.

It almost bounced me under before I could fling up an arm to catch a side rope and hang on. There was no sign of Jenny and my heart sank.

While being dragged along like a hooked fish, it was much more difficult to roll inboard than I'd imagined.

I was too close to Pelican's stern to be spotted from the wheelhouse. But if Helga should be on deck and chance to look over the stern rail, she couldn't fail to see me with the moon so bright.

After a struggle I hooked my right foot over and grabbed the thwart to give me leverage, and heaved myself over the side of the dinghy, fearing that any second I'd tip it over on top of me. Once on board, I attacked the taut painter with the broken hacksaw blade which snapped at once, leaving me with a bare two inches of metal in cold wet fingers.

I tried again, feeling the rope part, strand by reluctant strand until at last the dinghy's skimming motion ceased, and we settled gently in the Pelican's flattened wake.

Pelican herself motored onwards and it seemed that Poplar and Helga had not, so far, noticed anything amiss.

A small outboard motor was attached to the dinghy's stern, tipped forward on its brackets. I righted it and was thankful that it was a type I was familiar with. It started at the third pull and I set off in a tight circle and backtracked. The shore was just a thickened line on the horizon, and no pinprick of light showed anywhere. I headed that way in slow, shallow zig-zags, calling Jenny's name and praying for her to be safe.

Every pale flicker of a wavelet, every ripple of the surface became her face or waving hand.

Then, a hundred or so yards shoreward of me,I saw her: a darker shape on the dark waters, one arm raised.

I waved encouragement, opened the throttle and turned the dinghy her way.

I was leaning out to catch Jenny's tired arm when I realised that Pelican had turned back and was bearing down on us

She was still without lights, and from our position low on the water, a menacing shape, only slightly darker than the night sky.

I tried to ignore the threat, and concentrate on getting Jenny quickly inboard without capsizing us. The result was effective, if not graceful.

Through chattering teeth, she said: ‘Hurry, he’s getting closer!’

My outboard engine chose this moment to cut out completely.

I pulled the starter cord, and nothing happened. I pulled again, and this time, the cord refused to recoil. I heard my own breath sob, as I futilely jerked, and cursed the wet lanyard.

Pelican’s engine noise was close now, it’s noise making it almost impossible not to waste time in looking round. I jabbed a finger into the pulley housing and the mechanism flew back into place, almost, taking my finger with it.

The throb of Pelican’s engine shrank to a murmur, as Poplar hove-to, ten yards away.

He was too close to ignore now.

Another jerk on the rope: the motor spluttered and again the recoil jammed.

Another agitated poke with my finger to free it.

I was sweating, trembling with the frustration of it. From above came the sharp crack of a pistol shot – then another and a section of the dinghy deflated with a whoosh!

Then the outboard fired, roared, and the dinghy hurled itself vengefully at the Pelican, bouncing off her hull, and careering round in a tight, skittering turn as I grabbed desperately at the short tiller arm.

I inhaled the stink of petrol as we bore away from her side.

Either someone had been very careless with the jerricans or Poplar had been preparing our funeral pyre, unaware that we were on the loose.

I looked up to see Helga standing on the cabin top, the shotgun to her shoulder.

She fired the first barrel, and lead shot peppered the sea to our right. A split second later, she pulled the other trigger just as the Pelican rolled, sending the discharge harmlessly over our heads.

A fraction after the second barrel spewed flame, Pelican's deck ignited from stem to stern. Flames leaped high, turning Helga into a human torch.

I caught a glimpse of Poplar's screaming face at the open wheelhouse door an instance before the other petrol can went up in a welter of noise and light.

I pushed Jenny to the bottom of the inflatable, trying to shield her from the raining debris, only to jerk her up again, to help me rid the craft of the stuff before it melted holes in our rubber.

We looked back at the incandescent Pelican.

'My God! Just look at it!' Jenny said, 'we'll have to go back.'

We circled the crippled vessel as closely as possible without actually frying, shielding our eyes from the intense heat and sparks.

We found Poplar on the third circuit. He was face down in the water, and dead. With difficulty we got him athwart the inflatable's stubby bow.

There was an odd shaped mass atop the Pelican's cabin which could have been Helga.

As we watched, the cabin top collapsed and the shape fell through.

Years of accumulated paint, varnish and pitch, made sure there'd be nothing left above Pelican's water line, and my heart was heavy as we made a final circuit and headed shoreward.

I was surprised to realise that daylight was spreading about us ---a cold, blustery daylight, with grey clouds scurrying in from the south-west.

The shoreline became more distinct and my eyes, following Jenny's pointing arm, saw a distant orange wedge-shape, riding a white vee as it approached.

'Lifeboat!' I said, and altered course so that we wouldn't intercept.

There would be questions to answer, and then some. But that could come later: First I wanted a free hand for a couple of hours at least.

Poplar was a bit of a drag, and I was strongly tempted to tip him back into the sea. After all, it couldn't hurt him now.

Jenny balked at that, so I compromised by closing his eyes and leaving him stretched out above high water mark at the entrance to Helford river.

By now both Jenny and I desperately needed to get dry and warm. We made our way back to Windbeck, tied up to the jetty and broke into the house.

Strangely, the dog seemed glad to see us.

Chapter 19

Aunt Carrie sank into her high-backed chair with a pleased look.

'You and your Jenny will take over here, and Charlie and I will move into the flat in the west wing. I think, it will all work out admirably.

'I must say, I am looking forward — Yes Mrs. Beddows, what is it?'

'A man at the back door for Mr. Peterson, ma'am!'

It was Stoker. It couldn't be, but it was. He turned his head aside and blew away his fag end.

'I s'pose you 'aven't got one of them little cigars on you?' he said.

It was fantastic, I found myself laughing and shouting, as I dragged him by the arm down the passage to the drawing room.

I left him facing a bemused Aunt Carrie, while I fetched a new box of Charlie's cigars from the library.

I handed the box to Stoker who grinned and pushed them into the blue holdall he was carrying.

'I'll save 'em for later! he said, ' Have you got a light?' He took a quarter-smoked Woodbine from behind his ear, then looked at Aunt Carrie apologetically. 'Sorry ma-am, I wasn't thinking.'

'Oh please – do light it!' Aunt Carrie picked up a silver table lighter and held the tiny blue flame under Stoker's nose, 'And perhaps my nephew will introduce us.'

'Stoker Figgin,.' I said.

'Ronald Langon, ma-am,'Stoker said.

'Well I'm sure you know best, Mr.Langon,' beamed Aunt Carrie, 'And you seem to have had a remarkable escape. Michael was just telling me how you were drowned in mid-Channel. - Oh forgive me, do please sit down.'

Stoker chose a spindly chair and lowered himself carefully. He put the holdall between his feet.

'The douane boat picked me up,' he said through blue smoke , Did you hear about Dave and the others?'

'Some of it,' I said, 'Poplar said they'd done a deal.'

'Some deal! Him and Bennett locked 'em all in the cellar and set fire to the 'Four Eagles'.

'Oh *no*!' Aunt Carrie looked ill. 'Were they all --?'

She couldn't finish it, and my vocal chords seemed paralysed.

Stoker shook his head. 'Somebody saw the smoke and called les pompiers.'

'Thank goodness ... and they were in time to save-them?'

'Except for Dave. Bennett had shot him already'

Noting our expressions, he added quickly: 'Oh, he ain't dead. He's in a bad way but the 'ospital says he'll pull through all right.'

Dave Gregory's old van was standing in the drive when later I saw Stoker out by the front door.

'He said I could borrow it,' Stoker said.

'One thing still puzzles me, Stoker: When the war finished, why didn't you come out of hiding?

Stoker grinned. 'I'd signed-on for "twenty-one" just before the war. There was no way I wanted to complete that lot; I was too well settled. As far as the navy knew: I'd gone down with that torpedo boat.

'When the missus inherited the farm, she sold it and bought that bike shop... We do all right.'

'But you had four year's back-pay to come.'

'That went to the old feller, — my dad.'

He got behind the wheel, placing the hold-all on the passenger seat.

I eyed the coal-dust streaks on the blue canvas.

'Think you'll get past Justin with what's in there?'

'He's en vacance. If I catch the next ferry, my wife's cousin will be on duty.'

As the dust of his going settled, I walked slowly round to the stable yard, letting the peace of this place enfold me.

The future, – our future, -- Jenny's and mine, seemed assured. I stopped by the first loose-box; a long inquisitive nose appeared over the half-door, and snorted softly.

'I've decided to keep him: he's really rather sweet.' Aunt Carrie came from behind me and stroked Hot Potato's muzzle. 'Ralph is holding some eventing at his place next week-end and I was wondering if you might---?'

Ah well! I was used to living dangerously by now.

I thought about the gold Jenny and I had 'rescued' from Windbeck's cellars. Right now, the six genuine ingots that Poplar and I had fished up, plus part of another with rough hack-saw marks at one end were well hidden at Highfields, and only Jenny and I knew about it.

Somehow we had to find a way to dispose of it profitably without attracting unwelcome attention.

Dave Gregory would be entitled to a cut of course --- and Frank. Then there was Sam Wilkins --- and Stoker's old comrade, Smallridge and ---.

Aunt Carrie said something that I didn't catch, and hurried off in the direction of the vegetable garden, where Uncle Charles, accompanied by Poplar's boxer dog, was inspecting ranked broccoli.

There'd be plenty to sort out in the coming weeks: The police hadn't finished questioning Jenny and me by a long chalk; then there were bound to be difficulties with the Pelican's insurers

From here, I could see the window of my room, and I thought of that other, much smaller, treasure chest, that lay within.

Treasure chest? --- Or Pandora's Box? I made my way back there for another look at it.

I'd found it in Helga's room at Windbeck: a small, steel box with a brass padlock, and I'd taken it on impulse, resisting the urge to smash the padlock until later.

At first, the contents had seemed to be the usual family records: birth certificates, marriage lines, and other documents – all in German, and all dealing with the Oogmans and their relations.

And photographs, — many photographs.

Now I opened the box again, put aside the bulk of the contents, and once more removed the rectangle of cardboard from the bottom

My spine tingled as my fingers touched the envelope which had lain hidden beneath.

This envelope too, contained photographs, intimate family snaps, taken in gardens, by river banks, and some, more formal, apparently taken by flash in a living room.

The woman in the photographs was Helga: the Helga of forty years before.

In one, she held a child of a few weeks, shawled and sleeping.

I laid the photographs out on my dressing table and traced the child's progress to where he was a sturdy six year old, dressed in a miniature version of a storm trooper's uniform.

There was no mistaking the face of the man in all the photographs.

The man who had one arm round Helga as he gravely answered the boy's raised arm salute.

The strands of hair over the man's forehead, ---and the short bristly moustache, ---were imprinted on the memories of millions.

I wondered if I were the only person who knew the real identity of Henry Poplar: The man who seemed set to be our next Foreign Secretary.

The man who could well be a future Prime Minister.

****

Made in the USA
Charleston, SC
08 February 2013